Carl Weber's Kingpins:

Charlotte

Carl Weber's Kingpins: Charlotte

Blake Karrington

www.urbanbooks.net

Urban Books, LLC
97 N18th Street
Wyandanch, NY 11798

Carl Weber's Kingpins: Charlotte

ISBN 13: 978-1-62286-793-6
ISBN 10: 1-62286-793-9

First Trade Paperback Printing December 2016
Printed in the United States of America

10 9 8 7 6 5 4 3 2 1

This is a work of fiction. Any references or similarities to actual events, real people, living or dead, or to real locales are intended to give the novel a sense of reality. Any similarity in other names, characters, places, and incidents is entirely coincidental.

Distributed by Kensington Publishing Corp.
Submit orders to:
Customer Service
400 Hahn Road
Westminster, MD 21157-4627
Phone: 1-800-733-3000
Fax: 1-800-659-2436

Carl Weber's Kingpins:
Charlotte

by

Blake Karrington

Chapter 1

Strap bobbed his head to the new Yo Gotti CD as he drove through the familiar neighborhood. He was so ready to get to the last trap house for the night and then call King so they could hit the city hard. It was Friday, and definitely a payday, but Uncle Sam wouldn't be getting a damn dime of their money. He pulled his Audi SUV in front of the dope spot with 345 on the mailbox and parked by the curb. Strap scanned the street before getting out. He may have been feeling good, but not good enough to get caught slipping by some bitch-ass niggas. Strap always remembered what his granddaddy used to tell him and his cousins.

"Let your guard down and end up six feet in the ground, little niggas."

His grandfather was a real OG and ruthless as hell. The old man was in his sixties, but niggas in the hood were still scared of his ass. As Strap walked toward the drug house, the hairs on his arm stood up. Everything looked normal around the residence, but something felt off. He waited until he got by the big oak tree in the front yard and checked his gun. The only lights he could see in the house were on the side where the kitchen was located. He looked around again. There were no unfamiliar cars on the street, but he knew that didn't mean shit.

Gripping his Colt, he slowly walked up the walkway to the front steps of the house. As he reached the top step, he heard the stone gravel behind him crunch.

Strap felt an immediate chill go down his spine as he turned. A blue flash of light and a loud sound cut through the quiet of the night. Something stung his stomach and lower back, and then, he felt a burning sensation travel down his legs.

"Fuck!" Strap yelled as he fell back against the porch.

He scanned the street, but he couldn't see who had fired the shot. His phone vibrated in his pocket, and King's name flashed across the screen when he pulled it out. He hit ACCEPT, and as he looked back up, he noticed a tall, light-skinned nigga strolling up the sidewalk. Strap tried to pop off a shot, but his hand had suddenly stopped functioning. His gun and the phone fell from his grip.

"Hey, nigga, just relax and get ready to go to sleep. Night night!" the man said as he pointed the gun at Strap and pulled the trigger. The man's laughter echoed in Strap's head as his face faded into darkness.

The Queen City, known to visitors and the rest of the world as Charlotte, North Carolina, was named after Queen Charlotte of Great Britain. *The old bird would shit bricks if she knew that a black King was driving down the streets of the city named after her, and feeling this good*, King thought as he drove his new white Jaguar XJL through the center of his hometown. Usually, he would be checking his rearview and side mirrors for the fucking cops or some bitch-ass niggas that had beef with him or his crew. But tonight, he was riding on the high of it being Friday. Nothing but a good time was ahead. With the top down, the air caressed his freshly shaved face. He had just gotten the VIP late-night treatment from his barber, Don. It was after hours, and Don didn't do shit for anyone unless they made it worth his while. Dropping a c-note to ole boy had definitely made it worth it.

King checked his reflection in the mirror and smiled. His thin mustache was lined up perfectly, and his fade was cut very low. King's thick eyebrows highlighted his light brown eyes and long eyelashes. Genetics were a great thing; even when he was young, people would always compliment him on his looks. The summer after he turned thirteen, he'd had a huge growth spurt. He had shot up six inches, and his shoulders had broadened. He now stood six feet two with caramel skin and a sculpted body that turned the heads of women and girls.

Tonight, he was feeling himself. Usually, he was on ready-set-go, but, for a brief moment, he was going to allow himself to chill. He stopped at a red light, and a group of college girls walked by. They slowed down and seductively waved at King. He nodded at them and flashed his 1,000-watt smile as they smiled back. The light turned green, and he hit the accelerator. Resting his right hand on his steering wheel, he allowed his left hand to hang over the door. As he cruised, his mind drifted back to his teenage years, when he was just sixteen years old.

King was in the driver's seat of his father's Mercedes. They were listening to Frankie Beverly & Maze's "Before I Let Go," which was his father's favorite song. King bobbed his head to the music while his father ran down some facts about the family business of hustling. Reggie reached over and turned down the volume on the radio.

"Listen, Ronnie," Reggie said, calling King by his first name while looking out of the passenger's window. "Son, this life we in is like no other. These streets ain't got no love for no damn body. Games are for chumps, not for this business. This is some serious shit, and you can nev-

er underestimate a man's intentions when it comes to being on top. You feel me?"

King smiled as Reggie's face began to fade into the side glass of the downtown building. His heart ached as the pain of losing his father at such a young age began to resurface. King took a deep breath. As he exhaled, his current world came back into view. As his mind cleared of his father, he pressed the VOLUME button on the radio. JAY Z's "Heart of the City (Ain't No Love)" pumped through the Bose speakers. *Damn, Dad kept it all the way real*, King thought to himself.

He approached the top of the hill and dropped the car down into second gear. This was the perfect place to test out the power of his new toy. He looked at the clock. He had spent enough time bullshitting around. He was only about twenty minutes from his trap house. He needed to meet Strap, collect his money, and make sure those fools had everything bagged up. This was not the night to be running late. It was Friday, and the spot would have been booming all day with business. He didn't like to leave a lot of cash in the hood. It would tempt folks too much.

King took out his cell phone and called his boy, Strap, to make sure everything was ready for him to pick up. The phone rang several times before the voice mail came on. King dialed Strap's number again. It rang twice this time; then, there was silence on the line.

"Hey, yo, Strap. What up, fam?" King spoke as he turned down Milton Road. The silence erupted into loud popping sounds.

"Strap? Hey, Strap, what the fuck is going on? Strap!" King yelled into his Bluetooth. He heard several more shots, and then, the line clicked. "Strap, Strap!"

King hurriedly pulled over in front of the old Circle K and jumped out. He was only a couple of blocks away from the dope house, and he needed to get his gun out of the trunk. The biggest gang in the city, CMPD, was out heavy on the streets, so he knew he needed to ride somewhat clean, especially on a Friday. King wasn't sure what he was about to walk into, but he knew he'd heard some heavy gunfire when he called Strap.

He placed the glock in the back of his pants and jumped back in the car. Quickly, he popped it into gear and sped out toward the trap house. He killed his lights as he turned down Milton. The street was quiet as King slowly approached the house. He stopped two houses down from his destination, parked near some bushes that partially hid his car, and raised his top. The streetlights were shot out as usual; the power company had stopped replacing them. King double-checked his clip and quietly made his way up to the trap house. As he approached, he could see someone slumped on the front steps. He ran over to the body and saw his man holding his stomach and moaning.

"Ah fuck, Strap! Shit," King said, kneeling beside him. "Damn, brah, where you hit?" King asked while Strap coughed and tried to pull himself up. "Nah man, stay still. Who the fuck did this?" King asked, holding his friend.

King heard a gurgling sound come from Strap as he took a deep breath. He placed his ear close to Strap's lips.

Strap took another breath. As he exhaled, he whispered a name to King. "R-Red." After uttering the name, his head dropped to the left.

"Shit! Strap, come on, man. You going to be a'ight. Stay with me, brah," King said. He shook his friend, but the light had left his eyes.

King wanted to scream, but he knew he needed to get inside to survey the full damage. He closed Strap's eyes and stood. The screen door screeched as he opened it and walked inside the house. King kept his gun raised as he rounded the corner of the room. As he approached the kitchen, he could smell death in the air. Chris, Lil T, and Monster lay on the old cracked floor with bullets in the back of their heads and blood pooling around them.

"Fuck . . . Fuck!" King yelled as he scanned the room for any sign of his money or drugs. Nothing was there. All of it was gone.

In that moment, he didn't care about the money as his eyes fell on his fallen friends. He whispered a prayer to the God of his grandmother for their souls—the prayer of the thugs.

King stood and backed out of the kitchen. He left the house. He paused as the body of one of his closest friends lay on the steps. He hated to just leave him there like that, but he knew there was nothing else he could do for his man except make sure the people who took his life lost theirs.

"Brah, I got you. Them niggas gonna pay for this shit!" King said before jumping down the steps.

He sprinted back to the bushes and jumped in his car. He made a U-turn and headed back up Milton. As he drove up the street, he checked his rearview for any potential assailants or witnesses who may have been lurking. He was sure that the cops were only minutes away, and as he turned onto Plaza Road, he heard their sirens. Shifting gears as he made his way to Harris Boulevard, he felt his blood boil as he thought about Strap and his other homeboys. His heartbeat rang in his ears. He needed to get to somewhere quick so he could process everything, and he needed someone he could trust. His family was what he needed.

King headed toward his mother and stepfather's house. There, he would find sanctuary to piece together his thoughts and figure out what he should do next.

Chapter 2

Carlton, King's stepfather, had stepped up when his biological father passed away from a heart attack. King was eighteen when his father passed. That was nearly seven years ago and Carlton had been right there for him and his mother ever since. Carlton was his father's best friend, and in many ways, he was just like King's daddy. They both were old-school street dudes who knew the game and played it well. King had never seen either of them without a custom suit, a tie, and a starched shirt. King and Carlton were as close as two people who shared the same DNA.

As he pulled up to his parents' home, he checked the time. It was late, and King had a second thought about going inside. He didn't want to wake them up, but he knew that Carlton would be upset if he wasn't told about the robbery. Using his key, he let himself into the quiet house. He could tell that his mother had decorated, yet again. The living room that once had a country theme now had earth tone covers and African art on the walls, with little elephant, lion, and monkey figurines placed around the room. Hearing the TV, King shook his head and made his way downstairs to the basement.

Carlton was sitting in his favorite recliner watching an episode of *Law & Order*. "Hey, Son!" Carlton said, putting the TV on mute.

King gave him a weak smile as he sat down. He could see the butt of Carlton's Smith & Wesson on the side of the chair, and he was sure there was more firepower all around the room. The smile was short, and the anxiety of the evening returned.

Carlton took a sip of his Hennessey and slid to the end of the chair. “What’s going on, son? Talk to me.”

King looked up at him and dropped his head back down. “They dead. All of them . . . dead,” King stated, fighting back tears. He ran his hands over his face and laid back on the couch. As soon as he closed his eyes, he felt sick to his stomach when Strap’s lifeless stare entered his mind again.

“Who dead?” Carlton asked as he stood up.

“All my boys at the trap house—Strap, Li’l T, Chris, and Monster. They murked all of them and took the money and dope. Shit, Strap died in my damn arms. I know my nigga got a couple of shots off, for sure. Before he died, he told me this nigga name Red did it.”

Carlton could see the hurt in King’s eyes, and the fury. He sighed and sat back down in his recliner, shaking his head as he sipped his Hen.

King stood and walked over to the bar. He grabbed a glass and poured himself a drink. After swirling it around for a moment, he sipped it. Both men were quietly trying to process everything that had gone down.

“I’m going to get them niggas, though, and I’m going to start with Red’s ass. They going to get dealt with real soon!” King screamed.

“Son,” Carlton responded while lighting one of his cigars, “in our business, murder brings attention we don’t want or need. Murder results in bodies, and bodies result in investigation by the cops. I know you ready to wage war, but we gotta let this cool for a minute. You gotta be smart about your moves, and check your damn emotions. Keep it in your mind, but don’t act too soon. I know you want vengeance right now, but let’s just wait,” Carlton said, blowing circles of smoke in the air.

King shook his head and allowed the Hennessey to flow down his throat as he listened to his stepfather. "Yeah, let them rest easy for now. But believe me, I am going to have Red and his crew crying like little bitches when I'm done with them."

"Such language," a soft voice said from the stairs.

King managed to flash a smile at the beautiful woman that emerged from the stairwell. His mother wore a long silk robe with the belt tied tightly around her small waist, which accentuated her hips. The gold and diamond cross that she wore around her neck touched the heart shaped tattoo she had on her chest with "Reggie," the name of King's father, inside of it.

Yolanda, or Yogi, as everyone called her, was in her late forties but had the body of a nineteen-year-old. Her caramel skin was near perfect. She had large brown eyes, full lips, high hips, and long relaxed hair that flowed down her back. Yolanda was a natural beauty and a true southern lady. She was soft spoken, elegant, and graceful. She could enter a room without saying a word, and heads would turn. At least that was the Yolanda side of her. Yogi was the complete opposite. She was street-educated. She would always let you know just what she felt, and was ready to whoop some ass if anyone disagreed with what she was saying. King was her only child, and she had vowed to make sure he had everything he could ever want. She would do anything to make that happen.

Yogi smiled at them both and stretched her arms out to King.

Carlton stood and walked to the bar. He grabbed a glass and poured her a drink.

"Hey baby, I thought I heard someone come in. It's good to see you," Yogi said, hugging her son tightly.

King felt the anger and despair that had consumed him moments ago lift as his mother hugged him.

Carlton touched her back and handed her the glass.

Yogi flashed a smile at him and kissed his cheek. "Well, I will let you men get back to business," Yogi said, making her way toward the stairs. "Oh, and Sunday dinner will be served at four. I don't care how late you are out tonight, you better not be late."

King laughed and nodded.

His mother cut her eyes at him playfully and blew him a kiss.

"Night, Ma," King said as she walked back up the stairs.

Chapter 3

King blinked and looked at the time on the cable box. It seemed that he had just laid down, and now it was time to get up and get moving. He had literally done nothing but lay there. Sleep had not come to him at all. He had spent most of the night staring at the ceiling and thinking about the night before. R&B flowed from the speakers when he hit PLAY on his Beats by Dre iPod dock.

King sat there for a moment, feeling the depression creeping back in. He shook his head. "Nah nigga, buck up!" he said aloud. He changed the channel to a hip-hop station to get himself going. As he settled on Power 97.9, YG's "My Nigga" was just coming on.

I said that I'ma ride for my motherfucking niggas,
Most likely I'ma die with my finger on the trigger.

The lines seemed more than appropriate for this morning. He turned the volume up and danced to the bathroom. After he turned on the water in the shower, he checked himself in the mirror. He scanned his toned, tattooed body and flexed before opening the door to the shower. The steam from the shower was inviting, and the warm water soothed him as he stepped in. For a minute, he just stood there with his head down, thinking of his fallen comrades. The shower was set to pulsate. He allowed it to massage his shoulders and temporarily wash away the events of the previous night. He grabbed the AXE shower gel and was calmed by its scent as he lathered his body.

As his mind cleared, he remembered that he needed to pick up his best friend, Kareem. He had just come home after serving three years of a five-year bid for a pound of OG Kush and gun possession.

Kareem and King had been friends since the monkey bars in elementary school. In school, King was known to knock panties off on a regular, and he surely liked to kiss and tell. At lunch, he would keep the boys entertained with his exploits. Kareem would sit right there beside him, nodding his head and laughing while his friend entertained the masses.

Kareem would chuckle it up, but he didn't need to tell any stories of bedroom bullying. He had gotten his girlfriend, Tiana, pregnant in the eighth grade, and her pregnancy told his boys everything they needed to know. That was over eleven years and three kids ago for Kareem.

Kareem's incarceration had taken a toll on Tiana and the kids, but King and the crew had tried to make sure they were taken care of financially. He would personally check on her and the kids while Kareem was away. But during the last year of Kareem's bid, Tiana stopped accepting the help. She had made it clear to King that, when he came home, she wanted Kareem out of the game.

King could understand Tiana's fear, but leaving the game would have to be Kareem's decision. King knew that, like him, Kareem had been raised in the dope game and did not intend to leave it. However, if his boy had changed and was ready to leave, King would wish him the best. Secretly, though, he hoped he would still be his copilot in the streets, especially now.

King hoped that after pulling this bid, Kareem now understood how serious things were in the streets. He had always stayed on Kareem about being too lax about business. The day Kareem got busted, he was high, talking on the phone to Tiana with a pound of Kush and a gun in the car. The police pulled him over and smelled it on him.

Kareem was careless. He liked to play and joke; he was always either being the clown or the killer. He was never even keeled. Everyone in the crew was convinced that he was bipolar. The killer was the reason King and Carlton kept him around; neither would admit that, sometimes, the clown in him kept everyone in light spirits. Kareem's funny side didn't set too well with the judge. At his trial, he kept asking him if he thought something was funny because of the way he kept smiling.

The judge decided to make an example of him. He wanted to give Kareem more time, but King had paid a top lawyer to represent his boy, so, instead of ten years, he got five. King hoped that Kareem would now take life seriously and get his game up.

King turned off the water and stepped out of the shower, excited to see his boy. As he wrapped the towel around his waist, his cell phone whistled in the bedroom. He checked the text and laughed.

"Nigga you better get out from between dem hookers' legs and come get ya boy!" The text read.

King just texted Kareem back, "N.I.G.G.A."

He knew that he would understand. They were both Tupac fans and used the phrase all the time—Never Ignorant Getting Goals Accomplished. "Yeah, take that fucking word crackers used, and turn it into something positive, Pac," King said and went into his bedroom to get dressed.

***

King pulled up to Tiana's house and considered going inside but thought better of it. He did not want to hear Tiana's mouth. Today was a day of celebration, and he wasn't in the mood to hear her nagging. So, instead, he honked the horn twice.

"Nigga, lay off that horn. I ain't no trick you picking up for some ass!" Kareem said as he walked down the driveway.

King shook his head as Kareem jumped over the door into the car. "Nigga! Don't scratch my shit!" King said. "I thought Niggas got big when they go in. Your ass ain't gained an ounce!"

"Boy, you know I've been skinny with plenty all my damn life, nigga," Kareem shot back.

King reached out his hand. "Damn, homie, it is good to see your ass," he said as he pounded Kareem up.

"Nigga, fuck that, give your boy a hug!" Kareem screamed. The two men embraced each other tightly.

While letting go, King saw Tiana standing in the door. He waved, then, he checked his side mirror and pulled out into the street.

"Damn, how was the homecoming with your girl, brah? I already know she didn't like your ass coming out with me, huh?" King asked as he turned onto Ashley Road.

"Man, the same old, same old. I got her, though," Kareem said laughing. "So what's going on? I heard about Strap and them."

"Damn, nigga, how you get that shit that quick?" King asked.

"Man, niggas behind the wall know shit before it even happens. They been blowing up my phone all morning," Kareem said, shaking his head. "So, what we gonna do about this?"

"Man, thanks, but I ain't trying to get you caught up in this shit. You just got out and—"

"Nigga is you serious? Did your ass get soft while I was locked up? I know you ain't letting that shit Tiana spitting get to you," Kareem said, adjusting his .45 in his waistband.

Kareem shook his head. Although he was talking shit, Tiana's voice echoed through his mind. Every conversation they had while he was locked up was about him getting his shit straight when he came home. He would listen to her cry on the phone and tell him how much she and the boys needed him. When he said he was going with King, she threatened him. She told him that she would take the boys and leave if he didn't leave the streets alone. She refused to watch her boys grow up, while having to worry about them following in their father's footsteps. He loved her and his sons, but King had been with him since multiplication tables. He couldn't turn his back on his boy, and Tiana would have to just understand that shit.

"Dude, you know we got to handle this situation. You let this ride too long, and other hungry niggas will take it as a sign of weakness. You gotta set the example so they know and respect our game, homie," Kareem said, patting his .45. "Shit, you know Strap would expect no less, man. No fucking less."

King continued driving and listening to Kareem. Everything he said was true, but he knew Carlton was, also, right. Murder was bad for business, and no matter how much he and Kareem wanted revenge, it would have to wait until Carlton felt it was time.

King pulled up to his parents' house with Kareem, and they walked up to the door. King turned the knob, and the aroma of Sunday dinner filled his nostrils. The two men walked to the back patio and found Yogi and Carlton sipping on tea mixed with lemonade.

“Kareem!” Yogi said, smiling.

Kareem looked Yogi over. She wore a white denim mini skirt that showed off her toned thighs and a red lace shirt with a white cami under it. Kareem knew she was King’s mama, but damn, she was fine as hell. Beautiful face and that banging body made her a definite M.I.L.F. She gave him a hug, and he could smell her signature perfume, Jo Malone.

“Hey, Ms. Yogi,” Kareem said, slowly loosening his embrace.

“Kareem, so glad to have you home, baby,” Yogi said, touching his face and kissing his cheek. Kareem was like a second son to her.

“Hey boy! You look good, still skinny as hell,” Carlton said, pounding Kareem and giving him a brief hug. “Yeah, glad you made it out boy. Glad. Come on boys, let’s go to my office. We got some things to talk about,” Carlton said, referring to the basement.

The men walked down the stairs. Kobe, Carlton’s main security guy, was already sitting on the couch with a drink in his hand and talking on the phone. Carlton walked behind the bar and poured three glasses of Cognac.

He handed King and Kareem glasses, then raised his in a toast. “To freedom, friendship, family, and vengeance!” Carlton said, clinking his glass against King’s glass, and then, Kareem’s. The men sat down and sipped their drinks. Carlton took his seat in his recliner and waited for Kobe to get off the phone before he spoke.

“I had a night to sleep on this, and I’m thinking a quick response could be good in this situation. I had Kobe call our people downtown and check this nigga, Red, out. It looks like your boy been working with them people, so that’s probably what gave him the balls to think he could take from us. Word is that he done set up a bunch of people, so they probably got good protection on him, but that don't have nothing to do with the people around him. I say we send him and the streets a good message, and then, we wait a little while before we take him up out of here. That way, when he come up dead, it won't point right back to us," Carlton said, looking from Kareem to King. "What you thinking, son?" Carlton asked as he sat down at the bar.

"I think we need to make sure that every nigga in this state learn not to ever cross us like this again," King said and placed his Smith & Wesson on the bar.

When the family had finished Sunday dinner, King and Kareem excused themselves to continue the day King had planned for his newly released partner.

"Man where we off to?" Kareem asked, not sure what King had going on in his mind.

"Well, first, we about to swing by one of my little spots, so a couple of my side chicks can squeeze whatever cum you got left inside you after Tiana worked your ass over last night. Then, we off to the mall so we can get you out that damn Wal-Mart sweatsuit you got on, homie," King answered while trying to control his laughter.

"Fuck you, nigga. You know this some shit wifey had for me. It was either this or throw on some Rocawear I had from three years ago."

"Yeah, well I'm definitely glad you didn't put that on, but this shit ain't much better," King responded, still laughing.

Kareem looked down at what he had on, and he couldn't do anything but burst out laughing, himself.

"Yeah, you right brah. Good looking out. I definitely need the wardrobe update, but I'm going to pass on the strippers. I promised myself and Tiana that I was going to try to do better, and the least I can do is not fuck up on some busted-ass strippers. If I'm going to do something, it's got to be with someone worth something." Kareem spoke in a serious tone.

"Yo, I respect that, brah. . How Pac said it? My nigga 'hit the pen, and now, no sinning is the game plan . . . I ain't mad at cha.'" King stuck out his fist and Kareem pounded him up.

"A'ight, enough of that then. Let's go to the mall. But just know I'm going to swing by the spot and, at least, get my dick sucked afterward because them hoes already been paid," King added.

When King and Kareem pulled up to the mall, the shopping center was packed with people. Sunday was a day that everyone came to North Lake Mall to hang out. It was now considered the black mall since the city had shutdown Eastland Mall, which was where all the black people used to shop and hang out.

King and Kareem couldn't make it into the stores without being stopped by someone who knew either one or both of them. Charlotte was, indeed, King's city, and he made sure to stop and show love to all, almost as if he was a politician running for city council. King understood how important it was to have the common folks, as along with the street hustlers, on his team. There was no way to know when he would need either or both types of people. Many of the old Charlotte hustlers had beat cases simply because there were one or two black people on their juries who respected the hustlers that had shown love to them and their communities. King's father made sure he understood that.

When they finally made it to DTLR, King pulled the store clerk with chocolate skin and a million-dollar smile to the side. "Look, I need you to hook my dude up with all the latest shit. Now, I know him. He ain't going to want to spend no money because he cheap, even with my bread. So, don't say nothing about the price. Just put him a fly wardrobe together, and I'll take care of it."

King passed the lovely young lady three brand-new one-hundred-dollar bills. "This is just for you, so hook my boy up right. I'll be back."

King told Kareem he was going to run down to Foot-locker and see if one of his old flames still worked there. He hadn't seen Tiffany in a while, but he was in the mood for some of that masterful head game she possessed. If he played his cards right, he might convince her to use her lunch break to go to the parking lot with him and remind him of her talents in his SUV. That way, he wouldn't have to worry about the strippers that were sitting and waiting on the other side of town.

King's face lit up when he entered the store and saw Tiffany helping a group of young cats pick out some shoes. She was still looking good, and his dick was getting hard just thinking about her juicy lips and warm mouth around it. Their eyes met, and from Tiffany's smile, he could tell she was just as happy to see him. She asked one of the other sales associates to take over for her. Then, she made her way over to King, who was pretending to be interested in the display wall.

"Hey, stranger, long time no hear from," Tiffany said, interrupting King from his eye shopping.

King turned to her, smiled, and then, looked back at the display like he was really about to buy something. "Yeah, it has been a minute. I swung by here a couple of times, but you wasn't working. I wanted to give you my new number.

"King, stop lying. I'm a manager, so I work nearly every day. And why wouldn't you just text it to me?" Tiffany asked with a curious smile.

"Well, my phone was stolen, and I hadn't backed up the info. I'm telling you, I came by. I even asked homeboy where you was at." King pointed at a male associate who walked out of the stockroom. King signaled for the young guy, hoping that he understood man code.

"Hey, brah, didn't I come by last week looking for her?"

For a moment, the guy looked like a deer caught in headlights, but then, he smiled and shook his head yes. "Yeah, I thought I told you someone came by looking for you, Tiff," the young salesmen added, helping out King's story.

"You see that Tiffany? Now I'm hurt that you didn't believe me. Come on, where is my apology?" King asked as if he was in the right the whole time.

"Whatever, King, and whatever to you too, Tony," Tiffany responded.

King sat there for another twenty minutes trying to convince Tiffany to yield to his plan. It took her a while, but she finally broke down and gave into King's pleas. Deep down inside, even though she knew King might be playing her, she also knew that having someone like him on her side would pay off if, and when, she ran into financial trouble. Plus, she did like the bragging rights that came along with telling her girls she was fucking with King.

King hit the UNLOCK button twice on his key chain, opening all the doors on the vehicle. He and Tiffany climbed into the back. King wanted to have enough space to stretch out. He, also, wanted Tiffany to have enough room to do her thing. He started to ask her if she wanted the radio on but decided against it when he remembered that sexy noise she made while sucking him off.

Tiffany wasted no time. She unbuttoned King's pants and pulled them down in one motion. He assisted her by pulling his boxers to the floor. Tiffany looked up at him as she placed his half-hard pole into her mouth. She pulled and tugged on it with her lips, making a suction noise as King got harder and harder. Tiffany ran her tongue, first, down the left side, then, back up and down the right. When she got back up to the tip, she let out a drop of saliva and repeated the motion.

King just sat back and watched her work his dick. He couldn't remember what had been keeping him from coming and getting this weekly. He reached his hands down, grabbed one of her breasts and began rubbing her hard, long nipples. This must have excited Tiffany because she began to intensify her assault, moving from his dick to his balls and back up. She was now moaning with every suck and slurp. The mixture of the sight, sound, and feeling of her soft breast and hard nipple had King at his breaking point. He dropped his head back as he released his load inside Tiffany's waiting mouth. She kept going, making sure she didn't miss a drop.

King had to stop her before his shit got hard again. He knew if that happened, he would need more than just head, but he didn't want to take it there with Tiffany. He had always felt that if real sex wasn't involved, he wouldn't have to worry about the female getting her feelings caught up. To him, there was no way that could happen from just oral sex.

Trying not to make Tiffany feel like he had just played her, he sat and talked to her for about ten more minutes. Then, he reminded her that she needed to get back to work and he needed to find Kareem. King made sure he gave Tiffany his new number, and he pretended to put hers back into the phone, knowing that he had it already anyway. He walked back into DTLR, and the chocolate bunny was standing at the counter. He walked up to her and asked where Kareem was.

"He's in the dressing room putting on one of his new outfits. I told him he needed to throw this away," she said, holding up the all-grey cotton sweat suit.

"Shit, I agree. Get rid of that and ring everything else up," King responded.

"I already did, got it bagged and waiting," the young girl said with a smile, knowing her commission was going to be great.

"What's my damage, cutie?"

"Six thousand seven hundred fifty-nine dollars and nineteen cents," she answered.

King reached into his pocket and counted out seventy one-hundred-dollar bills. "Here's seven K. The extra is thanks for all your help."

Chapter 4

"Can I get a bottle of Cîroc? Damn, come on, Giant. What is taking so long?" Trixie yelled as she slammed her tray against the bar. Her feet were killing her, and the pleather bustier was beginning to stick to her nipples. Tonight was a fucking nightmare, and she was so sick of working at Nikki's. As much as these fools pinched, poked, and pulled on her ass, she may as well have been on the fucking pole.

"Calm down, love, I got you," Giant said, smiling at her. Giant was six feet six with blond hair and hazel eyes. He was from Scotland or somewhere like that; Trixie wasn't sure. She just knew he was a big white boy, working in a black strip club. He winked as he placed the glasses and the bottle of Cîroc on the tray.

"I mean, thank you, finally," Trixie said and walked back to the VIP area. She hated that she didn't put the damn insoles into the damn stilettos. She had left them in her purse and forgotten to place them in. Now, her feet felt like they were about to explode.

"Shit, we thought we were going to have to send out for your ass. Damn!" Tony said as Trixie placed the tray down.

"It's busy here tonight. Sorry about the wait." She forced a fake smile.

Tony nodded and Red sat back on the leather couch.

"Trixie, have you seen Peaches?" Red asked as he lit his blunt.

Peaches was Red's main girl, but she had been pissed at him for the last two weeks. She had caught him sleeping with this little young girl, Cara, who had turned eighteen only three months ago. Red had seen her at one of his parties, hanging with one of his young street dealers. She had long, naturally curly brown hair, large brown eyes, and full lips that would make a dude's toes pop when she put them on his pole. Along with all of that, she had nice round tits that sat up high, a little slim waist, and some thirty-eight-inch hips that were toned and tight from her running every day. Her body was hard to resist.

When Red saw her, she was wearing a two-piece red string bikini and walking around like a grown woman. He could tell she was not some hood chick. When he introduced himself to her, she simply smiled and thanked him for having her at his party. She had class and upbringing, which explained why she was with Dexter, who was a college kid just trying to pay his tuition.

Dexter was a nineteen-year-old college sophomore, and he had known Cara since high school. When Red told Dexter that he was not to see Cara again, the little nigga actually bucked at him. That lasted all of fifteen minutes, until Red had two of his guys persuade Dexter that it would be best for him to step aside quietly.

As soon as Cara became legal, Red made sure that pussy stayed wet for him only. He began taking Cara shopping, clubbing, and on out-of-town trips with him. Cara was young, but it was obvious that she liked to fuck; and she liked trying new tricks in the bedroom. Shit, she had almost turned Red into a bitch the first time she went down on him.

Cara, like many little spoiled girls, was rebelling against her parents. She had a strong will and a good head on her shoulders. One thing Red really liked about her was that she was about her business. She was in her senior year and had been accepted to several colleges on full scholarships. If he called her to come over and she had something to do that dealt with her education, she would turn his ass down quick. Yeah, Cara was something different for him, and she was making his ass slip on his female game. Shit, Peaches was his main girl, although he always had four or five other birds on the side. Since he'd had Cara, though, he only wanted her, well . . . her and Peaches. But Cara had been causing him to slip up on his main girl, and his slip-up may have cost him Peaches.

Peaches had shown up at Red's downtown apartment and found Cara naked in the kitchen preparing lunch. Red wasn't sure what was said or what happened exactly, but when he heard a commotion coming from the kitchen, he ran in to find Cara about to put Peaches' face in a frying pan filled with hot grease. Red grabbed Cara, and he had to struggle for a minute to get her to let go of Peaches. Red could not believe that this little refined girl had beat Peaches' ass. Peaches was a street chick. She had about twenty pounds on Cara and was ten years her senior. He had seen her shut bitches down and send their asses to the hospital, and now, she was lying on the floor, bleeding and damn near crying. The girl that put her there was from an affluent family in Lake Norman. He had struggled with Cara for a few minutes.

"Cara, chill out, baby. Chill out," Red had told her as he carried her to the bedroom.

It took some time to get her to calm down and stay in the bedroom, but she finally calmed down and went to take a shower. Red waited until he heard the water run and the shower door close before going back to the kitchen.

As he approached the kitchen, Peaches was pulling herself up from the floor. Red winced as he looked at

Peaches' face. Both of her eyes had begun to swell, her lip was split down the middle, and she was nursing her side.

"Damn, baby, you okay?" Red said as he handed Peaches a dishtowel to wipe the blood from her face.

"Fuck you, Red! Who is this bitch?" Peaches yelled, holding her side.

Due to the swelling, he wasn't able to see the look in her eyes, but he could tell she was fuming.

"You know what? I don't care. I'm done. I can't do this shit no more," Peaches said as she walked toward the door. She held her side as she grabbed her purse and keys.

Red didn't even try to go after her. He knew that, more than being mad, Peaches was embarrassed that she just had her ass beat by a pup. Peaches was raised on the west side of Charlotte. She had fought almost every day as a child and was known around the neighborhood as the chick you didn't mess with. Losing a fight was something that didn't happen to her, especially losing a fight to a rich little teenage girl.

Red had called and texted her a few times without any luck. Tonight, he was in a good mood. He had some extra cash, and he knew that with money and the right words, he could make Peaches forgive him.

"I haven't seen her in about two weeks. You can tell she ain't been here because the crowd has thinned some," Trixie said, looking at herself in the mirror. "I can go check and see if she back there, if you want."

"Nah, don't worry about it. I ain't got time to worry about that crazy girl. I got business to handle," Red said, nodding to Dover.

Trixie smiled and left the VIP room.

Dover leaned over close to Red. "Ok, man, we stepping our game up or being suicidal?" he asked, sitting on the edge of the leather chair.

"Yeah, dude, we robbed fucking Carlton and King. Them niggas ain't no light-weights," Texas said, sipping his gin.

"Man, fuck them niggas. Don't worry about that shit. I got back up if we need it. How much we end up with, anyway?" Red asked, while watching the dancer slide down the pole on the center stage.

"About two hundred and fifty stacks, and three bricks already bagged up," Texas said.

Red smiled and nodded his head in approval.

King, Kareem, and the rest of his crew sat at the kitchen table in one of their stash houses. They had been thinking, all morning, about the right way to strike back at Red and his squad.

"So, we know they are on their damn guard. We need to find a way to get our shit back, plus a pound of flesh. Fuck that, four pounds of flesh," King said, pacing the floor.

"You said Red did this, right?" Dirty asked and laughed. "Well, you know everything in life happens for a reason. Guess who my fucking cellmate was when I was in the joint?"

"Who, nigga?"

"Titus . . . and do you know who Titus is?" Dirty asked with a huge grin.

"Your cellmate?" King said, getting annoyed with the twenty-questions bullshit.

"Titus is Red's cousin, and Titus really liked to talk about how his cousin was taking over the city. You know when you are locked up, you either write, read, talk, or go crazy. Titus liked to talk, and he talked a whole lot. This nigga told me all about his cousin's houses, hangouts, and women. I think he got a girlfriend over at Nikki's.

Her name is . . . damn. What is her name?" Dirty said, tapping his finger against his temple.

"Nikki's?" King said, laughing. "The only dancer worth fucking with over there is Peaches."

"Peaches? That could be her name. I know her house is one of his stash houses. He got her in a place off Sugar Creek. He stashes his guns and dope there, from what Titus told me."

"He got his stash and ass in the same house? Damn he don't give a fuck about that bitch, huh?" King said, shaking his head.

"Nah, he care. He just makes sure that nobody know that he stash his shit there. Titus knows because he used to fuck Peaches until he got locked up. Red fucked her one night and fell in love with the bitch. Titus said he wasn't gonna fall out with family over no pussy," Dirty said and grabbed another beer from the refrigerator.

"What else did Titus tell ya, brah?" King asked as he sat down. "We need to get our shit back and give these fools some act right."

Panama, Kirk, Mike, and Trip stood in the parking lot of the old Harris Teeter. King had called and told them to meet him and Kareem there at ten. The four of them had heard about what happened on Milton, and Panama was ready to spill some blood in the streets. Strap was his first cousin, and he was the one who had to tell his aunt that her only son had been murdered. Each tear that fell from her eyes made his blood boil, and he wanted to go out in the streets and bring hell to Red. Even though his emotions were running high and he wanted Red's head on a plate, he knew that letting feelings run him in this game would end with him not breathing. Panama had joined the service straight out of high school, and one thing he knew was to study the enemy. When you attack the enemy, it is crucial to make sure that they can never come back. That was something that Red obviously didn't understand.

A pair of headlights cut the darkness of the parking lot. Panama made out King's Jaguar as he pulled into the parking space beside Panama's black Cayenne SUV. He pounded King and nodded at Kareem. Panama really didn't care for Kareem. The nigga was always cracking on people, and Panama's large facial features made him the butt of a lot of Kareem's jokes. But he also knew Kareem's street credit went deep. Niggas knew that he would put that work in, and his love and loyalty for King were undeniable.

"What's good, fam? You all know why we here," King said, leaning back on the trunk of his Jag. "Red done fucking robbed us and killed our brothers. We got to set this right and send a damn message to the streets."

"What you need us to do, King?" Panama asked, not in the mood for a speech.

The men discussed the plan for thirty minutes, then, they left the parking lot. Panama and Trip headed toward Fourth Street. Panama did not like using information provided by niggas he didn't know. He was sure that most niggas always left something important out. He had to check the area for himself to make sure they were not walking into some shit that would put them in body bags.

"You ready to do this shit, brah?" Kareem asked, checking his AR-15.

King nodded as he pulled to the end of the narrow road.

King's TracFone buzzed. "Yeah? All right, call me when we can move." King hit END on the key pad.

He had bought the temporary phone to make sure that no one could trace them. He didn't give a fuck about Red knowing, but he didn't need the cops being able to trace this shit back to him. He tapped his fingers on the trigger of his Colt. The car was silent. Both men were preparing to go in and send people to hell. They had shot his boys down like animals without a thought, and King was going to make sure that they felt exactly what his family felt.

Panama wiped the blade of his knife off on his pants. He had decided against guns, they were a little noisy and not as personal. He wanted these niggas to see death coming for them; and with the swipe of his blade across their throats, he would feel that he had avenged his cousin's death.

"I thought Kareem said there was only two niggas up here," Trip said, looking around.

"That is why we needed to check shit out for ourselves," Panama said.

It was early, and the hood was hot. The fiends were keeping the dope boys busy. Cars were going up and down the street.

"It's too hot here, bro, for this shit to go down tonight. Damn, and on a Sunday night too. This nigga got all this money being made, why the fuck he wanna come on our side?" Trip said as he watched the street with his night goggles.

"Shit, you know niggas greedy . . . but we gotta clear this shit tonight. We gonna need some more fire power. Get Shark and Marcus over here. I'ma call King," Panama said

Panama leaned against the wall of the building's roof.

"Yo, King, this block is on fire tonight. You sure you want to take this shit tonight?" Panama asked, while Trip continued to look down the scope of his rifle, watching the dope fiends and the hustlers.

"Yeah, I'm sure, fam. We might not get this chance again anytime soon," King responded.

"A'ight, man, we got you. I got Trip calling in some more peeps, just in case," Panama said before hanging up the phone. "So, did you get them on the phone?"

"Yeah, they just two blocks over at Chip's house. They on they way," Trip said, still looking through the scope.

"A'ight, we just waiting on King to give us the word," Panama said as he sat down on the concrete slab.

Red and his crew were still at the club. They had been drinking and smoking since the club opened. He and Texas watched the new dancer hypnotize the crowd with the movements of her full hips and thick thighs. Red's entire crew was quiet, which was a rarity for them. Miguel's "Adore" flowed through the speakers as the dancer floated down from the pole. "Floated" was the only way that Red could describe how she moved. The song ended, and the VIP room was quiet for a moment.

"Well, damn, Nikki's is getting some talent up in this piece," Texas said as he took a sip of his beer.

Trixie entered the room and began clearing the bottles.

"Trixie, who is that new bitch?" Texas asked, nodding toward the stage as the woman gathered her money from the stage floor.

"That's Mystic, she's new. She and her girlfriend just started. Since Peaches hasn't been here, Tigga scouted for some new talent and found them in some little place in Virginia. They do *shows*," Trixie said, making quotation marks in the air. "This is their second night, and the fucking line is wrapped around the damn block. I'll be back with your drinks, okay? And I hear that Peaches is here, Red, she just got here about ten minutes ago," Trixie said before walking out the door.

Red lit his blunt again and sighed. Although he missed Peaches, Mystic's performance had pushed her from his mind for the moment.

The lights flickered, and the scent of strawberries flooded the club. It mixed with the smell from the weed smoke in VIP. The stage filled with pink smoke, and Rihanna's song, "Pour it Up," came over the speakers. Trixie even stopped to see what was going to happen on the stage.

A silk, purple piece of cloth fell from the ceiling, and then, in time with the music, five additional silk cloth strands came down.

As Rihanna let out a "Throw it up, throw it up," two women descended from the ceiling, twirling themselves in the material.

"Watch it all fall out
Pour it up, pour it up
That's how we ball out
Throw it up, throw it up"

The women wore long black wigs with masquerade-type masks over their eyes. As the music flowed through the speakers, the women moved from the fabric effortlessly.

"Damn, you seeing this shit, Red?" Texas said, standing up.

The music stopped, and the material dropped. The women were hanging from a purple rope. Their legs were entwined with one another's. One of them had her hand on the rope, supporting the two of them. The music started again, and one woman flipped herself upside down, putting them in a sixty-nine position. The crowd went crazy.

"Woo, damn!" Texas said.

Trixie stood with her mouth open. Nikki's had never featured this type of act before. She looked at the flat screen TVs on the wall. The cameraman had zoomed in on the women. They had flawless bodies. Strong toned hips, thighs, flat stomachs, and full DD breast. The money began to rain down on them as they continued their routine. Their hands explored each other, and their facial expressions were making niggas' shit rock hard.

Red sat mesmerized by the women. It was like watching two fucking butterflies on stage. This shit was too high-class for Nikki's. This wasn't stripping, this was entertainment. The club went black for about thirty seconds, and one red light hit the stage. The women were arm in arm, each with one leg straight up in the air. They slowly lowered their legs and took a bow.

The club erupted again. Dudes and females began making it rain down on the duo.

Trixie had just witnessed her fucking tips getting better, cause these bitches were not only going to bring in niggas, they were going to bring some white money from Uptown Charlotte in the place. *Shit, we are going mainstream,* she thought to herself.

Panama and Trip watched the traffic on Fourth Street. They had been there for a little over an hour, watching the movement below. Panama was now satisfied that they would not have any surprises. There were three street workers, and from what he could see, there were maybe four or five people inside, including two women.

Panama called down to King to let him know the coast was clear.

"Did you say two ladies was in the house?" King asked with concern.

"Yeah, two hoes them niggas probably tricking off on."

"Well, we need to hold up until they leave. I ain't with killing women—"

"Brah, I thought you said this shit gots to go down tonight," Panama said, cutting King off.

"Yeah, I did, but I got a mother and a daughter. Like I said, I ain't with killing no innocent women, so we just got to wait!" King yelled into the phone, making his point clear.

Just as Panama was about to hang up, the two strippers came out the front door and started walking down the street. They were laughing and counting money, completely unaware of how close they had just come to death.

"All right, the bitches just left out. Are you ready?" Panama asked.

"Yeah nigga, we good," King said, looking at Kareem, who nodded at him.

Panama was watching from the roof of the tire building. He squeezed off two shots, quietly taking out two of the street boys with his silenced rifle. The two men fell to the ground without a sound. Panama waited for the third man to come out of the trap house. He had gone in to drop money and to get some product. As the third man walked toward the corner, Trip had him lined up in his sights. He exhaled as he squeezed the trigger, and the man fell perfectly in front of a tree.

King opened the door of the old Pontiac that he drove when he didn't want to draw attention to himself. He and Kareem walked down Fifth Street and jumped a fence to the house that was next to Red's trap house. Kareem held his AR, ready to pop anything that moved.

Shark and Marcus approached from the front.

On King's signal, the four of them stormed the house, and in only ten minutes, Shark had stripped every member of Red's crew. Marcus and Shark laughed as they packed up the money and the drugs. These fools had it out in plain sight, and their stash was in an obvious place under the tile in the bathroom.

"We got it," Shark said as he threw the backpacks on his back.

King and Kareem stood in the living room of the trap house. Red's cousin, Moose, was on his knees in front of King.

"Call your fucking, cousin," King said, throwing Moose's phone to him. The phone slid across the floor.

Moose spit on King's shoes and laughed. "Call him ya damn self, bitch," Moose said, struggling to get free from his restraints.

Kareem laughed along with Moose. As he laughed, he patted Moose on the shoulder. Marcus and Shark looked at King in confusion. A loud crack filled the air, followed by a scream.

"Aaahh, damn! Fuck . . . fuck. Nigga, you broke my nose!" Moose yelled as blood squirted from his nose.

Kareem continued to laugh. "Well, since you want to be a fucking comedian, I wanted to make sure your clown nose was beaming red. Now, you heard the man. Call Red, now!" Kareem yelled.

Moose whimpered. "Shit, man, I can't even breathe!"

Kareem raised the butt of the gun to deliver another blow.

"Stop, brah," King said as he walked over to Moose. "Now, nigga, this is simple. You can make the call, or die slowly right fucking now. Make the fucking call!" King said, holding the gun to Moose's shattered nose.

"Fuck it, press six," Moose said. He knew he was going to die, but he'd rather go quickly than have these fools torture his ass.

King smiled and pressed the six on the screen. He hit the SPEAKER option on the phone, and the line rang.

"What up, Big Moose? I thought your ass would be here by now. You missing a fucking circus here, nigga!" Red said.

Moose was silent for a moment. He looked back up at King and knew that his time was over on this earth. King raised the barrel of his Colt and pressed it against Moose's nose, causing him to yell out in pain.

"Moose, what the fuck is that noise? Moose!" Red yelled.

King pulled the trigger twice, causing Moose to fall backward.

"Oh, shit!" Red yelled.

"What's up, Red? You next, nigga," King said and laughed. There was silence on the phone. "You can't say nothing? See, I have some humanity within me. I killed your boy quick. Shit, I even let you hear his spirit leave his body. Take this as a warning. Don't fuck with me, and nigga you lucky I didn't make it rain up in Club Nikki's with bullets for you and your girl!" King hit END on his phone and nodded to Shark and Marcus to get going.

The men went out of the back door and disappeared into the darkness. Kareem checked the front door and scanned the street. Marcus and Shark moved the bodies of the dealers and placed them in one of their cars. The bodies of the two other men were in the dining room.

While Shark gathered the money and drugs, Marcus poured the kerosene from the heater over the bodies and throughout the house.

King took out the box of matches they had found on the mantle and threw them in the dining room, lighting up the two corpses. He took the remaining kerosene and doused Moose's body, and then flicked a match on it. He and Kareem ran out of the back door.

King stopped shortly to watch the house succumb to the orange flames that were leaping through the windows.

"Got 'em for you, Strap," King said as he turned to run behind Kareem.

Panama watched as the flames leapt from the roof of the house and lit up the street. He tapped Trip on the shoulder and motioned that it was time for them to leave.

"Well, that shit is done!" Trip said as he leapt from one level of the roof to another.

"Yeah, for now man, for now," Panama said, looking at the house.

Chapter 5

"Man, I'ma wipe your bitch ass off the face of the earth. That's my blood, nigga. That's my fuckin' blood!" Red was on his feet screaming into the phone. He couldn't believe what he had just heard.

"Red, what happened? Why are you hollering?" Dover asked. He could tell that some major shit had gone down with Moose. He knew that robbing Carlton and King was going to come back to haunt them.

"We out. Them niggas done touched my family. On my life, I'ma send they ass to hell," Red said, as tears poured down his face.

The three men left the club and got in Red's car. "Let me drive, man. You too fucked up," Texas said.

"Yeah, man, whatever. Just get me to the trap," Red said tiredly as he tried his damnest to stop his tears. He hated for his boys to see him acting soft, but Moose was more than a cousin; they were like brothers.

"Now, what the fuck happened? Who was on the phone?" Dover asked again.

"I got a call from Moose's cell phone. But when I answered, all I heard was him screaming. Then I heard two shots before that muthafucka King got on the line and started talking shit. Man, that nigga dead, I swear," Red said and punched the palm of his hand for emphasis.

"How they know it was us?" Texas said.

"Hell if I know. I know I bodied that nigga, Strap, and everybody else in the house. The street was dead, so I know that nobody saw me over there," Red answered.

“Damn, them niggas knew it was us, and they knew where our trap is. How the fuck they get all that in a day?”

“Shit, now that you mention it, King even said something about Peaches and coming to Nikki’s. How the hell this nigga know so much about us?” Red narrowed his eyes and glared at his comrades.

“I know you don’t think either one of us is out here running our mouth. Nigga, we been with your ass from day one,” Dover said.

“Man, fuck all that. Just get me to the spot. I gotta see what’s going on.”

When they turned on Fourth Street, the area near the house was blocked off. Police and fire vehicles were everywhere. Texas parked the car and they got out and joined the crowd that had gathered across the street. It took everything in him for Red not to run over and demand some information. He had to lay low because he didn’t want to draw attention to himself without knowing what was in the house.

After almost fifteen minutes, the fire was under control. A hush fell over the crowd as the bodies were carried out of the ruined house. Red sat on the curb and put his head in his hands. Not only had he lost his cousin and his workers, he had also taken a substantial hit to his money and work.

“If it’s the last thing I do, cuz, I’ma get them niggas for you. I’m gone get ’em.” Red blinked back his tears, got up, and walked over to his boys.

“We’re reporting live from the scene of a deadly house fire on Fourth Street, which claimed the lives of several men last night. As you can see, the house was completely destroyed, and the house next door was severely damaged. Police have also told us that they found two dead bodies in a car two houses down from this home. It is unclear if the house fire and the bodies are connected. Police are saying very little at this time, but as new details emerge, we will be right here to keep you informed. I'm Maureen O'Boyle, reporting for Channel Nine news. Back to you, Jeff."

King smirked as he watched the house burn. Whoever said that a life for a life would not make you feel better was lying. He sipped his Corona and let his mind travel back to the moment when he pulled the trigger on Moose. Now, when he closed his eyes, he saw his boy smiling at him instead of him lying lifeless in his arms.

King's phone rang, and Strap's face faded from his mind. King grabbed the phone and looked at the screen. Instantly, his head began to hurt.

"Dis trick," King said, looking at Yessenia's picture flashing on the screen. King almost slid his finger to IGNORE but thought better of it. "Yeah," King said as he stood up.

His stomach was growling. Thank God, his mother always packed leftovers for him when they had Sunday dinner.

"So, I need some money. The baby needs shoes, summer gear, and I got some bills I need to pay. You know bills, right? They come every damn month," Yessenia said, popping gum.

King could hear music blaring in the background, and females laughing and cursing.

"Bitches, y'all need to quit that damn cussing. My baby down the hall sleeping. Turn that damn music down!" Yessenia yelled.

"You gon' tell us to stop cursing, but you cussing," a woman said.

"Jan, go sit your big ass down," Yessenia said, laughing.

"Yessenia, what do you want? I got things to do."

Yessenia was annoying as hell. She had an identical twin sister who was away in law school, and they couldn't be more different. Her sister, Yasmine, was a good girl who wanted to have a family, career, and live peacefully. Yessenia had the same intellectual capacity as Yasmine, but she preferred to apply her skills to doing nothing. She was smart, quick-witted, and definitely, a chick you would want to have on your team—if she wasn't so lazy. She had tried to be there with King on his moves, but after his father passed away, King and the streets became closer lovers than he and Yessenia. His absence combined with her constant nagging and lack of motivation to get a job destroyed their romantic feelings for each other.

King continued to pay for the condo that Yessenia and his daughter lived in, and he made sure that the rent, utility, and medical bills were covered. If he could help it, he never put money in Yessenia's hands. Giving her money meant the lights would be cut off because she would spend the money on the latest kicks and freshest hairstyle. Truth be told, his main reason for keeping her up, aside from his daughter, was that he didn't want her fucking around with a bunch of niggas to get money.

King knew that many niggas in the streets would fuck with her just to dog her out so they could run around town, bragging about how they banged King's baby mama out. He couldn't have that on his name. Also, as much as Yessenia didn't want to get her own, King had to admit that she was a loving mother; and as lazy as she was, she made sure their daughter was book-smart and well-mannered.

Although she was commendable as a mother, housekeeping was not her strong suit. Walking into the condo, a person would have to run an obstacle course just to navigate through the living room. She would just place dishes in the sink, as opposed to loading the dishwasher; and the bathroom was something that made King's stomach burn whenever he thought of it. He couldn't stand knowing that his little girl was living in clutter and mess, so he made sure a maid service stopped by the condo once a week. He was mortified when one of the women from the cleaning service, who attended the same church as his mother, made it her business to call Yogi and tell her how filthy Yessenia's house was. His mother wasted no time calling him and giving him an earful about her embarrassment from having the church members gossiping about the horrible condition of the home where her only grandchild lived.

"What bill you need to pay, Ye? I pay all the bills, and if the baby needs shoes, I will stop by and get her to take her shopping," King said, trying to hold his temper.

"King, you not getting her. I hear you got some issues with Red, and I don't want my baby getting shot while you out there running around like you stupid. So, no, you can't get her."

King was quiet for a moment. He needed to count to ten in order to calm down. There was no way anyone would ever keep him from his daughter. If Yessenia wasn't his baby mama, he would put her face through a wall for saying some crazy shit like that. But in reality, although what she said had pissed him off, it was the truth. Maybe, right now wasn't a good time.

"What do you know about my business? If she needs something, then drop her off at my mama's, and she will take her shopping. The next time I tell you I want to see her, there ain't going to be no discussion. You got that?" King said, walking out onto his balcony. The phone was quiet for a moment. He heard Yessenia inhale, but he stopped her before she could speak. "Look, all you need to say is 'yes' and none of that other shit."

King waited for her to respond. He could hear Yessenia mumble and suck her teeth. He laughed as he envisioned what her face looked like at that moment. He really was just fucking with her at this point. He liked pissing her off from time to time, hoping that it would ignite a flame in her to get up and do something with her life. Yessenia was a beautiful woman, and she just needed to apply herself. She could go from street talk to corporate boardroom chat in a moment's notice. She had light brown skin with golden undertones, large brown eyes, 38DDD breasts, a slim waist, and full tight hips. She had curves that would make any man stop and look.

"King, why you got to be an asshole? You don't want me fucking with nobody else, but you don't want to give me nothing but enough money to live and take care of our child."

"Shit, I'm looking out for you. You know all these niggas want to do is jump up and down on you and keep pushing. Besides, I don't want these losers you be wanting to fuck with around my baby. So, like I said, call my mama, and she will take you shopping. And pull your lip in, I'll load some money on your PayPal card for you. This time, try budgeting," King said before he hit END on his phone.

King looked at the screen for a few moments. He thought about how he sometimes regretted ever putting his seed in Yessenia, but he had never regretted having his princess, Malani. He placed his phone on the counter and exhaled.

"That girl is exhausting, shit!" King said aloud.

King walked into his home office and sat at his desk. His eyes landed on the loot from the other night. It was still in the backpacks on the floor. King got up from his desk and went over to the backpacks. He unzipped one of them and began counting the money. As he counted, he felt his heart become heavy at the thought of Strap's mother and the way her heart must be aching. She had not only lost her son, but she had just lost a daughter to domestic violence two weeks prior to Strap's death. Jamica was married to, of all things, a police officer. Dude beat her ass on a constant, and every time Strap and King would try to handle things for her, she would beg them not to get involved. Her death was still under investigation by the detectives of CMPD, the same force where her husband was a detective. King was sure that they were not really working hard to solve her case.

King's stomach growled again, so he stretched and walked into the kitchen. He took the leftovers from Sunday dinner out and warmed them in the microwave. He needed to do something to get his head out of all the fucked up shit that had happened over the last few days.

The doorbell rang.

King checked the security monitor by the door and let Kareem in. He was laughing as usual. "Hey man, what's up? Look who I met outside."

Yogi stepped from behind Kareem smiling. "Hey baby, I'm on my way to get a couple of outfits for this weekend. I am going with the ladies to the mountains," Yogi said as she kissed King's cheek and walked inside. "I hope it's okay that I dropped by."

"You are welcome to drop by anytime, Ma," King said and hugged her.

Kareem closed the door behind him and headed toward the kitchen while King walked his mother into the den. She looked around and sat down on the couch.

"Hey man, bring me a beer while you in there scavenging in my fridge," King said, laughing. "Ma, you want something? I got juice, water, soda—"

"I will take a glass of ginger ale. Have you had breakfast? If not, I can take you two out and we can talk," Yogi said.

"Now, Ms. Yogi, you know I ain't gonna turn down a free meal," Kareem said, coming from the kitchen with her glass of ginger ale.

"That sounds good, Ma," King said, checking his phone. "Why don't you call Khristian too, I haven't spoken to her in a while."

"That sounds like a plan. Let me call her and we can be on our way," Yogi said as she took out her phone.

An hour later, King handed his keys to the valet as the other valet opened the door for his mother. Kareem pulled up behind them in the black BMW X6 that King had purchased for him. King smirked as the young valet eyed Yogi up and down. His mother flirted with the young man for a few moments while they waited for Kareem.

Kareem walked up and extended his arm to her. Yogi giggled and took his arm as King shook his head and opened the door.

"For you, Queen B," King said and bowed.

"Thank you, young sir," Yogi said and walked inside. The three of them walked up to the host stand.

The hostess had red hair, styled in a short pixie cut. She wore a white button-down uniform shirt, and HANNAH was on her name tag.

"Welcome to Brio, how many are in your party?" Hannah asked as she gathered the menus.

"I'm not sure, we have others joining us," Yogi said. "My daughter was with her friends, and I am not sure if they are going to come with her. So let's say eight, to be safe."

"Okay, a table for about six to eight people? Please follow me." Hannah led them through the dining area to the enclosed patio. "Will this be okay?"

"This is perfect, thank you," Yogi said.

Kareem pulled her chair out for her and, then, took his seat on the opposite side of the table facing her.

"So, boys, tell me what has been going on with you two," Yogi said as she looked over the menu."Yessenia called me this morning asking for money, saying she needed money for the baby and bills."

"And I know you gave it to her, didn't you?"

"Well, yes and no. I gave her a little money to hold her over, and I told her to bring Malani to you, and you could take her shopping."

"King, Yessenia is a selfish girl, but she is a good mother. However, someone needs to talk to her about her behavior. She needs to get a job and learn how to start living off what you have provided her. And she needs to learn how to keep a clean house, but as long as you keep giving in to her, she's not going to do what she needs to do. Now tell me, son, are you still sleeping with her?

"No, Ma, I'm not."

"Are you?" Yogi asked with a raised brow.

"No, for real. I'm not, Ma."

"Man, forget about him, Ms. Yogi. I got real baby mama problems," Kareem chimed in.

"Child, you ain't got no problems. As far as Tiana, she is only asking that you be around to help raise the children and stay out of jail. But you got to remind her that she knew what it was when she got into it with you," Yogi spoke while sipping her mimosa. "You boys got to learn that just because it looks good, doesn't always mean it is good for you."

"Hey, bro! Hey, Mommy!" Khristian said when the hostess escorted her to the table.

"Hey, sis, look at you." King embraced Khristian. "Come on, have a seat," King said, pulling out a chair for her.

"Thank you," Khristian said.

"Hello, everybody," Imani, Kristian's best friend said. "Hey, Ms. Yogi, I am loving that blouse!"

"Hey, baby, come on, sit down. I haven't seen you at the house in a while. How are your parents?"

"They are good. They're in Hawaii right now. My daddy had to go to a convention. I have been working a lot lately, which is why I haven't been by the house. You know I miss those Sunday dinners."

"Well, the two of you know you need to go to church with me and, then, have dinner. I know you are grown, but you still need family and the Lord in your lives," Yogi said, squeezing Imani's hand and looking at Khristian.

"Yes ma'am, I promise we will stop by soon. I am so glad we got together for brunch. So how is my niece doing?" Khristian said, looking at King.

"She's fine. You know she needs some clothes and shoes. Why don't you, Imani, and Mama pick her up and take her shopping today?" King said.

"That would be fun!"

King reached in his pocket and handed Khristian a stack of money.

"Dang, bro, she is only five. You want me to buy the entire mall? It's like five racks here."

"Nah, that's for all four of you. Have fun on me, sis."

Khristian squealed and hugged King. "Thank you, bro!"

King loved seeing Khristian happy. When his mother married Carlton, she was only eight years old. Khristian followed him everywhere he went, and King loved having a little sister. He never knew or asked about her mother, he just remembered her coming to live with them when Carlton married Yogi. Khristian had an innocence that was rare with an OG's daughter. She was always happy, smart, and giving. King and Carlton spoiled her as much as humanly possible, but she was far from being a brat. She was determined to make her own way in the world.

She was in college, had a job at a lawyer's office as a receptionist, and had her own apartment.

Occasionally, King would pay a utility bill for her not because she asked, but because he wanted to feel like he was helping. She had grown up so quickly, and much like Carlton, King just liked feeling needed by her sometimes.

Everyone ate brunch and caught up on what was going on in their lives. Khristian and Imani laughed a lot, and Kareem stared at Imani the entire time. Watching how her nose crinkled when she was amused and how she cut her food, he felt like he was seeing her for the first time. He wasn't seeing her as the friend of King's little sister, but as what she was, a beautiful woman.

Chapter 6

King sighed as he listened to the women's chatter. He had, somehow, been convinced to meet them at the house and drive them to the mall. Yessenia had dropped Malani off, and King was glad he had missed her before he arrived. He looked in the rearview mirror at his sister, Imani, and his daughter. His mother sat quietly in the passenger's seat looking out the window. He pulled up to the front of the mall near the food court entrance.

"All right, ladies, curb side service. I will meet you inside after I find a space," King said as he got out to open the doors for the women.

Malani giggled and jumped down. "Thank you, Daddy," she said. "Aunt Khristian said I can get a big sugar cookie!"

"Oh, she did?" King said, looking at Khristian. "Well, don't eat too much, okay? You don't want to ruin your appetite for dinner."

"Okay, Daddy," she said with her infamous pout.

Yogi laughed and held her hand out for her. "Come on, lady bug. Let's go get you some new clothes!"

King watched them walk into the mall, and then, he turned to walk back to the driver's side of the truck. As he opened the door, he noticed a black Monte Carlo slowly driving by. King felt his pulse quicken as he watched the car. He stepped inside the SUV, and watched as the car drove up an aisle, passing several empty parking spaces.

King checked his console for his Smith & Wesson and pulled away from the curb, looking for the closest parking spot he could find. He found a space near the front door and backed into it, scanning the parking lot for the Monte Carlo the whole time. The car seemed to have disappeared from sight. King took out his phone and sent a text to Panama. He wanted to ensure that if something popped off, he had some extra heat behind him. He put the gun in his waist and pulled his shirt over it.

"I can't have a damn moment's peace!" King said to himself as he opened the door of the SUV. He checked the lot once again and walked toward the entrance of the mall.

As he reached the mall, he caught the reflection of the black Monte Carlo in the large glass doors. He turned around, and the car window on the passenger's side began to come down. King could feel his blood flowing through his veins, and he placed his hand on the butt of his gun. The car stopped, and King swallowed. The Monte Carlo idled for a few seconds and, then, slowly pulled away from the curb. King could not make out anyone inside, due to the limousine tint that was on the windows. He pushed the glass door, and walked inside.

The aroma of the food court surrounded him. He did not realize that he was walking with his hand still on the butt of his gun until he reached the elevator and caught a glimpse of himself in the doors. He relaxed his arm and pushed the white button with the arrow pointing up. King held the door for a woman with a baby stroller before he pressed the number 3. His heart slowly returned to its regular beat, and he relaxed his shoulders.

As he exited the elevator, he took his phone out and texted his mother to let her know where he was located. He knew the women were probably knee deep in shoes or something by now. Sending his mother a text was the best way to get a response. He knew his sister and Imani probably were trying on the latest must-have fashions. Shopping was the only reason either of them would not respond to a text message within seconds.

King placed the phone back in his pocket and walked into Milan's Jewelry. He headed straight for the Rolex watches and diamond bracelets.

"Good afternoon, my name is Sloan. May I show you something?"

"Yeah, I want to see this Rolex right here," King said without looking up.

"That is a beautiful piece."

King sighed. He didn't need to hear anything about the craftsmanship or how many karats it was, he just wanted to see how it would look on his wrist. He continued looking at the other watches as she opened the display case.

"Okay, sir," the salesperson said.

King looked up as she held the watch for him to view. He felt a shiver go down his spine as he met the largest set of coal-black eyes he had ever seen. The red lipstick highlighted full lips and made her white teeth gleam. King's eyes scanned the face that was in front of him. He cleared his throat, hoping that his voice would return.

"Would you like to try it on, sir?" Sloan asked, unaware of the effect that she was having on King.

King shook his head and held out his arm.

She placed the watch on his wrist. "It fits you," she said. "Sir, are you okay? Do you not like it?"

"Umm, no . . . yeah, I like it," King finally said, looking at the watch on his arm. "Yeah, yeah it looks good."

"It is gorgeous, and it will go from casual to business." Sloan continued while King studied her lips. The words that were coming from them were inaudible to him, but their perfect shape mesmerized him.

"Yeah, umm . . . Do you have any crosses?" King asked, trying to get his thoughts together. "Something elegant but eye-catching."

"Yes, I think I have what you are looking for," Sloan said, taking the Rolex off his arm.

She placed it back in the case and walked over to a black case that displayed several necklaces with cross pendants. She opened the display and pulled out a beautiful gold cross with diamonds trailing down the center. "I can fit it to any chain you like," she said.

"You know, that looks like something she would like," King answered while looking at the cross. "I would rather have it on a bracelet but something unique."

"Well, I can have our designer come out and sketch something for you," Sloan added, getting her salesmanship on.

King studied her. She had a full bust line, slender waist, and full hips. She played her figure down by wearing a conservative white blouse and black pencil skirt. She was articulate and sophisticated.

"I'll tell you what, Sloan. You design it for me," King spoke, feeling his cool coming back.

Sloan laughed. "Well, okay. But, at least, tell me something about your wife, so I will know where to start," she answered.

"I can't tell you anything about my wife."

"You can't? Why?"

"Well, she hasn't agreed to come to dinner with me yet." Sloan had a puzzled look on her face. "So, Sloan, will you have dinner with me? That way, I can learn what my wife might like," King uttered in his smoothest tone.

Sloan's eyes widened then she laughed. "You are funny! Corny, but funny!" she said.

"So, corny, huh? Well, are you going to go out with this cornball?" King said, flashing his smile at her. "By the way, my name is King."

"I must say, you really have a sense of humor . . . King?" Sloan said, rolling her eyes. "So do you want me to have the designer come out?"

"No, I don't. I want you to design it for me. It is for a special woman, and it needs to be exquisite, and I can tell . . ." King said, looking over her body. "You understand style. I will, also, take that Rolex and your phone number." King handed her his Black Card, along with one of his business cards. Sloan giggled as she looked at his credit card.

"You were not joking about your name being King."

"No, why would I joke about that? That would really make me a cornball." King laughed

She shook her head and walked over to the register. "I need you to fill out this paperwork for your watch, and sign the order for the bracelet." Sloan placed the papers on a clipboard and handed it to him.

King began filling out the paper work as she rang up his purchases. She keyed information into the computer and the printer began to whirl.

"Okay, Mr. King, here is your paperwork, your card, and here is my card. I see you have an e-mail on your business card, so I will e-mail you when the bracelet is ready for you to pick up."

"And what about you?"

"I'm sorry?"

"What time can I pick you up?" King said as he placed his card back in his wallet. "I am serious about dinner. If you are comfortable meeting me somewhere, that is fine. How about Ruth's Chris tomorrow evening at six?"

"You don't stop, do you? Well, I can't. I have to work tomorrow."

"Right, right. Well, then, I will pick you up on Friday," King said, taking the bag from Sloan. "Or I will call you, and you can tell me where you can meet me."

"I tell you what. You can meet me at The Cup at nine on Friday. Do you know where it is? It's off of King Drive."

"Nine on Friday? I will be there."

"Mhmm," she said, walking away. "Have a good one."

"This is so cute!" Khristian said as she held up the little red sweater dress. "Come on, Malani. Let's try it on."

"I like that one 'cause it has a unicorn on the hood!" Malani said as she ran to the dressing room.

Khristian laughed and followed her.

Yogi shook her head and sat down in a large pink chair with purple and green hearts on it.

Imani continued looking through the racks of little rompers and dresses. Total Girl really lived up to its name. Everything was pastel-colored, frilly, and had plenty of little animals to make any little girl squeal with joy. Imani felt her phone vibrate. She smiled as she looked the screen.

> I can taste you right now. Can't wait until this evening, I want you now. Where are you?

"I know that look. You are smiling too hard, you're lighting the entire store up," Yogi said and chuckled.

"Oh, it's nothing, Ms. Yogi. Just a friend," Imani said as she sat down on the small white stool.

"Child, please, I may be old, but I know the look and the smile when someone is in love. So, who is he, where is he from, and what does he do?" Yogi asked, crossing her legs.

"Whoa, Ms. Yogi, you want his genetic code too?"

"Well, if you got that and his fingerprints, that would be a good start."

"Look, Nana!" Malani said interrupting the ladies' conversation.

Yogi twirled her around. "Don't you look pretty!"

"Yes, we do," Khristian responded as she joined Malani, who was, now, dancing and singing.

"Okay, okay. Let's get a few more things, and then, we can go to the toy store!" Khristian said, out of breath.

"Toys! I know exactly which one I'm getting. Come on, Auntie, help me get this dress off so we can go!"

"Slow down, good grief!" Yogi said to Malani as she zoomed by her to the dressing room. "The store isn't going anywhere, my Lord!"

Imani shook her head. She looked at her phone and sent a text back.

At the mall with fam now, but I can't wait to see you later. I bought something I know you are going to like.

I like you naked laying back on the bed with my face between them thighs.

Imani giggled. She felt her nipples becoming hard, and she was warm all over.

"So, you not going to give me details about this new man?" Yogi said, studying Imani.

"What man? Oh, you mean the one I still have not met?" Khristian said as she walked out of the dressing room, right into the conversation.

"Maybe she will tell you something about him because she is tight-lipped around me. I think he is either really old or ugly."

"Shut up, Khristian!" Imani said and threw a sweater at her.

"What . . . I mean, I haven't met him, and you have been out of town with him a few times. You never bring him to the apartment, and you guys are always meeting out. I mean, what is the big secret? Seems like you are sneaking around to me."

"Yeah, sneaking around," Malani repeated.

"Hey, watch your mouth, little girl!" Yogi said, tickling her. "Let's go pay for your pretty outfits." Yogi and Malani walked off, but Khristian continued the interrogation.

"So, you got another booty call from the mysterious man?" Khristian asked as she checked her lip gloss.

"It is not a booty call, and don't be jealous. When was the last time you had your walls rubbed by something that wasn't battery operated?" Imani said, not looking up from her phone.

"Woo . . . going for the jugular? He must be laying it down."

"Shut up, Khristian. You so stupid," Imani said and stood up. "Come on, your mother is ready to go."

Khristian and Imani walked out of the store with Yogi and Malani ahead of them. Khristian and Imani walked arm in arm, stopping occasionally to look in the store windows.

"Oh, that would be so hot on me!" Khristian squealed as she looked at a red cocktail dress.

"Yeah, that would look good on you," a voice said from behind them.

Khristian and Imani turned to see a tall young girl smiling at them. "Hi, Khristian, how are you?"

"Umm, hi, Cara. How are you?" Khristian responded.

"I'm great. Doing some shopping?" Cara asked, forcing a smile and looking at Imani, whose arm was still linked with Khristian's.

"Yeah, me and the fam came out to do some shopping. This is my best friend, Imani. Imani, this is Cara."

"Nice to meet you, Cara, and where did you get those pants? They are fire!" Imani asked.

"I got them from Mohawks on level two, and thanks. I think I bought the first pair they had. They were bringing them from the back, and they had a lot of different colors."

"Well, I want a pair! Did they have purple?"

"Umm, I'm not sure, but if they don't have them in the store, I'm sure you can get them online," Cara said, not taking her eyes off Khristian.

"Sweet!" Imani's phone buzzed. "Excuse me, I need to take this," Imani said and walked toward the railing.

"Well, you're looking good, Khristian. I haven't heard from you in a while," Cara said.

"Yeah, well, you know I got busy. I had papers to write and work. Call me sometime, and we can hang out. I need to get going," Khristian said as she turned to walk toward Imani. As she walked by Cara, she felt her hand on her elbow.

"I will call you, Khristian," Cara whispered as she slid her finger up Khristian's arm.

Khristian gently pulled away from her and quickly walked in the direction she had seen her stepmother and Malani walk in.

King sat near the window of the food court. He could see Panama sitting in a black Sonoma. He had parked in a space near the doors, right next to the handicap parking spaces. King knew that, if Panama was visible, the rest of the crew was lurking somewhere less noticeable. Hiring Panama had been one of the best moves he could have made. Although expensive, Panama brought talent and loyalty to his team—something that many other Kingpins didn't have. Panama's mother lived in Washington. She was the only thing or person that could make the man smile. Taking care of her was all he cared about. He would live on the streets under a bridge, as long as his mother lived well. Like King, Panama had lost his father, but he was not quite as lucky as King to have a stepfather who was a real dude. His mother had ended up with a broke ass African dude who liked to use her for boxing practice. He was Panama's first kill.

King sipped his coffee and scanned the parking lot. He didn't see any signs of the black Monte Carlo, but his instincts told him that some shit could still pop off.

He placed his ear buds in his ears and surfed his phone's music library. Soon, Maxwell's "Till the Cops Come Knocking" flowed into his ears. Music was the connection that he had to his father, and it always made him feel safe. It helped him clear his mind, and right now, he needed to be focused. The next few weeks would be critical. He had to move some weight from Miami to North Carolina. He also needed to obtain a new block for his business, not to mention the big concert that he had coming up. King was the owner of RK Entertainment Group. He was known for bringing the hottest hip-hop and R&B acts to Charlotte, and his state-of-the-art pre and postproduction music studio was a favorite among the local artists.

Some of King's best memories were of him listening to music with his father. They had their deepest conversations while listening to The Isley Brothers; Earth, Wind, and Fire; and Reggie's favorite, Frankie Beverly. King thought of how his father would ride around town with the windows down, some R&B playing, a bag of barbecue chips, and a cold bottle of grape soda. It would be just the two of them, riding around on a hot summer day, looking at pretty girls and talking.

"Boy, ain't nothing in this world that music can't cure. You can make babies to it, drink to it, and at times take niggas out to it," his father would say.

Young King nodded as he listened to his father.

King was twelve when his father had started letting him collect money from the trap houses. Learning the business from one of the biggest Kingpins in the southeast had made him what he was today. He remembered thinking that nothing and no one could touch his father. But Death is going to get everybody eventually. He learned that the hard way.

King later discovered that he had a real talent for putting together hot shows and throwing parties. Of course, it didn't hurt that the entertainment industry was one of the best places to clean money. Cleaning drug money was not an easy task; one had to be patient, smart, and willing to take chances.

King had opened Reggie's three years after his father's death. An old-school-style supper club catering to the grown and sexy, he brought all of his R&B shows there. Every third Thursday of the month, he held the popular "Reggie's Revue," an open mic night. Between Reggie's, his entertainment company, and his chain of barbershops, he had enough legitimate, cash-based businesses to clean his money with no problem.

"Daddy, Daddy, I got a cookie, and I bought you one too. Do you want it?" Malani asked, holding the red bag up to King.

King pulled the ear buds out of his ears, grabbed the bag, and then, grabbed her. She squealed as King tickled her. "No, Daddy," she said between giggles. "You have to eat your cookie. It's your favorite, oatmeal raisin."

"Oatmeal raisin? That is my favorite. Well, have a seat, and I will share it with ya," King said and kissed her forehead.

"No, no, ma'am. You have already had two of those cookies. No more until after dinner for you," Yogi said, walking up with her arms full of bags. She sat down in the chair and exhaled. "Whew, I think we got more than enough for this little girl. I don't think Santa is going to be able to make anything that you don't already have."

"Ma, did you get anything for yourself?" King asked, looking at the bags.

"Oh baby, I just grabbed some cleanser for my face. That is all I really needed."

King shook his head as he took a bite of his cookie. "So where are the Doublemint Twins?"

"We are right here." Khristian spoke. "Ready?"

"Yeah, if you guys are ready. Did you leave anything in the stores?" King said as he stood. He picked Malani up and they walked toward the large glass doors. King held the doors for his mother, Khristian and Imani, who still had her head down texting. Tommy pulled up to the curb with King's SUV.

"I didn't know the mall had valet service," Khristian said, taking Malani from King.

"They don't, but when you are riding with the King, you can get things other people can't," King said and winked at his sister.

"Shut up and drive, chauffeur!" Khristian said as she buckled Malani's seatbelt.

"We got everything covered, man. We had people on Red, and . . ." Tommy stopped talking, and sighed.

"And what, man?" King asked, closing the driver's door.

"And he here at the mall, man, with some chick."

King laughed and clapped his hands. "You mean the muthafucka in there now?"

"Yeah, we got Jinx following him. From what Jinx is saying, dude just shopping."

King leaned against the SUV and ran his hand over his face. "I don't believe in coincidences, Tommy," he said as he opened the door. "Keep an eye on the nigga. I'm gonna take the fam home."

"I told you, we got you, man," Tommy said, closing the door.

King put on his Tom Ford shades and looked in the side rearview mirror. He pulled out, and a white F-150 with limousine-tinted windows followed.

"Everything okay?" Yogi asked. She could tell that King was tense by the tightness in his jaw and the vein that was showing in the right side of his neck.

Yogi smiled weakly. Every day, he looked and acted more like his father. At times, when she glanced at him, she could swear that her husband was standing in front of her. She turned to look out of the window, found her shades, and put them on. Carlton was a wonderful husband, father, provider, and lover. She loved him as best she could, but her heart would always belong to her first love, Reggie. She touched her necklace and inhaled, thinking of how Reggie's laughter could make everything else in the world disappear; how he could tell her that everything was going to be okay, and she would believe it without a doubt.

"Hey, Ma, you okay?" King asked as he turned down Haven Road.

"Yeah, baby, just a little sinus problem is all," Yogi said, wiping her nose. "Thank you for today, baby. I really enjoyed it."

"Ah, anytime, Ma, and thanks for getting your grandbaby straight."

"No problem, baby. Oh, I love that song. That girl is singing about some pain," Yogi said as she turned the radio up.

All three the women sang along.

Last night I cried, tossed, and turned. Woke up with dry eyes. . . .

"That is a depressing song, Ma," King said as he pulled into the driveway of his parents' house.

"Baby, that song is not depressing. It is a woman's pain and a story of how she will love again! If you find a woman who can sing about her pain, and sing it with soul; well, you've found a woman who knows life!"

"Or needs some meds," King said, opening the door for his mother.

Yogi popped his arm.

King walked around to the back of his SUV and began unloading the bags. Today was a day that was few and far between for him. It was a day without gunfire or murder. He wasn't worried about his dope or picking up money from his trap houses. He had not gotten any calls from his crew about anybody being shot. So far, it had been what King imagined most people do every weekend—spend time with their family. King wanted more days like this.

Chapter 7

"Man, why the fuck do I need to bring Tiana with me tonight?" Kareem asked as he wrapped the towel around his waist. "I don't want to be nagged. Shit, I need to have some fun this weekend. Being with her is worse than being locked up at times. I mean, I got a damn job! It don't pay shit, either. I just need to blow off some steam."

Kareem had been stressed ever since Tiana got him the job at a paper warehouse. He worked in stocking for fucking ten dollars an hour. Most of the fools that worked there were clueless about having anything decent in their fucking lives, and they were breaking their backs for peanuts. Shit, when he went to work, he would have ten of his paychecks already in his pocket. Tiana bitched about him being in the game, but she didn't bitch about riding around in his luxury trucks with the kids and shit.

He didn't get Tiana sometimes. She didn't want him in the game, but as soon as he came home from doing a bid, she quit her job and told him she was going to school to become certified in home day care. He was happy to support his family and would do things Tiana's way . . . for now.

"Dude, just bring her. You should bring her out for a night on the town. At least, it will buy you some peace for a little while," King said. "Besides, this is a new club we are going to, and I need a good set of eyes and hands with me in case some shit jumps off."

"Nigga, I'll tell you who I should be bringing there tonight."

"Who?" King asked, curious to know who else Kareem could be talking about

"That girl, Imani. Brah, she done really grew up and filled out."

"Man, you tripping. She too young for you. Besides, she looks at us like we are her brothers."

"Naw, nigga, she look at you like that. That ain't got nothing to do with me. How Keith Sweat say, 'she maybe young, but she ready,'" Kareem continued while laughing.

"I ain't fucking with your thirsty ass tonight. Just finish getting ready, and holla at me when you outside the spot."

"A'ight, I got you. Meet you there in an hour," Kareem responded.

"Oh yeah, and afterward, I need you to head over to Hawthorne. I need my money from our trap. They been coming up short lately. Just scoop it up for me. Damn, I almost forgot. This club don't allow jeans, man, so you gotta put on your grown man shit to get in."

"Brah, you know I stays on my Ebony status shit, I got it."

"This is actually nice, Kareem," Tiana said, looking around the club. "Not what I expected from you at all."

"Your table is ready, sir. Please follow me," the host said as he extended his arm for Tiana. Tiana giggled and took the arm of the tall host. He flashed his smile at her and she felt a tingle in her spine.

"Right this way, madam. By the way, my name is Anthony."

Kareem shook his head as he and King followed Anthony down the stairs to a table close to the stage.

Anthony pulled the chair out for Tiana and placed three menus on the table.

"Your server will be with you shortly. Enjoy," Anthony said, winking at Tiana.

"This dude," Kareem said and shook his head.

"What? Jealous, baby? I am sure he does that with all the people that come here. It's part of the ambience of the place. Oh, I know what I want. I have never had one before, but I am going to order it."

King checked his phone. It was eight forty-five. He couldn't believe he had actually shown up early for a female.

"So, how did you hear about this place, man?" Kareem asked, looking at King.

"A friend told me about it. She should be meeting us here."

"A friend? What friend?" Kareem said, eyeing King.

"Nigga, you'll see. Just chill."

"Good evening, my name is Honey, and I will be your server tonight. Can I start you off with drinks?"

"Hi, Honey. You can. I would like a sangria," Tiana said.

"Sangria for the lady, and the gentlemen?"

"You can bring us whatever you have in dark beer," King said, looking at the staircase.

"Okay, and would you like some of our wings to start with? We have southern-style, garlic, and buffalo."

"You can bring us southern-style please, with hot sauce on the side," Tiana said with excitement.

King looked at Kareem. Tiana was acting and behaving like she doesn't get out much, which was actually true. Tiana, unlike so many chicks who had men locked up, had remained faithful to Kareem. She spent any free time she did have in church with her children. As soon as she had begun going to church, she started in on King about Kareem not coming back to the life.

King never argued with her, but he knew that it would be Kareem's decision to make. He was surprised when she stopped accepting money from him because he couldn't see how she was supporting the children on her CNA salary. Tiana was from the projects, so help from her family was out of the question, as well. King had planned to ask Kareem about it, but it had slipped his mind. Now that Kareem was home, he didn't see the point in mentioning anything.

The waitress returned with their drinks and wings. She placed a bottle of Texas Pete on the table, along with white linen napkins and cutlery.

"Thank you," Tiana said as she sipped her drink. "Oh, this is delicious. Taste it, baby," Tiana said, handing the glass to Kareem.

"Will you need anything else right now?" Honey smiled at Kareem.

Tiana was so caught up in the moment of actually being out of the house and on a date with Kareem, she did not notice Honey checking her man out.

"No, umm, not right now," Kareem said, returning the smile to Honey.

"All right, I will be back to check on you."

Kareem watched Honey walk away. The black leather skirt hugged her hips and thighs. The white shirt she wore only came down to her midriff, exposing her flat toned stomach and navel piercing. She had her hair pinned up in a messy, sexy ponytail, and her caramel skin shimmered in the low light.

King cleared his throat and broke the trance that Kareem was under. He checked his watch again. It was nine o'clock, and there was no sign of Sloan. He was a little offended that she had not shown up or called. *Chill, playa it's just nine. You're the early one*, he reminded himself and chuckled. King wasn't used to waiting; he was usually waited for.

Thirty more minutes passed and the room had started to fill up. People were eating, chatting, and laughing all around him; but Sloan still hadn't arrived or called. King laughed to himself. *This must be karma getting me back for all the times I have stood chicks up.* His phone buzzed on his hip and he looked at the screen. There was a text message from a number he didn't recognize.

Don't look so disappointed. I invited you, remember?

King shook his head. He tried to hide the smile that spread across his face, but it was too late.

You like being in control, huh? He texted back.

Always. Just sit back and enjoy.

King looked at the host stand. He scanned the crowd and searched the people at the bar, trying to locate Sloan.

"Yo, dude, you a'ight?" Kareem asked as he sipped a glass of beer.

"Yeah, man, I'm good," King said, still looking around the club.

"Good evening, ladies and gentlemen. Welcome to The Cup. I am Trenton, your host for the evening. For those of you who are regulars, welcome back. For those that are new, welcome. Here at The Cup, we see everything half-full. So, in order to fill your glasses up, I introduce to you Sloan Deveaux." The purple curtains opened, and a soft spotlight glowed on the center of the stage.

"I'm home alone again, and you're out hanging with your friends.
So you say, somehow I know, it's not quite that way.
It's getting pretty late, and you haven't checked on me all day.

When I called, you didn't answer.
Now I'm feeling like you're ignoring me.
I wish that you were home.
Holding me tight in your arms
And I wish I could go back
To the day before we met
And skip my regret
I wish I wasn't in love with you
So you couldn't hurt me . . ."

King's mouth fell open as the spotlight shone on the singer. Her hair framed her face in a curly auburn afro. She wore a dark brown lip gloss, a white halter top that stopped above her navel, and a long sheer pink skirt that flowed to the floor. Her dark brown skin glowed as the soft light shone on it.

"Damn," King said aloud. He felt heat rise from his feet to his head as she sang each note, effortlessly, with perfect tone and pitch.

The song flowed from her, and like a siren, she held him in her trance. She sang three songs, and at the end of the last song, the curtain closed, and the room erupted with applause and whistles.

"Damn, old girl can blow, huh?" Tiana said applauding. "Her hair is the truth."

King put the glass up to his lips and realized it was empty.

"She has a voice on her, for sho. Shit, Tiana might get some when we get back home," Kareem said laughing.

"Yeah, I'm gonna go get me another drink. Y'all want something?" King asked as he stood up.

Kareem and Tiana looked at each other, but King walked away before they could answer his question.

King found his way to the bar and sat down on a blue barstool. His body was still warm from being caressed by Sloan's sultry performance.

"Mr. King, I see you made it."

King inhaled and bit his lip to keep himself from smiling. He had never met a female who made him want to smile like this.

"Yeah, I made it. I have to say, I am impressed. You didn't tell me that you could sing like that," he said as he motioned for the bartender to come over. "Hey, man, I need two Coronas, a sangria, and whatever the lady is drinking."

"Hey, Tony, I will take my usual," Sloan said, sitting down on the stool next to King.

"So you drinking sangria?"

"Do I look like I would ever order some shit like that?" King asked, leaning back against the bar.

He couldn't take his eyes off her. Her skin was flawless; the only makeup she wore was the dark chocolate lip gloss. Her brown skin looked soft and kissable. King studied her body in a way that was foreign to him. He was not imagining himself smashing it, but he was actually admiring her.

"Is something wrong?" she asked as the bartender handed her a glass of clear liquid.

"No, ma'am, nothing is wrong. In fact, everything is right. Are you going back on again?"

"Why, you got a request?"

King looked at her and, then, back at the table where Kareem and Tiana were sitting. He was actually speechless. His mind was blank. He couldn't think of anything witty to say to her.

Sloan laughed and patted his hand. "Geez, why so serious, your majesty?"

"I like when you call me that," King said as he grabbed the two Coronas and the glass of sangria. "This might sound like a line, but I can help your music career. I have a studio, and I, also, hold events around Charlotte,

Atlanta, and Miami. I got a show in a couple of weeks. How would you like to open for me? Is this your band?"

Sloan studied him for a moment. She was about to laugh because she wasn't sure if he was joking or being serious. "A studio, huh? What kind of show do you have?" she asked as she sipped her drink.

King extended his arm to her. "Hey, can you bring those drinks to that table over there?" He asked, sliding a crisp big face to the bartender.

The bartender nodded to King.

Sloan looked King over again. She had to admit, she was enjoying her word dance with this man. He was enigmatic, funny, and seemed to have himself together, at first glance. But Sloan knew that first impressions could, sometimes, be misleading. She had learned that lesson the hard way with her last relationship.

"Kareem, Tiana, this is—"

"The girl that can blow!" Tiana said. "Sit down, girl, sit down." Tiana patted the seat of the chair next to her.

Sloan took the seat, and Tiana hugged her.

"Babe, stop, you gonna scare her off, damn. Hey, I'm Kareem, and yo, you got a set . . ." Kareem paused as he looked over Sloan's full bust. He cleared his throat. "A set of pipes on you. Woo, yeah, King need to get you on his team," Kareem said as the waitress placed the drinks on the table. "Yeah, you know he got a big show coming up in couple of weeks, some pretty big names will be there."

Sloan looked at King, who sipped his drink as he used his phone.

King handed her his phone with a web page pulled up for her. Sloan searched the site and scanned the Getty's photos of King with Keyshia Cole, Anthony Hamilton, J. Cole, and other celebrities. Some of the females were really hanging on to him. King's handsome face stared at her from the small screen. She looked up and met his eyes, cleared her throat, and handed the phone back to him.

"So, are you from Charlotte?" Tiana asked Sloan.

"No, I'm from Jersey."

"That's what's up. Well, girl you sure can blow. If I could sing like that, you'd never get me to shut up," Tiana said and laughed.

"So, you never said whether you had another set or not," King said to Sloan as an old Xscape song came on.

Tiana grabbed Kareem's hand and pulled him up. "I love this song. Come dance with me."

"Girl, you know I don't dance to that shit."

"Come on, Kareem, it's just a dance . . . please?"

"Nah, nah, I'm going to get me a drink," Kareem said and pulled his hand away from Tiana.

King shook his head as Kareem walked toward the bar where the cute server was picking up drinks. Kareem was far from faithful; he had a wandering eye, but Tiana never argued with him about it. Her arguments were always about saving his life and his soul so that he could be there for their two children. Every female King had ever brought around loved Tiana, and some were still friends with her. Tiana could be a handful, but she had truly been loyal to Kareem, and sometimes, King wished that Kareem would treat her a little better.

King was shocked when Sloan grabbed Tiana's hand.

"Come on, girl. I'll dance with you. This my joint too." Sloan smiled and winked at King as she walked Tiana out onto the dance floor.

King just sat back and admired Sloan's dance moves. She was sexy without being slutty, and she and Tiana had all eyes on them as they danced and enjoyed themselves. King couldn't help smiling. The evening was a success, and he couldn't wait to get to know Sloan.

***

Deshawn hated this fucking place with these stuck-up-ass niggas, but he would sit in the pits of hell to hear Sloan sing. He sat at his usual table on the second floor, staring down at her as she talked to some slick-looking nigga. This one was different from the other shirts that frequented the club; he had an edge about him. As he took a sip of his cheap Cognac, he searched his memory for the dude's face. He took his phone out, zoomed in on the young gentleman, and snapped a picture. The face of every man she'd talked to since they had broken up was saved in his camera. Being a police detective, he had access to anyone and everyone's lives. It would only take him a few minutes to find out all he needed to know about this one.

Sloan was a smart girl, and he thought, by now, that she would understand that she wasn't going no damn where until he felt like letting her go. His cell phone rang, and Janet's face showed on the screen. He placed it back in his pocket. He had been married to Janet for five years. She owned a successful boutique in the South Park area of Charlotte and two more in Atlanta. She was the perfect wife—great for his image, supportive, financially stable, and when they were out together, they were seen as an attractive couple.

Deshawn loved the life he had with Janet, but he didn't really love her. Making love was more of a duty than a pleasure for him when it came to her. She was sexy as hell, and she had a body that would make a dude cream just by watching her walk away, but she had no idea how to use her assets in bed. Deshawn never hesitated when he had the opportunity to beat down a chick in bed. He had kept one or two on the side the entire time he had been married to Janet. That was, until he met Sloan.

She had put a spell on him that made him put the other side chicks down. For the first time, Janet actually had competition on the other level. Not only was Sloan a beast in the bed, she was smart, educated, and she had Deshawn under a spell. He had taken so many chances with her—using vacation time to take her out of town on trips and spending money he didn't have, buying her studio time. If Deshawn had a free moment, he wanted it occupied by Sloan.

Deshawn watched Sloan dance with the unknown man. She would pay for letting another man put his hands on her. The last time he had actually seen and touched her was the night she broke up with him at Carolina Sundries. She had been quiet through their dinner, barely looking at him. When she finally made eye contact with him, he had known something was up.

"What's up, beautiful? You been quiet all night," Deshawn had said to her, attempting to take her hand. Sloan pulled her hand away from him and sat back in the chair.

"Don't touch me, Deshawn, especially with that hand," Sloan said, crossing her arms. "I mean, isn't that the hand you are supposed to keep your wedding ring on?"

Deshawn felt the air in the room grow thicker, and his pulse began to quicken. He started to speak, but Sloan held her hand up. "No, no, please, spare me whatever fantastic lie you have to tell me. I don't even care." She stood and grabbed her purse.

As she turned to leave, she stopped, reached in her purse, and threw two twenty-dollar bills on the table. "I pay my own way. I would never take money from another woman's house. Please, don't call me. Just forget you ever knew me. I know I will be forgetting you." Sloan turned and walked toward the door.

Deshawn had wanted to run after her, but his legs felt like they had cement blocks tied to them. Days later, he had attempted to contact her. He stopped by her job; sent roses, begging for forgiveness; and had lost his mind in the process. She finally answered his call but only to tell him that, if he did not leave her alone, she would go to the police chief and file harassment charges against him.

A new song came on, bringing Deshawn out of his reverie. He almost jumped out of his seat when Sloan put her arms around the guy's neck and slow danced with him to Jaheim's "Anything." That was their song. She was taking this shit too far.

In his mind, she only threatened him because she was hurt. She just needed time to cool down, and then, they could be together again. In the meantime, he would watch her and keep her safe from these trifling niggas trying to talk to her. She needed him, and soon, she would realize it.

Chapter 8

Imani sighed as she slid the card in the hotel room door. The green light beeped, and she pushed the handle to let herself in. After she pulled her suitcase inside and placed the door key on the table, she walked into the bathroom. The four-hour trip was grueling, but Imani had actually made it in three without being pulled over. She hated that she had to travel so far, but she knew spending time with him would be well worth it.

"Damn, I got to pee." She sat down on the toilet and began checking her text messages and e-mails.

When she finished in the bathroom, she made sure the room door was secure and opened her suitcase. The lavender-colored lingerie that she had bought last weekend on the shopping spree with Khristian and Yogi immediately caught her eye.

Imani grabbed her shower gel and lotion and headed for the shower. While the water ran, she pulled her long, dark hair up into a ponytail and looked at herself in the mirror. "Yeah, you a bad bitch," Imani said and winked at her reflection.

She stepped into the shower and allowed the hot water to flow over her. As she washed herself, her stomach growled. She was starving, but she knew that she would go somewhere special after she had pleased her man. Imani placed the sponge between her legs and rubbed her lips gently.

"Woo, girl, slow down. Save it for your babe." Imani rinsed herself off and grabbed the large white terrycloth robe that was on the hook by the shower.

"This is going to be a weekend he will not forget any time soon," Imani said as she began to apply apple-scented lotion to her legs.

Imani hummed to herself as she prepared for her night of lovemaking. After she was properly oiled, she put on the lavender corset and ruffle skirt set. The lace-embroidered bust area had her girls sitting up beautifully. Imani lit the last candle and spritzed the air with her perfume. She walked over to the mirror and checked herself one last time before she heard the latch on the door move.

"Showtime," she whispered before positioning herself in the middle of the large king size bed.

"Babe, you here?" a man said as he entered the room.

"Yes, I'm in the bed." She heard his footsteps and laid back. "Hey, Daddy," Imani said, smiling seductively.

"Well, damn, you are beautiful."

Imani kneeled on the bed and reached for him. He dropped his bags and kissed her deeply, sucking lightly on her tongue. He slid the strap of the corset down and licked her collarbone.

Imani moaned as his warm mouth found her hard nipple and teased it with his tongue.

"Oh, Carlton. Damn, babe. Mmm . . . I been thinking about this all damn week."

Carlton slid the zipper of the corset down, freeing her other breast and exposing her navel ring. He licked her left breast while spreading Imani's legs wider. She bit her bottom lip.

"You want me to taste that pussy, don't you?"

"Y-yes, taste my pussy," Imani said.

"Your pussy? That ain't your pussy is it? It's mine. Now you gonna have to be punished for that," Carlton said, rubbing his thumb inside Imani's moist walls. She moaned. "You better not cum, you little bitch. Hold it, or you won't get what you really want."

"Please, let me cum. I'm sorry, this is your pussy. It's yours! Please, I can't hold it, Daddy!"

"No, no, you better hold it."

Carlton smiled as he watched Imani's face. She had tears forming in the corners of her eyes, and her hands were wrapped around the sheets. His dick stood at attention as he slowly slid his thumb out of her hot cavern and licked it.

"Don't you move," Carlton said as he slid off the bed.

He pulled his shirt over his head and unbuckled his belt. Then, he took off his pants and boxers. Imani watched as he walked around the bed, looking at her. Her legs were spread wide and her nipples were hard and pointing toward the ceiling. Her pussy was throbbing, begging for Carlton's touch.

Carlton stood at the foot of the bed and began stroking his thick dick and squeezing his balls. Imani's mouth began to water; she wanted to feel his thick pole slide down her throat. Carlton was more than twice her age, but the man had a body on him. His muscular thighs and hips were the source of his ability to make her body shiver and explode.

Imani moaned remembered how he had made her body respond the first time they were intimate.

Yogi and Khristian had gone to the store, and she was downstairs with Carlton playing pool. She'd had a crush on him since she was sixteen. She had intentionally worn a short skirt and tight shirt to show off her legs and breasts. Her mind traveled back to how she had placed one leg on the pool table, exposing her lower lips to him as she pretended to get ready for her shot.

"Five ball in corner pocket," she had said to him. Before she could touch the ball with the cue stick, Carlton had slid inside her from behind. She remembered how he made her bite down on a pillow as he carried her around the room while thrusting inside of her.

That was a year ago, and she had enjoyed every moment that she had spent with him. Her desire for him outweighed any guilt she may have felt in the beginning for sleeping with her best friend's father. Sometimes, when Ms. Yogi was around, she felt a little awkward, but Carlton had made it into such a game, that it actually felt more exciting now.

"Turn over," Carlton commanded.

Imani turned over and raised her ass in the air. She felt a sharp sting. "I didn't tell you to get on your knees, you little slut! Crawl to me."

Imani obeyed him and crawled to the edge of the bed. Carlton slid his rock-hard member across her soft, full lips. She moaned, as she looked up at Carlton. He nodded to her, giving her permission to taste him. Her full lips encircled the tip of his rod. Carlton's head dropped back as her mouth began to slide up and down his thickness.

"Yeah, yeah, that's it babe!" Carlton pushed her back on the bed. His dick was shiny from her beautiful mouth massage. "Put that ass up in the air for me, sexy."

Imani quickly flipped over on all fours and spread her legs. She felt the tip of his dick dip inside her cavern, teasing her walls. Carlton loved her plump ass; he smacked the left cheek and watched it ripple. He separated her cheeks and watched his dick moving in and out of her hot box. Imani grabbed the sheets; Carlton's low grunts were driving her over the edge with each thrust.

"Oh, Daddy, it feels so good." Imani loved the way he felt inside her. She tightened and released her muscles with each thrust, causing her cream to cover his dick.

Carlton began to pound her as he listened to her breathe and gasp when he hit his favorite spots inside of her. She bounced up and down on his rod as she pulled her nipples.

Carlton closed his eyes and enjoyed the ride.

Sloan walked briskly down the dock. For some reason, she was mindful of how loud her heels sounded on the wood. The lake air caressed her face, which would've been fine if she had not just spent an hour flat-ironing her hair. King had offered to pick her up, but she decided it would be best to meet him. She had only known him a short time, and this was their official first date. Although they had spoken over the phone, met a couple of times at King's studio, and Skyped each other in the last week, she still wasn't comfortable with him knowing where she lived. History had taught her against giving out that type of information too early.

"Miss Deveaux, welcome to the Lake Noria. My name is Phillip, and I will be your host this afternoon," a short white gentleman with snow-white hair said to her and extended his arm.

Sloan smiled. She took his hand and stepped up on the boat. She could smell the scent of his after-shave as the breeze continued to gently blow. Phillip chatted politely about the menu and the weather. Sloan loved his Australian accent. He was quite the charmer, and he made her laugh with his little quips about taking her around the world if King did not behave the way he should.

King stood as they approached the table. He smiled at her and kissed her cheek.

"You look . . . mmm, you're wearing that dress, and the shoe game is on point," King said, walking around Sloan.

She pushed him playfully and shook her head. "If that was a compliment, thank you," Sloan said as Phillip pulled her chair out for her. "You should take notes from Phillip on how to speak to a lady." Sloan winked at Phillip.

King laughed. "What, you fell for that crap Phillip spews? Please, he was thinking the same thing I said to you."

"Yeah, but he had a lot more tact. Take notes," Sloan said.

Phillip kissed her hand and nodded to King.

"You a dirty old man, Philip," King said laughing.

"Yes, sir, I am."

Sloan's mouth fell open and the three of them laughed.

"I will have Edward bring out your wine." Phillip walked down the steps. Sloan turned to King, who was studying her face. She was beautiful, smart, talented, and had class; she was the polar opposite of the women he usually dated.

"So, how was your evening?" King asked as he sat down.

"It was good, I got a lot of writing done, worked out, then, wrote some more. How about yours?"

"Just another day, nothing major. Took care of some things, then, I just relaxed. So, tell me some more about you. Do you have brothers or sisters?"

"No, I don't have any siblings. It is just me," Sloan said, sipping the white wine that the petite Hispanic server had poured for her. "I'm an only child. I guess I was more than enough for my folks!"

"Is that right? So how long you been singing?"

"For as long as I can remember having a voice. I used to sing to anything that I heard, country, opera, rock, R&B. Whatever had a melody or beat, I would sing to it."

"I didn't hear you say Gospel," King said. Sloan rolled her eyes. "What? Hey, I'm a southern boy, and even though I don't go like I should, I was raised in the church. Most artists say they learn how to sing by singing in Church."

"Not everybody believes in God, you know," Sloan said looking out at the water.

King was silent until he saw Sloan's shoulders shaking from laughter. "I'm joking. You should see your face. You better believe and lean on Him daily if you want to have any type of life here on earth, boy! My grandfather was a minister, and my grandmother actually sang back-up for a lot of Motown artists. So music is in me. What about you? What made you get into music?"

"Well, it damn sure wasn't the ability to sing. My voice has been known to make dogs howl. My father, he loved music. And it seemed like no matter what was going on, we would jump in his car, turn on the radio, and just cruise, listening to all types of songs."

King looked into Sloan's eyes. He thought back to his father putting him in the back seat of his red Cadillac, kissing his mama on the cheek, and telling her that it was man time. They would listen to Keith Sweat, Gerald Levert, Sade, and some hip-hop. Once he was old enough to ride in the front seat, his father broke out the classics. With the older music, every song told a story, and Reggie would sometimes use the song lyrics to teach him life lessons. King missed him, especially on Sundays. Sundays were their days.

Sloan touched King's hand. "Hey, you okay?"

"Yeah, yeah, I'm good. Just thinking about my Pops is all. He died when I was a teenager."

"Oh, I'm sorry, King."

"Yeah, well, you know things happen, right? My mom and I were lucky that Carlton was there to step in, but even with him there, I still missed my father. But anyway, he loved music and always talked about opening a club and bringing his favorite artists to Charlotte. That is why I got into promotions and started my company. I may not be able to perform it, but I know what I like when I hear it. You blew me away when I heard that instrument of yours," King said and caressed Sloan's palm.

They were quiet for a moment, as Phillip appeared with their salads and bread.

"Thank you, Phillip," Sloan said, "this looks so good." She bowed her head to say grace. "How old is your daughter?"

"She is five, going on twenty-five," King said smiling. "She has invited me to her dance class later this evening for daughter daddy day."

"Ah, are you going to wear a tutu? That is going to be adorable. What color are you going to wear?" Sloan joked.

King shook his head. "I will not have on a tutu, but if she asks me to wear one, I guess I will. I find it hard to say no to her. She is the one constant joy in my life and the best thing I ever created," he said smiling.

Sloan felt warm as she watched his eyes twinkle at the mention of his daughter. She could see the love he had for her and the pride he took in being a parent which, for someone his age, was rare. Sloan, personally, wasn't thinking about having children, but she did appreciate his love for his daughter.

As the boat sailed around the lake, the two of them talked about their childhoods, schools, and favorite music artists. When the boat docked, King felt a rumble in his stomach at the thought of having to say good-bye to Sloan.

He took her hand as they walked down the dock. King wondered if, maybe, this was the feeling his father told him he would one day feel for a woman. When King asked him what had made him marry his mother, Reggie had initially thought the question was odd, until King explained that none of his other friends' parents were still together.

Chapter 9

Red held the smoke in his lungs and slowly puffed out perfect circles. Music was playing, but he wasn't paying attention to the words of the song. King had hit him hard. Red expected him to bite back, but he had underestimated the nigga. King had taken out some of his top soldiers, and not only had he taken back his product, but had lifted all the product that he had in the stash house. His ego was telling him to strike back at the nigga, but his brain told him to lick his wounds and recover first. He could not be sure if King would strike again, so he moved his shit to different locations.

It had been a week since the funerals. Things were slowly returning to normal. Peaches had come to Moose's funeral, but she still refused to speak to Red. It didn't help that Cara was there, by his side. He had truly begun to cherish her. She was proving herself to be a real ride-or-die. They spent time together every day, and he had even started to expose her to his business.

Red now realized that he had made an amateur mistake by not going after King or Carlton. He should have cut off the head so that the body would die. Instead of weakening their empire, he had only pissed them off and hurt his own business in the process. Red was by no means finished. He was just going to bide his time and build his arsenal, so the next time he struck, there would be no one left standing to retaliate.

"Baby, baby, are you hungry?" Cara waved her hands in his face.

"Nah, I'm cool, baby."

"Where were you just now?

"Whatchu mean?" Red asked.

"I have been calling your name for the last five minutes. You were a million miles away."

"My bad, boo. This shit still has me fucked up in the head. Every time I think about my fam being carried out of that house, it pisses me off all over again. I should've clapped at that nigga when I saw him at the mall."

"Well, no, baby. That wouldn't have been a smart move. The mall was too crowded, and you were with me. I can't be involved in no shoot-out before I even start college," Cara said.

"That chick you went and spoke to while we were shopping, how do you know her? I saw her get in the car with that nigga."

"Oh, she is just someone I know from school," Cara quickly answered. "Well, baby, since you are not hungry, I am going to go and finish my paper, okay?"

"Cool," Red responded and put out his blunt.

Red stared into space as he thought about all that had been taken from him. King, Carlton, and all of their crew were as good as dead. He would just have to be patient and lay low for a while to let them get comfortable. Eventually, they will slip, and he will be right there to ensure that they stayed down.

Sloan smiled as King opened the door to the club for her. She took his hand as he led her inside.

"So, are you going to tell me who I am opening for next week?" Sloan asked.

The last two weeks had been like a dream come true for Sloan. King had provided a place for her to practice, a live band, and unlimited access to his studio. She had been working on new material nonstop since meeting him. He shared with her his extensive knowledge of the music industry. He had been all business. Sloan had been in the studio and working so much that she barely had time to sleep or eat. True to his word, King had booked her to open for a major artist that he was bringing into town. She had been rehearsing like mad, but he had refused to tell her who the mystery artist was.

"This is who you are opening for," King said, pointing to the large poster with a picture of Jill Scott. Sloan's head shot was also on the poster that read: AND INTRODUCING, NEW R&B SENSATION, SLOAN DEVEAUX.

"What? Oh my God, you are kidding me. Are you serious?" Sloan squealed. "Jill Scott! She is beyond amazing!"

Sloan jumped up and down and, then, hugged King. Amazingly, this was the first time that they had actually touched each other in an intimate fashion.

King played himself well with her, holding back and restraining himself. He felt her soft breasts against his chest, and her lips were only a few centimeters away from his. His lips ached to taste hers.

"Thank you, King, I—" before she could finish speaking, King covered her soft lips with his, exploring her mouth with his tongue, and lifting her off the floor by her hips.

Sloan wrapped her legs around his waist, and he could feel the heat coming from her center as her cavern pressed against his stomach. She moaned as he cupped her ass tighter and kissed her neck.

"Damn . . ." King said as he looked into Sloan's eyes. "Woo, boy! Mmm." King loosened his grip on Sloan's ass, but she tightened her legs around his waist, causing his member to touch his navel. "Shit!" King said as he carried her back out the door to his SUV.

She laughed as he practically threw her inside and ran to the driver's side. "What are you doing?" Sloan asked.

"I am canceling rehearsal, that's what I am doing, babe," King said as he drove out of the parking lot.

It seemed to only take seconds to get to King's building. He pulled into the garage and jumped out of the car, not even waiting for the parking attendant. He jogged around to Sloan's side and opened her door. The flash of thigh that he saw as she stepped out had his dick hard as steel.

They were quiet as the elevator ascended to the fifteenth floor. The temperature inside the small space seemed to be on low hell, and the elevator was going slower than usual. When they finally arrived, King grabbed Sloan's hand and practically dragged her down the hall. He opened the door and pulled her inside.

She laughed at him and pushed him away. "Umm, is this your place?" Sloan asked.

"Yeah, why would you ask that?"

"Because the alarm is going off. I think you better stop it."

"Ah shit," King said as he ran to the keypad to punch in his code. Although he didn't have anything in his place, he didn't need the police up in his spot. "Good call. Well, come on in and have a seat."

Sloan looked around at the African art on the walls and on the shelves in the living room. It smelled of citrus and mint.

"Would you like something to drink?" King asked as he grabbed the remote from the coffee table and pointed it toward the window.

The blinds rose to the ceiling, and the Charlotte skyline appeared.

"Whoa, what a view. It's beautiful," Sloan said as she opened the doors to the patio. "You can see the entire city from here. How can you even stand to leave this? I would be out here all day and night writing music."

King encircled her waist with his arms and pulled her close to him. He kissed the back of her neck and caressed her stomach. She relaxed her head on his shoulder and pressed her soft hips against his crotch. He tasted the soft spot behind her left ear and gently caressed her right breast.

"Mmmmm . . . King," Sloan moaned as he slid his hand under her shirt.

She began to grind against him. King matched her movements; his dick threatened to burst through his zipper. King slid her panties down. Sloan kicked off her shoes and kicked her panties on one of the patio chairs. He placed both of her hands on the rail, bent her over, and pulled her dress up to her waist. Licking his lips, he knelt down behind her; her ass was right in his face. It was smooth and soft as he kissed each of her cheeks, inhaling the scent of the cucumber lotion she used. With both of her mounds gripped firmly in his large hands, he slid his tongue over her anus.

Sloan gasped as his tongue explored her. She had never had anyone put their tongue inside her there, and the sensation was almost too much. King continued sliding his tongue in and out of her tight ass as he opened her hot, wet pussy with two fingers and massaged her walls.

Sloan moaned loudly and gripped the railing. "Ooh, that feels so good baby. Oh, King."

King buried his face between her soft cheeks and sucked her ass. As he licked, he opened her lips wider and massaged her clit with his middle finger. Her legs shook and her body began to jerk as she yelled from the top of her lungs. Her whole body trembled as her fluids hit the concrete.

"Fuck! Fuck!" Sloan said breathlessly as she collapsed against the railing.

King stepped back and looked at her from behind—the dress pulled up to her waist, her toned brown thighs, her round ass, and her thick pussy lips. "Don't move, stay like that," King said as he sat down in the chair.

When he heard her breathing return to normal, he stood and took off his pants, and then sat down again in the large blue chair. "Walk back to me slowly."

Sloan looked back at him.

"No, turn around. Just walk backward. Take off that dress." Sloan began to unzip the dress. "Do it slow, babe."

Sloan obeyed him and eased the zipper of her dress down. She held the dress to her body with her hand, and the purple cotton material slowly moved down her body.

King stroked his member as he watched her run her hands over her smooth skin. "Walk to me, but don't turn around. Walk straight back. Take your time, and sing something to me."

Sloan took a deep breath, and the words that came from her were shocking.

"I am ready for love,
Why are you hiding from me?"

With each line of India Arie's song, she took a step. King's dick throbbed as she sang to him. The girl's voice was angelic, hypnotizing.

Sloan closed her eyes as she sang the words to the song. She had no idea why it popped into her head. The last couple of weeks had been the best weeks for her, professionally and personally. King made feelings inside her bubble to the surface, and it terrified her. She had only known him a short time, but he had managed to crack the darkness that she had surrounded her heart with for safety.

As she approached the chair, King closed his eyes as she sang the last verse.

"Tell me what is enough . . . to prove, I am ready for love. . . ."

King caressed the outline of her body; he traced her spine while he kissed her back and pulled her to him.

"Damn, baby, you taste so good. Open your legs and sit on my lap." Sloan paused. King laughed. "Look," King said. Sloan turned around to see the condom on his beautiful ten inches. "I wouldn't do you like that, babe."

Sloan shook her head and mounted him. She slid down on his thick pole with ease, her pussy sucked him inside of her like a starving woman reacting to her first taste of food in days. She glided her pussy up and down on him. King gripped the arms of the chair as he felt her pussy tighten around his dick. She stopped, turned to him and smiled.

King looked at her questioningly. She wrapped her feet around the calves of his legs, leaned forward and placed her hands on the ground. King looked down at her ass, and without saying anything, Sloan began pounding her pussy on his dick.

"Ah baby! Yeah!" King said as her beautiful pussy loved his dick, making it harder with each bounce of her soft ass.

King had been with many women. Some were champions in bed, but it was rare to find one who really knew how to ride a dick. It was especially rare to find someone who seemed like she was making love to his dick, not just sexing it. Everything about this woman was intriguing to him.

Deshawn sat in the parking garage across from the condo building downtown. He felt his head begin to spin as he watched Sloan fucking that King nigga. Never, in a million years, did he imagine another man would be inside her like that. He gripped his gun, wishing he had a scope and an automatic rifle to take the nigga out and make his brains explode all over Sloan. The worst part was the bitch looked like she was enjoying fucking him! Through the binoculars, he could tell she was fucking the shit out of the nigga. He put the binoculars down and punched the dash of his car, nearly cracking the plastic.

"No, no, no!" Deshawn yelled as he continued punching the steering wheel.

He had been watching King over the past two weeks. He knew that he had a drug business, but for the last two weeks, he had been at the studio and his club on the east side. It didn't matter. He knew that it would only be a matter of time before King made a move that Deshawn could use to his benefit. He would get his woman back and make some cash in the process. He fought the urge to continue watching them through the binoculars and started the car. Still cursing under his breath, he pulled out of the parking garage.

He needed to head to the other side of town. His wife had made plans for him with her parents and siblings. As he pulled out of the garage onto the street, he turned on his radio. He hoped the noise would help him block seeing Sloan fucking another dude from his mind.

His phone rang. He hit the PHONE button on his steering wheel. "I am on my way, babe. Got held up with something," Deshawn said, turning onto 277.

"Okay honey, hurry up. Love you," Janet said.

"Yeah, I'm on my way," Deshawn said, accelerating.

The line was silent for a moment.

"Is everything okay?" Janet asked.

"Yes. Damn, I said I was on my way."

Deshawn hit END and dialed another number.

"Yo," the voice answered on the other end.

"I need to holla at you. Meet me at the spot tomorrow at noon. The streets are talking, and I hear we got a common problem. Maybe we can help each other."

"The streets are talking? Whatchu—"

"Tomorrow at noon," Deshawn interrupted. "Don't make me come get you."

He disconnected the call and turned the radio up, hoping the music would erase the last thirty minutes from his mind's eye.

Chapter 10

Sloan straightened her dress as King opened the door. She walked inside, and the aroma of food engulfed her. King held her hand and led her to the kitchen where Yogi was stirring a pitcher of tea.

"Hey baby!" Yogi said, kissing King on the cheek. "Hand me that lemon over there, please." King handed his mother the lemon quarters and took a piece of cheese from the tray on the counter.

"Ma, this is Sloan. Sloan, this is my mother," King said, smiling.

"Nice to meet you, Mrs. King," Sloan said.

"That's not my last name anymore, how about you just call me Yogi," Yogi said, forcing a smile. "King, your daddy is downstairs in his usual place, why don't you go see if he wants anything."

"All right." King kissed Sloan on the cheek and opened the door to the basement.

"So, is there anything I can help you with?" Sloan asked.

"No, I think I have everything under control. So where did you meet King?"

"I met him at the mall. He came into the jewelry store that I work in."

"The mall, huh?" Yogi said as she opened the oven. "So are you from Charlotte?"

"No ma'am, I am from New Jersey. Morristown, New Jersey."

"Oh, a Yankee! Well, what brought you down south?" Yogi asked as she poured a glass of wine.

"I finished my music degree at the University of North Carolina and kind of stayed here," Sloan said.

Yogi sipped her wine. The silence in the room seemed to echo. Sloan was a bit taken aback by Yogi's coldness. King had described his mother as sweet and soft spoken, but she seemed to dislike Sloan immediately.

King opened the door and looked at Yogi then Sloan. He pulled her to him and slid his arms around her waist. "So, did I interrupt some girl talk?"

"I was just getting to know Sloan a little. The table is set, so go have a seat." Yogi opened the basement door and yelled down to Carlton.

"I can help you bring in the food, Ms. Yogi," Sloan said.

"No, no. You go have a seat. I like to take care of my things. I been doing this for years, and I like things done a certain way. So, you go have a seat. You are a guest."

Sloan followed King into the dining room just as the doorbell rang.

Yogi went to the door, and let Kareem in. "Heeyyy Yogi, it's your Boo Boo bear, Kareem, and I brought company."

"Yogiiiii!"

"Oh my God, what are you doing here? When did you get into town?" Yogi said, hugging David.

David squeezed her and swung her around. "Girl, you have not aged a bit. That damn Carlton snuck and got you before I did, and I know that smell. Is that your macaroni and cheese?"

Yogi blushed and smacked David's arm. She took his hand and led him into the dining room.

"Uncle David?" King said.

Carlton turned around.

David smiled at him. He had lost weight since the last time Carlton had seen him, two years ago. Although

Carlton didn't make it to see him, he had kept his books straight for him over the last ten years. David was Reggie's younger brother and had spent the last ten years in prison on a drug charge.

"Man, why didn't you tell me they let you out?" Carlton asked, pounding David.

"You know me, I make my own way."

"Come on and sit down," Carlton said, pulling out a chair for David.

"Well, I am going to get the food," Yogi said. "Kareem, why don't you come and help me?"

Sloan felt a chill go down her back. "Are you sure you don't want me to help, Ms. Yogi?" Sloan offered.

"Umm, no. Like I said, you are a guest. Kareem is family, and he can help. You just sit tight."

Sloan sat down and listened as the men chatted. Dinner was full of conversation about things that Sloan didn't understand. Her attempts to talk with Yogi were met with one-worded answers. Dinner and time seemed to drag on, and she was relieved when King finally decided to leave.

"Ms. Yogi, dinner was delicious. Thank you."

"Well, you have a good evening," Yogi said. She kissed King on the cheek and hugged him. "You make sure you take care of yourself, okay?"

"Okay, Ma. Hey, excuse me a second, babe," King said as he turned and walked over to Kareem. "Hey, man, where is Tiana?"

"She went out of town. She paid a sitter and said she had some business to take care of. I am telling you, I'm enjoying the peace with her being gone, and the kids are handled. Shoot, I been hanging out with that waitress from the club."

King shook his head. "What kind of business does Tiana have out of town? You better hope she ain't setting your ass up to catch you." King laughed.

"Hell if I know," Kareem said. "I was just happy to get the time to myself without all of the nagging. I didn't ask no questions. Anyway, enough about that. Is everything cool for the show?"

"As cool as it is going to get. Now, for my other business, I sure could use my right hand man watching my back. I know that damn job ain't paying you shit."

"You right, but for right now, I told her I would try this straight thang. She did hold me down when I was locked up. So, for the kids, I'm gonna try this shit for a minute. But I already told her I'm not going to sit around and starve. So the first time a bill collector calls, talking about taking something back or turning something off, she know this deal is done. You feel me?"

"Yeah, I feel you on that. You straight on money, brah?" King asked.

Kareem wanted to tell him that he didn't have two pennies to rub together, but his pride stopped him. "I'm straight dog, I'm straight."

King dapped Kareem. He smiled at Sloan, who waved to Kareem and opened the door.

Yogi watched them walk down the driveway to King's SUV. King opened the door for Sloan and waved to her. Yogi waved back and inhaled. She didn't like Sloan. She wasn't the type of girl that her son needed. She was too soft around the edges, and she didn't seem to have much survivor in her. She knew that, at the first sign of King's lifestyle, which she could tell Sloan had no idea about, the chick would bail on him.

Chapter 11

Three weeks later. . . .

Sloan examined herself in the full-length mirror of her dressing room. She could not believe she actually had a stylist! King spared no expense for her big night. She applied the lip gloss and closed her eyes.

Her eyes flew open when Jimmy knocked on the door. "On in five, Lady."

"Thanks, Jimmy." Sloan stood. The red cocktail dress she wore sparkled in the light. She walked to the stairs and had a brief moment of prayer. As she opened her eyes, King was there smiling at her.

"You ready, babe?"

"As ready as I'll ever be. I been dreaming of this night all my life."

"Well, it's here now, sexy. And I know this is the first of many."

Sloan shook her head. King always seemed to have the right words. She grabbed the mic out of his hand and headed for the stairs near the stage.

King clinked glasses with his staff, Kareem, and Sloan. Everyone had shown up except Yogi. She had something to take care of, so she sent Carlton and Khristian to represent the family.

"Young lady, I would have never thought that a voice like that was inside such a pretty package. Damn, you can blow!" Carlton said while Imani and Khristian high fived Sloan.

"Girl, you actually gave Jill a run for her money. They gave you a standing ovation! I want to be in your video when you make it," Khristian said, hugging her.

"Shit, I'm starving. I say we go get something to eat," Kareem added, while keeping his eyes on Imani.

"Yeah, I'm with you on that, brah," King responded while tapping Kareem to let him know that his gaze was too obvious.

As they exited the building, there was still a large crowd standing outside. King had parked his car in the rear, while everyone else was up front in VIP.

"You want me to give you a ride around back, homie?" Kareem asked.

"Nah, we good," King answered while showing the butt of the pistol in his pants.

King held Sloan's hand as they walked around the side of the building through the crowd.

"Yo, Ma, let me holla at you! You did your thang in there tonight," one guy yelled out of a crowd full of men.

Sloan and King just kept walking. The entire crew looked like they had been drinking heavily, so King was going to give him a pass.

The tall dark-skinned man with long dreads did not take the hint; he walked up and grabbed Sloan's arm. "Damn, bitch, didn't you hear a nigga giving you a compliment? You can't say thank you because you with this corny-ass nigga, playing Puffy and shit."

King stopped walking and turned to the man. "Nigga, what did you say?"

"Nigga, you heard me."

King let go of Sloan's hand and reached in his pants. Before Sloan could say anything, King had pulled out his .45 and smashed the gun across the bridge of the man's nose. Blood shot out, and the man screamed. King hit him again in the forehead.

Sloan screamed as she heard something crack.

People began to yell. The commotion made Kareem, Carlton, and David come running around the building, just in time to draw their guns.

The man's crew stepped back.

King was stomping the man until Carlton and David pulled him off.

"That's enough, nephew," David told him. "He got the message."

"Yeah, we need to get out of here," Carlton added.

Sloan did not recognize King. His face was dark and angry as he grabbed her by the arm and quickly headed toward his truck.

"Sloan, babe, listen to me. Take this, and hide it for me. I'm going to ride with my pops, just in case the police come. I will meet you at home later." He took Sloan's purse, placed the gun inside and opened the door to his SUV. He watched her pull out of the parking lot.

"Yo, man, get out of here before the police show up," Kareem said. "You fucked old boy up, come on."

"Nah, dawg, you don't need no heat on you. You go on ahead. I'm going to ride with Pops," King said.

"A'ight, call me."

King walked down the sidewalk, trying to blend in with the crowd leaving the club. As he approached the intersection and was about to jump in Carlton's sedan, the cops swarmed him.

"Put your hands on your head, and get down now!" an officer yelled.

King dropped his head. His temper had, once again, gotten him into a mess. It would have been easier to just ignore the nigga, but he could not allow that kind of disrespect, especially in front of people. "I said, put your hands on your head, and get down!"

King sighed and complied. The officers rushed him and placed handcuffs on him. The larger officer lifted King off the ground.

"What is the problem, officer?" King asked smugly.

"You are under arrest for assault, King." King looked closer at the officer. He had a bald head, broad shoulders, and a goatee. King laughed aloud when he recognized who was arresting him.

"What up, Pool?"

"That's Officer Pool, nigga. Come on!" Pool said, twisting King's wrist back as he walked him to the patrol car.

"Man, you actually gonna take me in over some bullshit?" King asked as he sat down in the cruiser.

"You pistol-whipped a man in front of at least twenty people, and some even recorded it. You ain't getting out of this one!" Pool said, laughing.

King shook his head. Pool had been after King since high school. He had always been a big ass dude, whose family never had the money to dress him with any style for his size. His pants and shirts were always too short, and the fool couldn't even play basketball worth a damn. As a matter of fact, he didn't play any sports. Just a big-ass nigga, who had always hated King and his crew. Kareem, always a comedian, used to call him Lurch and clown his clothes, which didn't help soothe Pool's dislike of them. After high school, the nigga went off to college and came back to Charlotte to join the police force.

"Yeah, you going down this time, Mr. Big Dope Man."

King shook his head. He knew that Pool was trying to bait him. He sat back and looked out the window. He was relaxed, and he didn't care what kind of video they had. He had a team of fucking lawyers on speed dial, and he would be out before they booked him.

Sloan gripped the steering wheel as she checked her side and rearview mirror. What the hell just happened? She was shaking. The gun on the passenger's seat in her purse made her pulse quicken. What the hell was she doing? Why would King beat that man like that? Shit! Sloan was too scared to cry. She just wanted to get back to the safety of her own apartment and forget the night ever happened.

"Shit, I gotta get rid of this!" Sloan closed her eyes and took a deep breath. She turned down Kimble Avenue and drove into the old Winn Dixie parking lot. The parking lot did not have any lights, and there were no open stores in the strip mall.

Sloan looked around and turned off the headlights. She drove around to the back of the strip mall. On wobbly legs, she got out of the truck and walked toward a wall lined with dumpsters. Her cell phone provided a little bit of light as she tripped over broken beer bottles and other debris on her way to a large dumpster. It was full of trash, which she found odd.

She used the tail of her dress to pull the gun out of her purse. "Good riddance," she muttered as she threw the gun into the dumpster.

Sloan ran back to King's SUV and jumped inside. Her heart was beating one hundred times a minute. She looked around for a moment then turned the key. She drove blindly from behind the store and turned onto Pairston Road. As she approached the stop sign, she turned on the headlights and continued toward the interstate.

***

King sat on the steel bench, pissed the hell off. His wrist had gone from throbbing to numb. He knew that it was, at least, sprained, but these muthafuckers were not trying to hear that he was injured.

"Come on, nigga." Pool growled as he led King to have his mug shot taken.

"Damn, man, why you so hostile? Was that your brother or something?" King laughed.

Pool stopped walking for a moment. "You and them niggas always got jokes, huh?" Pool said. He elbowed King in the side.

King fell down as the air escaped his lungs. "Hey, hey, everything all right?" a detective asked as he walked over to King and Pool.

"Yeah, I think he just tripped, is all," Pool said, pulling King up. "I got him. No problem here."

The detective studied Pool. Then, he looked at King, who was trying to catch his breath.

"A'ight," the detective said, walking away and looking back at King.

King felt his head begin to spin due his rising blood pressure. Police or not, he would not forget what the fuck had just happened with Pool.

Sloan pulled into the parking garage of King's condo building. She had not stopped shaking since she left the parking lot of the club. Finally, she turned off the engine and rested her head against the steering wheel. She inhaled, trying to calm herself down. As she exhaled, tears flowed down her face. Her entire body shook as she sobbed. She could still hear the sickening crack as the butt of the gun hit the guy's head. It seemed to be playing on a continuous loop in her head.

She grabbed her purse and got out of the car, heading toward the elevator. As she passed a row of parked cars, something grabbed her from behind. A hand covered her mouth, and she was lifted off the ground. She tried to scream, but as she inhaled, a strong chemical smell flooded her nostrils and her mouth. Her head felt light, and then, darkness followed.

Sloan woke up in King's bed. She jumped up and looked around, but the room began to spin, causing her to fall back onto the bed.

"Shit," Sloan said, closing her eyes and massaging her temples. "Oh, my head is banging."

"Hey, baby, I got something for your head."

Sloan felt her blood chill in her veins. Her heart seemed to slow down as she opened her eyes. When her vision focused on the man standing beside the bed, her heart began to pump faster. She screamed when she saw Deshawn standing beside the bed holding a glass of water and a bottle of Tylenol.

"Shh, shh, I'm not going to hurt you, baby. Calm down, calm down," Deshawn said as he sat down on the bed.

Sloan's head was pounding, but she quickly jumped out of the bed. "What the hell are you doing here, Deshawn?"

"Saving you, baby. I'm saving you from this mistake you've made," Deshawn said as he stood and walked toward Sloan.

She stepped back against the wall and looked toward the door. The remote was right next to her on the nightstand, so she grabbed it and threw it at Deshawn, hoping his dodging it would give her enough time to make it to the entrance. As she ran by him, he grabbed her by the waist and slung her on the bed. He covered her mouth as she attempted to scream.

"Shut up, shut the fuck up!" Deshawn said, placing his weight on her.

Sloan's lungs began to burn from the lack of oxygen. She stopped struggling, and he slowly moved his hand from her mouth and shifted his weight to allow her to breathe. "Damn, baby, you are so beautiful. You blew them away tonight. You were better than Jill. They didn't even ask for an encore from her, like they did you. I love hearing your voice, but you know that, don't you?"

Sloan shook her head in agreement.

He caressed her face and traced her lips with his fingers. When he leaned in to kiss her, she turned her head.

Deshawn laughed and rolled off her. "Really? You would deny me a kiss, after fucking a damn low-life like Ronnie King? Someone who put you in danger and, then, just abandoned you?"

Deshawn stood and walked over to the large black duffel bag that was on the small table.

As Deshawn unzipped the bag, Sloan began to cry.

"Calm down, damn! Can't you see I would never hurt you? Stop crying!" Deshawn yelled.

He turned around with a large Ziploc bag. As Sloan's eyes locked on its contents, Deshawn smiled at her.

"You see? I told you, I'm going to always protect you, always. All you gotta do is listen to what I tell you, and you will never be unhappy or unsafe."

Sloan sat up slowly. She stared at the gun in the bag and, then, turned her gaze to Deshawn.

"What do you want, Deshawn?"

"You not going to even try to deny that you threw this away tonight? Good girl, I knew you were smart, you just made a bad decision." Deshawn shook his head and placed the gun back in the duffle bag. "Sloan, look at you. Hiding guns, obstructing justice. When did you become that kind of girl? As these street niggas say, you ain't 'bout that life."

Sloan pulled her legs into her chest and buried her face in her hands. How did she get here? Last night was one of the best nights of her life, and now, it had turned into a nightmare.

Deshawn caressed her face and grabbed the bag. "I will be in touch with the time and place we need to meet." He pulled her face closer to his. "Sloan, I understand why you left me, but you didn't give me a chance to explain. I forgive you, and don't worry about this," Deshawn said, patting the duffel bag. "All of this will disappear, okay?"

Deshawn kissed her forehead and walked out of the room.

Sloan sat on the bed and listened for the alarm to beep twice, signaling that he had opened and closed the door.

Yogi parked her car beside King's SUV and took off her sunglasses to allow her eyes to adjust to the darkness of the parking garage. It was two o'clock, and her baby had been locked up for hours. He had not been allowed to make a phone call until this morning when he spoke to Carlton. This bitch had not even called to check on him.

She slammed the car door and began walking toward the elevator. This was the shit she was afraid of with this girl. Shit, she couldn't stand Yessenia, but at least the bitch knew how to handle herself and would have gotten King a bond by now.

She pressed the UP button and waited for the elevator. The doors opened, and a tall, slim man stepped out. He held the door for her and nodded.

Yogi smiled politely at the stranger and pressed the button for the fifteenth floor. King always chose the wrong type of women, but this time, he went and got himself a weak little uptown chick who thought she was the next big thang on the stage.

Yogi wrinkled her nose at the strong chemical smell that greeted her when the elevator doors opened.

For all the money he is paying to live here, the hallway should not stink, Yogi thought as she walked down the hall. She stopped at King's condo door. She took out her key and unlocked the door.

As she entered the apartment, the alarm began to blare. She ran to the keypad and put in the code, but the alarm continued.

"Shit," Yogi said as she searched her cell phone for the code. She heard something click behind her and froze. She swallowed and turned slowly, only to be met by a barrel of a Smith & Wesson.

"Oh shit, Ms. Yogi!" Sloan said as she lowered the gun and walked over to the keypad. "I almost shot you!"

Yogi looked at Sloan. Her hair was in a messy ponytail, and she had on one of King's T-shirts. Her eyes were swollen and red, and she had been chewing her bottom lip so badly, it was split and chapped.

"Kareem called already and told me he was going to bail King out, Ms. Yogi. He told me he didn't want me coming down there seeing him like that. Whatever that means," Sloan said as she sat down on the couch, still holding the gun.

Yogi waited for her heart to return to her chest. The last thing she expected from this girl was for her ass to actually be strapped up. "Umm, okay, why don't we put the gun down? Have you eaten anything?"

Sloan stared off into space for a moment. She stood and placed the gun on the small glass table and walked out onto the patio.

Yogi looked around the apartment. She had never seen it so organized, clean, and comfy. Nothing was out of place. She walked out onto the patio and sat down in the blue chair.

"I . . . I should have called you, I know," Sloan said, looking out. "It just all happened so fast, and I couldn't think straight. I have never seen that side of King before. I don't even really understand what happened. We had an awesome night. We danced, had some drinks, and were leaving the club. The next thing I know, King banging on this dude's head with his gun. Shit, I didn't even know he carried a gun!" Sloan said, sitting down on the blue chair opposite Yogi.

Yogi took out her cigarettes and tapped them on the arm of the chair. She lit it and sat back as she inhaled the smoke and released it through her nose, trying to calm her nerves. Right now, she wanted to throw this weak-ass bitch over the damn balcony and be done with her stupid ass. She really fell for the whole music producer bit that King gave her?

"When King handed me the keys and the gun . . ."

"Whoa, what? He gave you the gun? Where the hell is it?" Yogi asked, sitting up.

Sloan studied her for a moment. She narrowed her gaze and sat back in the chair. She knew that Yogi was definitely not her biggest fan. She could feel the coolness from the woman at dinner a couple of weeks ago. Sloan had to contain herself for the moment because this woman had the nerve to look at her as if she wasn't good enough for her son!

"I got rid of it, Ms. Yogi. I am not stupid, nor am I as naïve as you think," Sloan said, not dropping her eyes from Yogi's.

"Really? So, where is the gun?" Yogi said, now leaning forward.

"It is gone, and that is it. It has been . . . Taken care of," Sloan said, standing again.

Truthfully, she was terrified that Deshawn had the gun in his possession. She had no idea what or how he intended to use it. She knew it would only be a matter of time before he would come seeking his payment for keeping her secret. The alarm beeped, and the women looked at each other.

"Babe, babe?" King yelled as he walked through the door.

Sloan ran inside. She threw her arms around him, and for a brief moment, the events of the night disappeared. His touch made her feel safe. She sobbed as he kissed her cheeks.

"Hey, hey, what are the tears for, babe? I'm fine, everything is okay," King said as he held her. "Hey, Ma, what you doing here?"

"Boy, you're gonna stand there and really ask me that? What the hell were you thinking? They say that boy laid up in the hospital! Mouth wired shut."

"Good, he shouldn't have shot it off to me and called my babe a bitch. You know I ain't letting no one disrespect her like that," King said, kissing Sloan on the forehead and walking into the kitchen.

"Disrespect her? Is that what this is about? What do you think your father would say to you right now? Seeing you act stupid like this over some girl?"

"Damn, babe, we ain't got nothing here to eat?" King said, ignoring his mother's last statement. He walked over and began looking through the refrigerator.

"Umm, I can run to the store," Sloan said and walked to the bedroom.

Yogi rolled her eyes and turned to King. "This, this right here ain't gonna work. She isn't made from the right stock to be with you, baby. Why in the world would you give this little girl the gun to get rid of? Why?"

The door opened and Sloan walked out wearing the same T-shirt and a pair of skinny jeans. She slid her feet into a pair of brown flats, grabbed her keys, and walked out of the door without looking at either of them.

"What did you say to her, Ma?"

"I didn't say shit to her, King. Right now, she is a freaking non-factor. We need to clean this mess up. One of the things that made you so successful in the game is that you managed to remain under the radar of the authorities."

"I got busted for assault, Ma. It will go away in a few days. Bolter will have it fixed, stop worrying."

Chapter 12

Red watched the video of the fight that had taken place at King's club on the screen. He shook his head and slammed the laptop closed. He stood and walked out onto his patio. The Jacuzzi was at the right temperature. He was sore from playing basketball, so he stepped gingerly into the hot water and slowly descended into the whirlpool.

"How you doing, Red?" a man asked as he walked over to the hot tub.

"Yo, what's up, Officer?" Red responded to one of the many police officers who he supplied information to about what was going on in the streets.

Deshawn had been one of the first he ever cooperated with when he was busted years ago. His information had allowed Deshawn to rise through the ranks from a uniformed officer to a detective. Deshawn had, also, helped Red's rise on the street by taking out most of his competition and sometimes, even selling Red cocaine that had been recovered when those busts went down.

"Well, I'm trying to see what the fuck is taking you so long on handling the situation with this nigga, King," Deshawn said angrily.

"Look, man, I told you the nigga stay guarded up, and I got to make sure I cover myself. I'll get to it when I can," Red responded.

He was tired of Deshawn calling him every day about the same shit. Hell, he wanted King dead, too, but Deshawn was taking this shit to the next level.

"Yeah, that's what I figured."

Deshawn laughed and stepped closer to the hot tub. He made sure that the hoodie covered his face at all times, but he wanted the security camera to catch everything he was about to do.

"Man, I said I got you. And why you sneaking around my spot anyway? It's too damn late for all this. Damn, I am trying to relax before my girl gets home."

"Red, you know I never really liked you. You not that smart, and I should have known that when I asked you to do this job for me. Since I knew there was already bad blood between the two of you, I thought offering you the chance to get rid of his ass and pick up his business would have got you going. I guess you can lead a horse to water, but you can't make him drink. Anyway, shit has a way of working itself out, and I think I will handle King myself," Deshawn said, laughing.

"Damn, you really got a hard-on for that nigga," Red said jokingly. "What he do to you? Fuck your girl?"

Deshawn's vision became slightly blurry for a moment. He had to concentrate on his breathing and focus on Red's face. As his vision cleared, Deshawn pulled out the gun that he had taken from the dumpster. He made sure the Rolex on his wrist was on display for the camera, and he fired two shots. One shot hit Red in his left eye and the other, in his chest. Brain matter and blood sprayed back on the gun and the watch.

"Yeah, nigga, he did." Deshawn laughed as he ran out the door toward the large wooden fence that enclosed the property, and he dipped down the street into the dark.

He made sure he dropped the Rolex in the bushes. He had carefully removed a pin, making it look like the watch fell due to an issue with the clasp. He threw the gun into some bushes a little further down and jogged to his car, which was three blocks over.

"Now, how does it feel to be King?" Deshawn said, feeling higher than he had in a while.

Carlton held Imani's head and exploded down her throat.

"Fuck yeah! Yeah, babe, swallow that shit!" Carlton yelled as he pulled her hair.

Imani winced as her scalp stretched from all of the tugging. He loosened his grip and wiped the tip of his dick across her lips. She smiled at him; she loved when he was satisfied.

He walked over to the couch and grabbed his underwear.

Imani slid off the bed and kissed his back. "You leaving? I thought you were going to stay a couple of hours today."

"Nah, baby, I got some business to handle."

Imani pouted and walked into the kitchen.

Carlton had recently rented this place for them, so they could get in some quick visits during the week without the risk of being seen during hotel visits. It was a one-bedroom apartment on the north side of Charlotte. She opened the refrigerator and took out the cranberry juice as Carlton continued getting dressed.

"A'ight, babe, I will catch up with you later," Carlton said as he kissed her on the cheek.

The door closed, and Imani sighed. She walked over to the couch where she had placed her purse and pulled out a white sheet of paper. She sighed again and sat down. Things were about to get real, very soon. She had hoped her period was late only because of the stress of her final exams. However, the test results she received from her doctor confirmed that the stress was just beginning.

Chapter 13

Two weeks later. . . .

King sat in the large leather chair and watched the faces of the producers as they listened to Sloan's demo. He knew he had them when they kept adjusting themselves in their seats.

There was a knock on the door of the studio, and Panama entered. He leaned down and told King that he was needed outside.

"A'ight, gentlemen, I will return in a few moments," King said as he stood.

He opened the door and walked out into the lobby where six men were waiting. He knew they were cops by the way they were positioned.

Panama walked closely behind King with his right hand twitching.

"Ronnie King?" the shortest of the men asked as King approached.

Two of the other men tried to walk behind King, but Panama wasn't going to let that happen.

The short man pulled out his badge and smiled at King. "Mr. King, you are under arrest."

King looked back at Panama and laughed. "Arrest for what?" King asked, waving at Panama to stand down.

"You are under arrest for the murder of Travis Indigo," the detective said as the other detective placed the handcuffs on King.

King felt the cuffs click and tighten on his wrists. The detective patted him down and, after finding that he was clean, pushed King toward the doors.

"Who the hell is Travis Indigo?" King asked as they opened the door.

The detective just shook his head and read him his Miranda rights as he walked him toward the unmarked police car.

"Yo, King, I'ma call your Pops!" Panama yelled to King as the detective closed the car door.

King sat back in the seat, trying to figure out what the fuck was going on. He wanted to ask the detective again who Travis Indigo was, but he decided it would be best to stay quiet and wait for his lawyer.

As the car pulled off, King looked back at his studio and mumbled to himself, "Damn, man. Even when you try to do right, wrong won't leave you alone."

Chapter 14

Deshawn smiled as he watched King through the one-way mirror. His plan had gone off without a hitch. He couldn't have wished for it to go any smoother. King was right where he wanted him—in a cage, far away from Sloan.

"Okay, okay," he said to himself, trying to calm down before going into the interrogation room.

Deshawn couldn't believe Sloan had stooped so low and gotten a street nigga. He closed his eyes and took a breath as the image of her having sex with King on the balcony resurfaced.

"Hey Detective, you okay?" an officer asked as he walked by.

Deshawn took a deep breath and relaxed his hands. "Yeah, yeah, I'm cool. Just trying to think of my strategy with this guy," he said, forcing a smile.

He opened the door to the interrogation room and went inside where King was already sitting, awaiting the million and one questions he knew he was about to be asked by Charlotte's finest.

King shook his head and smiled when he saw the African American undercover cop. He knew how these crackers liked to play. They always loved to use your own kind against you.

"Hey, man, I didn't think I would see you back here so soon," Deshawn said, pulling out the metal chair.

King shrugged and sipped water from the small Styrofoam cup. The officer wasn't dressed like a normal detective with a suit and tie, which was why King assumed he was a vice cop. It was clear that he was trying his best to blend in with the hood in his True Religion jeans, white Polo T-shirt, and Timberlan boots. On his head rested a newly purchased New York Yankees fitted cap.

"Damn, King, what's up with you?" Deshawn asked, taking a seat on the table instead of the other chair.

"Look, homeboy. I'ma save you the time and the trouble and tell you, just like I told the other cops. I want to see my lawyer," King responded, leaning back in his chair.

"Ease up, my brother. I'm not here to interview you. I was just checking up on you, partna," Deshawn responded with a smile, staring down at King.

Deshawn wasn't the arresting officer; he wasn't even on the case. That would have been too obvious. King or someone else would have figured out that he could have had something to do with the murder and setup. So, today, Deshawn was there for one reason and one reason only—to make sure he was the first person to see King's face when he found out he was being booked and charged with Red's murder. The only thing that was currently messing the moment up for him was the fact that King didn't look worried. In fact, King was quite relaxed for a man facing a first-degree murder charge. Deshawn figured he would add some info, hoping that he could get a rise from King.

"Look, man. These guys are going to come in here in the next few minutes and chew that little alibi of yours out the frame. That lawyer you keep calling for ain't gonna be able to do jack shit. I hope you got yourself a good piece of pussy before they picked you up because it's going to be a long time before you have some again."

"Hold up. Fuck do you mean, my alibi?"

King still didn't have the slightest idea who Travis Indigo was or why he was being charged with his death. He had even thought about a couple of his old bodies that could have come back to bite him in the ass. It seemed that he was only going to be able to find out what was going on if he entertained the interrogation. Maybe, he could extract some information from the detective.

"Yeah, murder raps are hard to beat around here, so don't play around wit' ya life," Deshawn added. "If it was an accident, then, just say that it was—"

"It wasn't no fuckin' accident because I didn't do shit!" King yelled, slamming his hands on the table.

The look that Deshawn had so desperately wanted to see on King's face finally appeared. It was a look of anger, with a hint of fear. This was the same way he felt when he saw King and Sloan together. He was mad as hell, and at the same time, it hurt to know that he had really lost her. Small as it might have been, it was a great sense of retribution seeing King in the predicament he was now facing. For the next few minutes until the lead detective on the case arrived, Deshawn was going to enjoy every second of it.

Sloan wiped her mouth and checked her teeth. Her dentist appointment was in fifteen minutes. Most of the night and early morning, she'd spent waiting for a call from King about his meeting with the producers for her album. She grabbed her keys and slid her feet into her Donna Karan slingbacks. When she opened the door, a large white envelope was on the floor. Sloan looked around before she picked it up. It had her name printed on the front. She tucked it under her arm continued on to the elevator.

“Hold the elevator, please!” A heavyset white woman yelled as she trotted. She stepped inside, causing the elevator to go down slightly. “Whew, thank you! Good morning.”

“Good morning,” Sloan said.

She took the envelope from under her arm and opened it. Inside were photos from the last photo shoot that King had set up for her. Things were really starting to fall into place for her career, and it was all because of her man, a man who she felt she only knew part of; but for right now, that was enough. Deep down inside, Sloan knew what the other side of King’s life entailed. She, also, felt that getting her singing career to the level she wanted would take King’s record label to the same level, and all the street shit could be left behind.

Sloan slid the photos back into the envelope as she walked to her car. If she didn’t hurry, she was going to be late for her appointment. Her cell phone began to vibrate as she got into her car. Noticing it was an unknown number, she hit IGNORE and turned her focus to the road and the time on the clock. As she drove to her appointment, she considered calling King, but the last thing she wanted to do was nag him. Sloan knew, all too well, how easy it was to lose track of time while in the studio. She put King out of her mind for the moment and rushed from her car into the dentist’s office.

“We know you did it. Just tell us what happened,” Detective Kobb yelled, standing up and punching the table where King was sitting.

Deshawn had handed King off to the two lead detectives who were assigned the case. His partner remained outside, watching the interrogation through the two-way glass and waiting to impose the good cop, bad cop routine if needed.

King wasn't paying Kobb any attention. The whole time the detective questioned him, King sat, twirling his thumbs. At one point, he reached down and acted like he was really reading the Advice of Rights form. King knew that at any minute, his lawyer would show up, and he just needed to buy some time until that moment came.

After another twenty minutes of the same questioning, there was a knock on the interrogation room door.

Before Detective Kobb could reach the flap to see who it was, Thomas Bolter, King's lawyer, entered the room.

King smiled at the look on the white detective's face. His attorney's presence had sucked the bullshit out of the room.

"Go ahead, and take a break, Kobb. You did a good job today," Bolter told the detective, patting him on his shoulder and leading him to the door.

Bolter was so arrogant but so good at what he did. There wasn't a cop in the city of Charlotte who didn't know him or who hadn't at least heard of him. With well over a hundred trials under his belt, and an 85 percent average of "not guilty" verdicts, he was the lawyer to have if you were a major coke boy in the city. His prices were high, but his performance in the courtroom was amazing.

Attorney Bolter's loyalty went all the way back to King's father, who had given the young lawyer his first major drug case. After defeating the feds on a major RICO charge against the elder King, Bolter's name had been cemented in the streets of Charlotte amongst the high-level hustlers, so, he was guaranteed top rates.

"So, what the fuck are these people talking about, I killed someone? I don't even know who the hell this dude is they are talking about," King said, standing up.

Bolter sat down and placed a manila folder on the table.

King opened the folder and his blood stopped flowing through his veins for a moment as he stared at the photograph. King stared at the picture of Red's lifeless body lying in the hot tub. "Fuck, somebody smoked this nigga? Shit, I can't say I'm upset, but damn! Look, Bolter, somebody got to this fool before me. Why are they so sure I killed this nigga?"

"They say they have evidence they can link back to you. Look, I need you to tell me where you were the night of June sixteenth, and I need names of people who can back up what you say. Right now, this ain't smelling too good."

"Bolter, I ain't did shit to this dude. Right now, I need you to get this shit fixed and get me out of here," King said, walking over to the two-way mirror.

King stared at his reflection. Although he had planned to eventually take Red's ass out, this shit was blowing his mind. If Red was bold enough to fucking rob one of his houses, there was no telling who else he had pissed off.

"Trust me, I'm trying to. I spoke to the Chief of Police, and he said that they have enough evidence to charge you in the murder."

He walked near King and continued. "The only evidence they have told me about is the murder weapon. Since they didn't take it off of you, I'm not too concerned about that. What does concern me is what they haven't disclosed, so if it's anything, and I mean *anything*, that I need to know before I move forward, let me know."

King looked over at Bolter and shook his head. Not being able to think of anything, he looked his lawyer up and down and couldn't help but to laugh.

Bolter looked at his clothes then back at King. "What?"

"What in da hell are you wearing?" King joked, pointing to the multi-colored flower shirt he had on.

"I was in the middle of Caribbean night at Michelle's, for crying out loud. I had two Hawaiian girls shaking their bodies in front of me when you called," Bolter playfully answered. "I could be balls-deep in some vagina right now."

They both chuckled at his comment. Laughter was something that King really needed right then. Now, he felt very comfortable, knowing he had somebody like Bolter on his side. King had total confidence in his lawyer and felt, beyond a shadow of doubt, that Bolter would fight tooth and nail for him in any courtroom, any time, at any place.

"But on a serious note," Bolter said, getting right back to business, "more than likely, you'll be taken to the county in a few hours. Your bond hearing won't be until next week sometime, after you are arraigned. This is a murder case, so whatever properties you have to put up, make sure you have ya mom bring the paperwork to my office on Monday," Bolter instructed.

King stood from his chair and stuck his hand out for a shake. At this point, he knew nothing else needed to be said. Bolter was on his job, so, for now, all King could do was wait it out and hope to get bail next week.

Sloan arrived home and tried to busy herself while she waited for King's call. She was so anxious to hear how the producers had liked her demo that she just couldn't sit still. Her phone began to ring. Looking down at the screen, she noticed it was another blocked number. Sloan hit the IGNORE button again. If someone was calling her and blocking their number, then, that was someone she didn't need to speak to. She put the phone back on the coffee table and hummed softly as she continued to sort the magazines on the rack beside the low-back couch. The phone went off again, interrupting her from going over the lyrics to a new song she was formulating in her head.

"Damn, this better be my baby," Sloan uttered under her breath as she grabbed the cell for the second time.

Disappointment immediately hit her face when she realized, once again, that it wasn't King calling. This time, at least, the number wasn't blocked.

"Hello, who's calling?" she asked in a professional manner.

"Hey, Sloan. What's good, sis? This Panama. I wanted to hit you up and make sure you knew Bossman ran into a little problem late last night. The cops came and picked him up, and . . ."

"Wait . . . What you mean the cops came and picked him up? What happened?"

"That's why I'm calling you. I'm not sure what they got him on, but I called his pops last night and left him a couple of messages, so I'm sure Carlton is on top of it. I just wanted to give you a heads-up in case you was wondering where he was. I figured the nigga would have hit you by now."

When Sloan heard the last statement, the blocked calls she had been getting all morning popped into her head. She was about to ask Panama if he had spoken with Yogi when her phone got another incoming call.

"Hold on," she instructed and hit the ACCEPT INCOMING CALL button.

Before Sloan could get a word out, she heard a female voice yelling on the other end.

"What the hell happened to my son?" Yogi asked in a demanding voice.

"Hello? Excuse me?"

"Child, I don't have time for your dizziness right now. What happened to King? I just got word that he was arrested late last night at the studio. Have you spoken with him?"

Sloan let the dizziness remark slide off her back. She understood Yogi was concerned about King, and this wasn't the time to call her out on her inappropriate comment.

"Ms. Yogi, I just got the call myself, and I have Panama on the other line, now. He said he called Mr. Carlton last night and left him a few messages, and he should be already on top of everything."

Hearing Carlton's name somewhat eased Yogi's mind for two reasons. For one thing she knew how much Carlton loved King. He was sure to be already working on getting her baby out. Secondly, Carlton had not come home or called last night. She had assumed he was up to his old bullshit—somewhere lying up with some bitch while claiming he was working. But it looked like she was wrong. He was out, taking care of their family.

"Okay, that's good to know. Well, you get ready. Either way, we need to be there when he gets out. I'll call his daddy and see how close he is to having him released, and then, I'll be on my way to pick you up," Yogi instructed.

Sloan agreed. Although she and Yogi weren't the best of friends, she was going to stand by King's side, even if that mean getting along with his mother, a woman she knew didn't like her. Sloan was at the point where she would do just about anything for King, and in time, her love would be put to the test.

Carlton awoke to the smell of pancakes cooking in the small one-bedroom apartment where he and Imani had their love sessions. The young girl had been fucking him all of last night and most of the morning. He would need to make sure he went to the Caribbean store to re-up on the Black Ant pills he had been taking. If he wasn't careful, Imani was going to give him a heart attack. *Shit, that wouldn't be a half-bad way to go—up in some tight, wet, twenty-year-old pussy,* he thought to himself with a laugh.

Imani jumped on the bed, pulling him back to reality and reminding him that he had not checked his phone since they began their fuckfest late the previous night.

"Hey, babe, be a sweetie and reach big daddy his phone," Carlton instructed while tapping Imani on her soft, round ass.

"Okay, but don't stay on it too long. I cooked us some breakfast. I want us to sit because I have something special I want to share with you, and I need the mood to be just right," she responded while handing him his phone.

Carlton didn't mind taking a break to talk because, even though the pills were keeping his dick hard, his body was exhausted, and he was feeling a little sore from all the positions he and Imani were putting each other in. As he reviewed all of the missed calls, the two that stuck out were from Yogi and Panama. He hadn't gotten his lie together for Yogi, so he figured he would hit Panama first.

"P, this Carlton, what's going on? I thought you and King was music moguls for this weekend, what's up?"

"Damn, Unc, I thought you had got my voice mail. They picked King up last night."

"Who's they?" Carlton asked, now sitting straight up on the side of the bed.

"I couldn't tell if it was the feds or local, but they was wearing suits, so I'm guessing it's something serious."

"Goddamnit, let me check with Bolter and see what my boy done got himself into this time. I told him to lay low after that last incident. . . . Okay, thanks for the call, I'll get back with you."

Carlton hung up and continued scrolling through his missed calls. He had a few unknowns on the list, so he figured King had tried to call him. Knowing that, and with the chance that Yogi had already been contacted, he figured he better get himself down to the police station. As he stood up and quickly put on his clothes, he could hear Imani in the kitchen working hard on the brunch she was preparing. He knew she would be disappointed, but she would just have to get over it.

Chapter 15

Deshawn pulled up to the corner of Walton Road and parked. A few females were standing outside, along with a couple of dope boys who were watching the trap house a few houses up the block. Dax didn't recognize the car Deshawn was in, so he immediately pulled the chrome .45 from his waist and held it down by his side.

"Who da fuck is dat, cousin?" Dax's boy asked, pulling his weapon from his waist and doing the same thing. "Dat mafucka 'bout to get wet up."

The dark tinted window of the 2013 Cadillac DTS rolled down, and a familiar face popped out. At first, Dax didn't know what to do. He thought about running since he knew Deshawn was a cop, but when he saw that he was by himself, he stayed put. One thing he did know about Deshawn was that he was as crooked as they come.

"Dax, let me holla at you for a second," Deshawn yelled across the street.

He just stood there. He wasn't really big on talking to the police. He didn't care how crooked Deshawn was.

"I'm not asking you," Deshawn shouted. "Put ya piece up, and get over here," he demanded.

Dax let out a frustrated sigh but tucked his gun back in his waist and proceeded to walk across the street to Deshawn's car.

Deshawn rolled up his windows and unlocked the doors so Dax could get in.

"Damn, Dax, you act like you don't know who I am. Me and ya boy was doin'—"

"I know who you are. I'm just tryin' to figure out what you want wit' me," Dax said, cutting him off.

"Yeah, well, ya peeps, Red, left me wit' some coke. I don't really fuck wit' a lot of niggas, but he spoke highly of you, and I was hoping me and you could continue doin' business since Red is dead," Deshawn said as he looked out the window at the constant crackhead traffic going up the block.

"Nah, I'm cool, brah. I really don't need ya kind around here," Dax spoke.

"You don't need my kind around here?" Deshawn shot back with an attitude. "How da fuck do you think Red lasted this long? If it wasn't for me, this corner would have been shut down. All of y'all stupid mafuckas would have been in jail by now," Deshawn snapped. "If I wanted to, I could lock ya dumb ass up right now, and ya dumb-ass friends."

Deshawn was talking real reckless, but he was speaking the truth, and it didn't take long for Dax to catch on. There hadn't been a police raid on Walton Road in over six months, and the police weren't messing with any of the other corners Red owned, either. No cops meant more money could be made, and the longer Dax sat there and listened to the services Deshawn had provided for Red, the more Deshawn convinced him that he was needed in more ways than one.

"So, just tell me what the numbers look like, and I'll see what I can do," Dax said.

Deshawn looked over at Dax and chuckled. Dax had no idea that it wouldn't be as simple as a payoff. A lot more was required from him, and he was about to get a clear understanding of what he was about to get himself into, messing around with Deshawn. The cost of hustling freely wasn't going to be cheap.

***

King woke up to the sound of his cell door being popped open. By the time he was transported to the county, fingerprinted, and processed, he was tired as hell. He still didn't know who his celly was or how he looked because once he got to his bed, he went straight out.

"Chow!" the guard yelled out to the pod.

King jumped down from the top bunk and stood by the door, checking his surroundings before he went out. He slept with his shoes on, so all he had to do was tighten up the strings and stretch his body out a little. This wasn't his first time in the county, and he knew that it could go down at any minute. Drama from the streets didn't stop once you got to jail; it only intensified, especially between rival gangs.

"Aye, celly, you gettin' up for breakfast?" King asked, looking over at the small body hidden under a bunch of blankets.

A grey-haired old man peeked out from under the covers with one eye open. "Nah, young blood. I don't do the breakfast around here," he answered then threw the covers back over his head. "We'll do the formal introductions when you get back," the old man yelled from under the blanket.

As soon as King walked out of the cell, he stood with his back against the wall and watched as the other convicts walked past him. Within seconds, he noticed his man from the block, Will, walking down the tier with Fats, another familiar face.

"Fat Man," King yelled out, getting the two men's attention.

Shocked but happy to see King, they both walked over and showed him love. It had been over a year since King had seen either of the men. They were locked up for homicides themselves and were about to start trial in a couple of months.

"Yo, I appreciate everything you did for me, yo," Fats said, giving King some dap.

"Yeah, me too, my nigga," Will added.

Not only did King pay for their lawyers, he also made sure they had money on their books every month. King wasn't able to visit, but he made sure his boys were not forgotten in the hood. He made certain they got pictures and mail at least once a week, and every now and again, he would shoot them a quick kite from himself. That's the way King was. He made sure that he looked out for the people in his circle at times of hardship and at times of ease.

"So, what it do?" King asked, wanting to know if there was any beef he needed to know about.

Will wasted no time going in on how the East Side Boys had the jail on smash. King and his crew had always had beef with the East Side Boys, and it didn't matter where they saw each other, a brawl popped off on sight.

"What about us? How many of us is in the jail?" King asked, trying to assess the situation.

Will pulled up his shirt and showed King the multiple stab wounds he'd received from the East Side Boys during their last altercation. "Not enough," he answered. "But they definitely know we ain't bitchin' either," Will said, patting the handle of the whack he had on his waist.

Will didn't just get stabbed, he'd, also, put in some big work and made it known that he wasn't a sweet victim. King was feeling him, nodding his head in respect, then, giving Will some dap. It was respected, and at the same time, it was a reality check for King. He understood how easy it was for him not to make it out of there. Because of that, he was going to stay on point.

"Make sure you get me some steel. It don't matter if it's sharp or not. I'ma make it do what it do," King said as they walked to the chow hall.

***

Dax placed his revolver on the counter, walked over to his bar, and poured a glass of Cîroc. He stared at the glass. Although his heart was heavy about Red's death coming so soon, his mind was ready to get down to business. The streets were already talking about King's arrest for Red's murder. It amazed him that the fucking pigs of CMPD had actually jumped on something so quickly. In his mind, King didn't deserve to be locked up, he deserved an eternal nap. Dax was well aware of the rules of the street, and Red had fired the first shots, but Dax thought the shit was over when King killed their boys on the block.

His phone chirped. Peach's picture flashed on the screen. Dax was not in the mood to be putting up with her bullshit. He needed to get things in order before they fell apart. The crew was already rumbling about Red's death and the direction they would be taking the business. Red was sloppy with his business, and Dax always tried to help him keep things on track. Red was a reactive nigga, which meant that he didn't always think things through; and now, his ass was six feet under because of it. His phone chirped again, it was a text message from his boy, Chub.

Yo man, I see this King nigga coming through the line now for grub.

Dax shook his head. Red had many niggas that were locked up. Some dudes he took care of, some he let rot. Dax had always made sure everyone had their books straight, just for cases like this. He knew the value of having an ear to the wall. Those niggas knew more about what was going down on the streets than the dudes actually in the street. Dax texted Chub back, telling him to just lay low for a minute. He needed to plan shit out in his mind. With Red in the ground and King's ass locked up, Charlotte was about to see a new Kingpin rise.

Dax's doorbell rang, and he checked the security monitor. A petite girl wearing a short black cocktail dress was standing outside. Dax walked to the door, opened it, and smiled at Cara.

"Come on in, Cara. How you holding up?" Dax asked, closing the door.

"I'm okay, I guess. Today kind of made everything sink in that Red is really gone."

"Come on, have a seat," Dax said, pointing to the den.

Cara looked around. Dax had African art throughout his house. As she walked into the den, she was impressed by the print of Shaka Zulu that hung from the ceiling to the floor. Dax had never struck her as a man who appreciated history or art, but from the way his home was decorated, maybe there were other layers to him.

"Wow, your home is beautiful," Cara said, looking around and taking a seat on the large leather sectional.

Dax laughed. "You act as if you are surprised!"

"Honestly," she said, crossing her long, lean legs, "I am. This is not what I expected."

"What were you expecting? A futon, some black magazine pics, and the house to smell of ass and weed?"

"Umm, yeah," Cara said laughing.

Dax shook his head. "So, do you want something to drink?"

"No, I'm good. I just didn't feel like going home yet."

"Yeah, I understand that, lady. I understand that," Dax said, sipping on his drink.

He knew what this was really about. Cara had gotten used to being a hustler's girl, and now that Red was gone, she needed a new baller to take his place and make sure she was financially straight. Although he thought Cara would have waited at least a month or two and found someone who wasn't so close in Red's inner circle, he understood the game. Truth be told, he had always wanted to see if that young college pussy was everything Red had bragged about.

Red had also given him the 411 on Cara being willing to eat some pussy every now and then, something that Dax would have her doing on the regular if she wanted to be a part of his team.

"Where you goin'?" Carlton asked as he watched Yogi standing in front of the mirror getting dressed.

Yogi cut her eyes over at him, then, rolled them back toward the mirror. When she and Sloan had arrived down at the police station before Carlton, Yogi had the confirmation she needed about what her husband had been up to lately. She was pissed about his lying and cheating, but she was more upset with the fact he wasn't there working to get her son out. No one had talked to King since his arrest, and Bolter had told them that he was already shipped to the county, where he would await a bail hearing.

Yogi knew that Panama had called Carlton in enough time that, if he wasn't somewhere putting his dick up into something, they could have been down there, and Bolter could have gotten them in to see King before he was transported. If something happened to her son because of his bullshit, Yogi swore that Carlton would have hell to pay.

"Damn, what's all this about?" Carlton asked, getting out of the bed and walking over to her.

He tried to wrap his arms around her, but Yogi pushed him away. He tried again but got the same results except, this time, Yogi turned around to face him. Looking at him face to face made her even more upset. She was tired of holding back the way she felt.

"You know what, Carl? Get the fuck out my face," Yogi said, grabbing a handful of his face and mugging him.

Carlton grabbed her wrist before she could let go of his face. He held his hand up like he was about to slap the shit out of her.

Yogi looked at him like he was crazy. He had to be crazy if he thought about putting his hands on her.

Carlton had to think about it himself, and instead of slapping her, he simply pointed his finger at her.

"What da fuck is you talkin' about?" he uttered though clinched teeth.

"You don't think I know what the fuck you doing? You must think I'm a fuckin' fool," she snapped. "Get da fuck off of me," she yelled, yanking her hand away from him.

"Man, I don't got time fa da bullshit," Carlton responded.

"No, you right. You don't have no time for your family, but you seem to find plenty of time for those dirty-ass bitches you out there fuckin' wit'. I swear you better not bring me no fuckin' STD," she said, pulling her hair back into a ponytail.

Carlton felt some type of way about her last comment. He always prided himself on taking care of his family. He walked up to her in an aggressive manner, towering over her as she sat on the bed.

Yogi shot up off the bed, ready for whatever.

"That's the second time you acted like you was about to do something to me. Next time, you better do it because if you don't, I'ma force ya hand. Now move the fuck outta my way so I can go see my son," Yogi said, brushing past him.

As bad as he wanted to grab her, he knew that the repercussions behind it could be great. Yogi didn't make idle threats, and with King on her mind, she was liable to do anything. Instead, he just sat on the bed, knowing that the argument was his own fault. All he could do, for now, was chalk it up. He was wrong for cheating, and before he could get upset with Yogi's reaction, he had to check his own behavior.

Sloan hurried to get herself ready. She had to meet Yogi at her house. Today was the day they were going to finally be able to visit King. She put on one more coat of lip gloss and gave herself a final look over in the large standing mirror. Grabbing her red leather Brahmin handbag, she headed for the door. She was startled when she almost ran into Deshawn, who was standing in the doorway about to ring the bell.

"What the hell are you doing here?" Sloan asked, looking around to see if any of her neighbors were outside watching.

Deshawn hadn't seen her in a few weeks, at least not up close and personal. She was still as beautiful as they came, and for a minute, he forgot what he had come there for.

"Damn, babe, how have you been?" he asked, reaching out for her waist.

Sloan quickly grabbed his hand and threw it off her waistline, showing her disapproval. She couldn't stand his touch, and now, she wondered how she could have ever gotten involved with such a lunatic.

Deshawn tried to pull her closer, thinking that if she could just feel his embrace, Sloan would, maybe, remember the connection they once shared. But Sloan wasn't having any part of it; she had come to the end of trying to be nice. She needed Deshawn to understand that she didn't want or need him anymore. The very sight of him sickened her, so with a strong push, she let him know her thoughts.

"Don't come around here again," Sloan told him, pushing him back and locking her front door before heading down the steps.

Deshawn could feel her hatred, and he knew he only had one card left to play.

"Yo, I can help him," he said, following her down the walkway. "I can get King out of jail, if that's what you want," he offered, getting Sloan's undivided attention.

Hearing that, she stopped in her tracks and turned around to face him. One thing she knew about Deshawn was that if he said he could do something pertaining to his work, nine times out of ten, it would be done. She, also, knew that he had a catch-22 with just about everything he did.

"And why would you wanna do that for him?

"I wouldn't be doin' it for him," he responded.

"So, what is it that you want from me?" she asked, shaking her head, knowing he was on some bullshit, and already having an idea of what he wanted.

"I want you to stay with me for one night. I wanna make love to you one last time. After that, you'll never have to worry about me bothering you again, and I'll make sure the evidence they got on King disappears for good," Deshawn added with a straight face.

All Sloan could do was continue to shake her head. She couldn't believe he would be so upfront with his request, and although it seemed disgusting coming from his mouth, it was something Sloan had immediately began to consider. She loved King and would do just about anything for him, but at the same time, she didn't want to degrade herself or betray King's trust.

Sloan looked at Deshawn and walked off. She wasn't going to rule out his proposal right then and there. It was something she, unquestionably, had to think about further, and if she did decide to go along with it, she knew that King could never find out.

***

King sat in the cell looking at the wall. It had been over forty-eight hours, and he still had heard nothing from Bolter. There was a tap on the bar of his cell. He turned to see Boyd Simpson staring at him.

"Hey, Detective Simpson, how are you?" King said standing.

"Looks like I'm doing a lot better than you," Simpson said, crossing his arm.

Simpson was somewhat a friend of the family. King's grandmother ran one of the most lucrative whorehouses in Huntersville, North Carolina back in the sixties and seventies. Huntersville was only ten minutes from Charlotte, it was known for its rednecks and crooked-ass police. Back in the day, Simpson was one of her best customers. In exchange for keeping his pecker deep in some chocolate, he made sure that she was protected, and law enforcement never bothered her. Over the years, Simpson had managed to maintain a relationship with the King family. Even after the death of King's grandmother, Simpson would stop by and check on Yogi. He was in his last year on the force, and had been put on desk duty, which was fine with Simpson, who now suffered from arthritis.

"I hear they got you in here on murder charges. Now why you go and do something so stupid?" Simpson said, leaning against the bars.

"I didn't do this, Detective. I have done some shit, but this one isn't mine. What kind of evidence do they have?" King asked.

Simpson was about to speak when the CO walked up. "Hey, Detective Simpson, how are you? What you doing down here?"

"Just talking to King is all, just talking to King," Simpson said without looking at the guard. "I will talk to you later, boy, and keep your nose clean," Simpson said, walking away.

The CO laughed and unlocked the cell door. "What his racist ass doing? He fucking with you?" the guard asked, placing the cuffs on King's wrist and ankles.

King smiled to himself, thinking of how Simpson had portrayed himself in the department. He had taken down so many dirty-ass cops, just by pretending to be a racist-ass cracker.

"Nah, not too bad," King said, walking out of the cell. "Where am I going? Is my lawyer here?"

"No, you got two visitors," the deputy answered as he led King through the large metal doors.

They made a right down a long hallway. King shuffled his feet as he tried to walk. They stopped at a white door. The guard opened the door to a small room with a glass partition. Yogi and Sloan smiled at him from the other side of the thick Plexiglas. King took the phone down. He laughed as Yogi wiped the receiver with a disinfectant wipe.

"Hey, baby, how you holding up?" Yogi asked, touching the glass.

Yogi's heart was breaking. She had seen King's father and Carlton locked up before, but to see her baby made her stomach ball up in knots.

"I'm good, Ma, have you heard from Bolter? What is the hold up?" King asked, leaning forward.

He could see the pain in Sloan's eyes. She was uncomfortable and looked out of place in the visiting room. Part of King was ashamed that she was even seeing him behind the glass. His lifestyle and the truth about his business had been rammed down her throat without any preparation. Yet, she sat there with his mother. Although she looked uncomfortable and terrified, she was still there for him.

"Bolter is working on it, baby. He said it is a mess." Yogi stopped and studied King for a moment. "You didn't . . ."

"Look, Ma, I have done a lot of things, but this is one thing I didn't do. I didn't kill Red. Believe me on this, I swear on—"

Yogi raised her hand. "No, don't swear on anything. Your word is all I need."

Yogi turned to Sloan, who had not taken her eyes off King. She took Sloan's hand and placed the receiver in it. Sloan put the phone up to her ear and cleared her throat. She had no idea what she was supposed to say to him.

"Hey, bae," King said smiling. "Don't look like that. I'm going to be fine. I will be out soon."

Sloan licked her lips and swallowed. "Are you really okay in here?" Sloan asked.

The door behind King opened, and Deshawn walked in.

Sloan's heart stopped. A chill ran over her body, and her vision became blurry.

King could see the terror on her face and turned around.

"Time's up," Deshawn said with a smile.

King turned around and looked at him like he was crazy.

"Yo, partner, I just got down here," King snapped.

"I didn't ask you anything, and I'm telling you, time is up. Now, get up!" Deshawn shouted back, knowing he had the upper hand and wanting to put on a show for Sloan.

King was about to buck, but he looked at the iron around his wrists and the shackles on his ankles. Even if he tried, there was no way he could win, although he felt in his heart that Deshawn was a true lame and would buckle if the press was put on him. Rising from the chair like Deshawn instructed, King turned back to his mother and Sloan and mouthed the words "I love you."

Yogi blew a kiss to him and watched as he was escorted through the door. She placed her arm around Sloan's shoulder and hugged her.

"Hey, things will work out, baby girl. Trust me. Come on, let's go get something to eat. You are pale."

Sloan shook her head in agreement and followed Yogi out. She paused for a moment and looked back at the door. She had fallen in love with King, and now, because of her, he was in the pit with the devil, Deshawn.

Dax drove down White Hall Drive and turned into the parking lot of NC Power and Energy. He had to cut the visit from Cara short to go and try to get off the dope Deshawn had put on his back. He didn't like dealing with cops, and he knew if he came short with the money or took too long, he would find himself locked up quickly.

He stopped to allow the two conservative looking white women to cross the street. It was late in the evening and the parking lot was busy with people heading home for the day. These were Dax's uptown customers; the ones he had kept hidden from Red. It took a certain type of finesse to deal with these white folks. Dax had tried to convince Red to take his business from the streets to the suites of uptown, but Red wasn't trying to hear him.

Dax had continued to help Red with his business, but at the same time, he was a businessman. He had grown up in the game on the streets of Houston. His mother had been murdered when he was ten, and his father ruled a section of Houston's drug ring. However, Dax did not have the typical upbringing of a hustler. His father was a thriving dealer who wanted his children to be successful. He paid for private school, piano lessons, and everything that a child would need to become a well-adjusted adult. Dax was not only a smart child, but also an observant one. While he had all the education provided to him of an affluent adolescent, he always watched his pops make his moves in the streets. Having the best of both worlds, Dax planned to build a strong empire, and it was starting with these uptown white boys.

Dax parked his car in the parking garage. The upper levels were under construction, which meant the cameras were not yet functioning. He checked his watch. It was 10:35, Corey had five minutes to meet Dax, or he would leave. In dealing with these types of folks, one had to set rules to let them know that they were not dealing with a low level dealer. Dax was about to lie back and relax when he heard the sound of a car engine. A few moments later, a white mini-van pulled in beside him. Corey was a slim white guy who stood right at six feet tall. He had on the normal nine to five working man's gear of brown khakis and a white button down.

"Hey, Dax, my main man, hope you got something good for me today. I don't mean to complain, but the last powder you gave me, I nearly had to sniff all of it to get a high, and all my customers were complaining. I have some major clients coming into town, and they are used to that Hollywood type expensive shit."

"Corey, I got you, my favorite white guy," Dax responded with a large smile.

He hated fucking with the garbage dope that Deshawn was making him sell. That bullshit was fucking up his name with his clientele. Dax knew that he was going to have to do something, and do it quick. His first thought was to try to touch base with Red's connect, Chin, and hope that he would intervene and offer some assistance, especially since Deshawn's actions were taking money out of his pocket as well.

***

Sloan walked into her bathroom and patted her face with the wet washcloth. She had finally stopped trembling from seeing Deshawn take King away. Her cell phone rang with a number she didn't recognize, so she swiped IGNORE. A few moments later, it rang again. Sloan sighed and answered, remembering that it could be King trying to call.

"Hello."

"Hey luv, you left without saying good-bye," Deshawn whispered.

Sloan was silent. She steadied herself against the wall and took a deep breath.

"I love your hair pinned up that way, Sloan. Of course, you could be bald-headed and still be the most beautiful woman I have ever seen."

"What do you want, Deshawn?" Sloan said, trying not to let him hear her voice tremble.

"I want us to be happy, Sloan, like we were before all this stupid shit. Before you decided to fuck a low life like King. You are better than that and you know it. You wouldn't give me a chance to explain anything to you. . . ."

"Deshawn," Sloan said, trying to control her anger. "What have you done to King? He is the only thing I care about, and I know you had something to do with his arrest. I don't want to hear anything from you about what you didn't get to explain. There is nothing to explain. I don't love you, I'm in love with King. You are a married man, why don't you be happy with that? End of discussion."

"You are young, Sloan. You don't understand that life can sometimes be difficult. My marriage has been over for quite some time."

"I don't care about you or your marriage, Deshawn," Sloan interjected. "King is all I care—"

"King, King, King . . . That's all you care about . . . that motherfucka is in my damn house now, and I can do whatever I want to him. You want to act like you run shit just 'cause you with a little dope boy?" Deshawn asked laughing. "Let me show you how it is in the big world, baby girl."

The line went dead, and Sloan stared at the screen in despair. She sat down on the green cushion, feeling sick to her stomach and dizzy. Her life could not be more wonderful and horrific at the same time. Her career was progressing, and she had a man that she adored who was a protector, provider, and friend. King had his faults, but at his core, he was a great guy. Sloan inhaled; she walked over to the mirror and applied a coat of chocolate lip gloss. It seemed that anytime her life was going well, the devil always sent his warriors to cause chaos.

King sat at the metal picnic table. Doogie sat beside him smoking his Newport and glaring back at some dudes across the yard.

"Yo, King, you good, man?" Doogie asked as he blew smoke out his nostrils. King nodded, looking over at the dudes who had Doogie's attention. "I got you, man, ain't nobody gonna do shit with me here. Dom and them here too."

King had some of his dudes that owed him for holding them down placed around him, but he had more enemies than friends in this shit hole. He had been locked up for five days now. Bolter was not earning his damn money. All he kept telling King was that he was working as fast as he could to get him out. He found out that they had found a gun with his prints, and his Rolex at the scene of the crime. It was a complete mystery how any of that shit could even be possible.

Doogie spit as a female CO walked by. She stopped and looked at him, then turned her attention to King and walked over to their table.

"Get your ass off the table, Jennings," the officer said, kicking Doogie's feet off the seat.

Doogie took a deep breath and sat down on the bench. She smirked at him, and eyed King. King shook his head.

"You got something to say, King?"

King tried to keep his temper under control. There was no need to start any trouble, since he wouldn't be there too much longer.

He looked away from her and mumbled, "No."

"No, what?"

"No, I don't have nothing to say," King said, clenching his teeth.

"You think you royalty for real, huh?"

Bump and Doc walked up and sat down with King and Doogie. King dapped them as they sat down, ignoring the officer's last comment.

"What up, man?" Bump said, pulling out a pack of gum.

Bump had been locked up for three years, and his time was about up. He had been arrested at King's club because he beat a dude down for trying to rob the bar. The dude ended up in a coma, and Bump was charged. Bolter had gotten the charges reduced to assault, but because Bump was on probation, he had to finish out his bid.

"Nothing, man, trying to get out this bullshit I'm in," King said, turning around to talk to his boys.

The CO cleared her throat and tapped the table with her baton.

"I asked you a question, King."

The yard's volume lowered.

King exhaled and turned to her. She had an afro pulled back off her face, and her skin was a deep chocolate. She was short with a wide butt, and it was not the kind of butt that would make a brother look. It was just wide and flat. Bump was about to say something to her when King motioned for him to step back.

"Look, Officer Frump, is it? I don't want any trouble, okay?" King said as humbly as he could, but he had purposely mispronounced her name.

The guys laughed.

"You Kevin Hart now, oh no, you the King of Comedy?" Officer Trump said, pushing the baton into King's ribs.

King flexed his hand. He had always prided himself on never hitting a female, but this bitch was putting herself in a man's place. Taking a deep breath, he memorized everything about her. He would have one of his females handle her ass when he got out. She huffed at him and walked away.

"Ratchet-ass bitch," Bump said. "She just wanna suck your damn dick, man. This the only place she can get some pipe."

"And even these niggas make her pay for it in here!" Doc said laughing. "So, nigga, why you in here? Rumor is you smoked Red's punk ass. Glad you got to him before I got out. I heard he fucking with one of my associate's daughter."

"Who that teenage girl he was messing around with?" King said.

"Yeah, her people had sent word they wanted her away from his ass. I was about to get it handled when the nigga was found floating in his hot tub. I should have known you weren't going to stand for what he did to old boy, and robbing you," Doc said.

Doc was old school and had run with King's father back in the day. He was the kind of dude that would take a contract, do the job, and move on like a ghost in the night. He got caught up on being a felon with a gun in a routine traffic stop.

"Doc, I didn't get to his punk ass. Someone else took his ass out and set me up."

King stopped talking. He didn't want to sound like a punk-ass nigga whining about being set up. He couldn't do shit about it right now from where he was sitting. What he had to do for the moment was survive being in the same hole as his fucking enemies. These dudes were circling like lions around him and his crew, just waiting for one of the COs to slip up so they could slit King's throat. King smiled to himself. If they were going to come for him, they would have a fight on their hands, with or without his boys on his side. He was going to survive this shit and find out who was setting him up.

Chapter 16

Yogi sat in the passenger's seat listening to V101.9. They were playing the best of Frankie Beverly and Maze, and she was floating with the music. She needed a distraction today. Her son was in jail, he was dealing with a weak-ass broad, and to top it all off, she had found some text messages on Carlton's phone from some chick named Veronica.

"Hey, I need you to stop by and take care of me, Papi," is what the urgent text read.

She had looked up the number, and it went to some stylist at a salon on Central Ave named Honey Blossoms. The bitch sounded Hispanic on the phone when Yogi had called her. She made an appointment to get her hair done with the trick. She would make sure that Veronica was taken care of and not in the way she wanted.

The more Yogi drove, the angrier she got. By the time she made it to the salon, her temper was on lava level. She walked into the hair shop, sat down, and waited for the woman to walk out into the lobby to bring her back to her station.

Yogi smiled at her as she walked around the corner. Veronica wore a black latex top with black leggings, her breasts were on display, and she had cherry-red lipstick on. Her long curly hair was loose and cascading down her back. She was young enough to be dating King, not Carlton.

"Hey, you Misha?" Veronica asked Yogi.

"No, bitch, I'm Yogi, Carlton's wife."

The girl stared at her for a moment, but before she could say anything, Yogi hit her with an uppercut that sent her flying back against the glass doors of the salon entrance. Yogi dragged her by the hair through the salon. The girl was screaming and kicking, but Yogi kept punching her in the stomach, knocking the wind out of her. She found the restroom and threw the girl inside.

"Look, you little bitch. I don't know how you met him, and I don't care, but you better stay away from him. This will be the one and only fucking warning to you. You hear me? Keep your fucking ass away from my husband or the next time I come back, somebody will be calling the ambulance for your ass." Yogi gave her another smack across the cheek and added, "Don't make me have to come back down here again!"

With that, she opened the door. One of the male stylists was standing there holding a flat iron. She jumped at him, and he dropped the iron and stood back. As Yogi was leaving, she looked at the station where the stylist worked. There was a picture of the Dominican woman with a handsome young man and a little girl. Yogi shook her head and walked out of the salon.

She was so hurt by Carlton's betrayal with this girl. She really thought he loved her, and would never do something so dirty. Why would he cheat on her? Yogi knew she looked damn good, and her bedroom skills were well above average. Did she bore him now? What in the hell had she done to send him out in the streets with this young girl? Yogi just wanted forget about the entire day.

She pulled into the BMW dealership. Maybe this was a good time for her to reward herself for putting up with the bullshit that came with being a hustler's wife. She had been with men like Carlton and King's father all her life, and she knew that they all had wandering eyes. Deep down inside, though, she had hoped that, when they got older, that shit would stop. Well, it looks like that was just a hope. The only thing that comforted her when she was younger was to make them pay in their pockets, and maybe, buying a new car with Carlton's money would help ease the pain.

"Push that shit back on me, baby," Carlton shouted while trying to catch his breath.

Imani was on all fours while Carlton was bent over her like a wild dog, fucking her from behind. The white glaze that coated his large pole was erotic to him, and he could feel his thick liquid making its way up from the bottom to the top of his broad shaft.

"Where you want it at, babe? Daddy is 'bout to cum for you," he exclaimed while pumping her tight walls faster and stronger with more deliberate strokes.

"Cum inside me," Imani yelled back, knowing exactly what Carlton sought to hear.

He cherished cumming inside of her and, then, watching her thrust all of his semen back out of her pussy. Imani wanted to make sure he enjoyed himself fully because today was going to be the day that she gave the big news she had been wanting to tell him for so long. She couldn't wait to see the joy on his face when she told him she was carrying their baby.

Carlton gave one final deep stroke before shooting his hot load inside Imani's awaiting womb. He fell over onto the bed, completely exhausted after the extreme fuck session.

Imani, then, rolled over on her back and positioned her pussy to where he could get a full view. She flexed the interior muscle of her vagina with enough force to have cum dripping out, drop by drop.

Damn, Carlton thought to himself. This young girl was everything that he needed. Not only was the pussy good, she was a pure freak, and she obeyed every command he gave.

After giving Carlton his final show, Imani got up and went to the bathroom to retrieve a washcloth. She placed it under the faucet and let the hot water run over it until the rag was good and warm. She applied a little bit of soap and began washing the remaining sticky substance from between her legs. Imani rinsed the cloth again before taking it back to the bedroom to clean Carlton. She laid down on the bed and meticulously cleaned his dick. After she had given him a full cleaning, balls and all, she tossed the rag onto the floor and turned around to look Carlton in his eyes.

“Baby, I wish we could lay like this forever,” she said as she lay inside his arms.

Carlton gave her a warm embrace. Although he loved every minute of the physical relationship that they shared, he knew that wish could and would never happen. But he also understood that Imani was a young girl, and young girls had dreams like that, so he didn’t burst her bubble.

“Carlton, can I ask you something?” she said with a big smile on her face.

He raised his brow, pretty sure she was about to ask for some money or some type of expensive gift. He had no problem giving to her either one, just as long as she didn’t ask to go another round. He did not have any energy left in him. Imani raised up in the bed, making sure she was directly in front of him.

"I have something that I really need to talk to you about."

"Whatever it is, baby, you know you can talk to me, and daddy will make it okay."

"Well, *Daddy*, I think maybe I'll show you the letter."

Imani got up, went over to the dresser and opened the top drawer to retrieve the paper that the doctor had given her as confirmation of her pregnancy. She walked back over to the bed and handed it to Carlton. He sat up, took the paper, and began to read. The very first line with the doctor's address and heading piqued his curiosity, but his heart sank and he felt nausea when he looked at the next section that read, "Pregnancy results for Imani Davis." All he could do was hope to see "Negative" somewhere on the page, but he had no such luck. When he looked down further and saw a positive result, he quickly stood up.

"What the fuck is this?" he asked as his anger rose.

Imani saw that he was becoming upset but couldn't figure out why, so she asked him, "Wuz wrong, babe? Isn't this great news? I'm carrying *our* child."

Carlton looked at the ignorant young girl and shook his head. *She could not be this stupid*, he thought to himself. She had to know, if Yogi found out, what could possibly happen to her. Obviously, she was not thinking rationally. Whatever the case, he knew he needed to quickly bring her back to reality.

"Listen, baby, as much as I know that you love me, and as much as you know I love you, what are your thoughts about having this baby? You know you are too young to be having a child. You have so much more living to do."

Carlton figured he would try the sweet before giving her the sour. Hopefully, he could convince her to do the right thing. He thought that if he told her directly to have an abortion, she could take the whole situation wrong and possibly expose him to Yogi. So, instead, he felt like he should try this gentle-hand approach first.

"Baby, you know that we had plans of traveling. We had plans of doing so many things. Maybe, now is not the right time for a child." Carlton was pulling out all the stops, hoping that he could convince Imani to have an abortion. But looking into her eyes, it didn't seem like she was buying any of it.

"Carlton, I could never consider killing something that was a part of you and me," she said with her hands on her stomach. "I know one day we are going be together, and will be able to raise our child just like a family," she continued.

Carlton now knew that the nice way wasn't going to work. He would give her some time to come to his way of thinking, but if she didn't, he would have to take more extreme measures.

Kareem turned the wrench one last time until he could no longer move it. The bolt was tight, and his shift had finally ended. Marty walked over and slapped his shoulder, and they both walked toward the terminal to their lockers.

"Hey, man. Me, Natalie, and the kids are going out for pizza tonight. You want to join us with your family?" Marty asked as he began packing his things.

Kareem shook his head. Marty was a straight type of dude. As far as he could tell, he had never been in any trouble; and he loved his wife, kids, and this piss ass job. The thought of becoming Marty made Kareem's skin crawl, and yet here he was working for fucking pennies and actually about to have a damn conversation about a family night. Not that he had anything against spending time with his family. It was more of the fact of not being able to do it without the worry of spending money. It seemed as if everything was always about a budget if they planned anything. The last time he and Tiana had taken the kids to the amusement park was before he started working for King. It made him feel like half of man, standing there watching his children share drinks and food while the other kids enjoyed their own meals with all the extras.

"Nah, man, I think I am just going to sit my ass in front of the TV tonight. We can get up next week, though," Kareem said as he slung his bag over his left shoulder.

"A'ight, you want me to give you a ride home?" Marty asked.

"Nah, man, I'm good. Wifey on her way to get me," Kareem responded.

He knew that something was going to have to give, and quick. Tiana had convinced him to give the truck back, and somehow, they were making it, even though he wasn't making shit. That was mainly because of Tiana's grant checks that kept coming through at the right time. It wasn't just about money, though. He was really missing the life that came with the money. He couldn't keep a side chick because he couldn't afford one; and as much as he loved Tiana, he didn't want that to be the only pussy he would ever get for the rest of his life. The thought of some pussy made him think about the waitress' young, fine ass. See, if his money was straight, he would have that young ass of hers in some fly spot, waiting on him to come through on a day like today.

The sound of Tiana blowing the horn brought him back to reality. Kareem grabbed his bag and tossed it into the back seat.

"Hey, honey, how was your day?" Tiana asked in a soft voice. She knew how hard Kareem had been working to stay on the straight and narrow.

"It's all good. Where the kids at?" he asked.

"Oh, I dropped them off at my girlfriend, Sharon's. She's doing a little party for her son, so we got a couple hours of free time. What you want to do?"

Kareem looked at the time on the clock. He still had time to make it down to Spectra Drive, where the county jail was located. The visiting hours on Thursday were from 5 to 7 p.m. He had not been able to see King yet because he, either, got off too late or had all of the kids. There was no way he was trying to take all of them down there for a little thirty-minute visit. He had only spoken to his boy twice since King had been locked up, mainly due to Kareem not being able to add the minutes he needed to get collect calls from the county.

"How about you take me over to the jail so I can get a quick visit in with my boy?" he asked.

Tiana knew how much the two men meant to each other, and she wanted to check on King herself, so she agreed that was the best way to spend the free time they had. It only took about fifteen minutes to get to the jail, and when they pulled up to park, the line was already starting to form. They got out and made sure they left everything in the car except their licenses and the car key. Tiana hated coming to this place. She had gotten more than her fair share of it from dealing with Kareem.

Once they were inside and seated in the last booth on the end, Kareem sat in anticipation of seeing his best friend come out the large steel door. When King finally arrived, shackled up like a runaway slave, Kareem noticed that his boy looked scruffy. He grabbed the receiver at the same time King did.

"What's up, homie? Niggas not cutting no hair in this joint no more?" Kareem asked.

"Nah, playboy. The one nigga that got some skills, he repping the other side. The cat that's riding with us, I done seen him fuck too many nigga's hairline up. And you know I ain't letting him get on this good shit," King responded playfully.

Kareem laughed. "So, on the real, how's everything going, fam? You good?"

"As good as a brother can be behind these walls. Tell wifey I said what's good," King added while cracking a smile in Tiana's direction.

Kareem delivered the message and then went right back to trying to gauge what the situation looked like for his friend. Quickly falling back into their old habit of speaking in code, they talked for about ten minutes before the CO told everyone to wrap up their visits.

King looked into Kareem's eyes after scanning over the work clothes his partner had on. The overalls were dingy and dusty-looking.

"How you holding up with the j-o-b? You need any money or anything?" King asked.

Kareem dropped his head for a minute before looking back up. Here King was, locked up and shackled, asking him if he needed anything. Kareem knew, without a doubt, that if he would have said yes, King would have moved heaven and hell from inside the prison to make it happen for him.

"Nah, brah, I'm Gucci," he lied.

Kareem and King both placed their fists on the Plexiglas, before saying, "I love you" to each other. That was one of the crazy things about being in prison; it seemed like that was the only time black men could say, aloud, that they loved each other. The whole ride back to pick up the kids, Kareem sat and thought about how he needed to be out on the streets, helping his brother find out who was setting him up and making sure he had all the money he needed, just like King would have done for him.

Carlton was sitting at the red light less than two blocks from his house when his cell phone began to ring. He looked at the screen and quickly hit ACCEPT, seeing that it was one of the locations he had weed delivered to via FedEx. He had just been over there about two days ago, so he knew another shipment wasn't due for at least a week.

"Veronica, how you doing?" he asked.

"Mista Carlton, some woman came by, trying to fight me. She said she ya wife, and she going to kill me if I keep working with you!" Veronica screamed frantically.

Carlton was trying to make sense of the conversation, and at the same time make sure Veronica wasn't saying anything that could get him a case if the feds were listening.

"What you mean my wife?"

"The lady said she ya wife, and she going to kill me for texting you," Veronica repeated.

Damn, Carlton thought to himself. Yogi must have gone through his phone and seen the text from Veronica earlier in the week. He knew something was up because Yogi's ass had been over his shoulder for the last day or two. As upset as he was about what she had done to Veronica, he was just glad that she hadn't found out the truth. If she knew who he was really fucking with, all hell would break loose.

Carlton assured Veronica that he would handle everything and told her not to worry about Yogi coming back around there. He, also, let her know that he would bring some extra money by to compensate her for the inconvenience and whatever damages Yogi had caused. After he hung up the phone, Carlton sat in the driveway for a minute to sort his thoughts out. This situation was just further confirmation that he needed Imani to hurry up and get rid of the child she was carrying. He made up his mind that he would have to fall back from seeing her until shit settled down.

Chapter 17

King stared at the ceiling of the cell. He had been locked up for two weeks now, and Bolter was no closer to having him released than he was the day of his arrest. The COs were fucking with him on the regular. Being locked up was causing him to think about everything that had transpired in his life up until this point.

He had contacted Max to ensure that Sloan would be taken to meet with Pitt from BMI Records. Pitt worked with artist development and was one of the top producers in the country. He had promised King he would work with Sloan. Not that she needed polishing, but artists had to know how to conduct themselves in interviews, meetings, events, and other things to be successful. Sloan had the talent, and he wanted to ensure she understood the business. The music industry was more dangerous than the street hustle at times. Even though he was locked up, he wanted to make sure that Sloan was straight.

The cell door opened, and King stood to go through the normal routine of being shackled. The CO pulled him out of the cell, and he joined the other inmates. Doc nodded to him as he exited his pod. King nodded back and waited for the line to move. Out of nowhere, King felt something cold around his neck and his body being lifted off the floor. He felt blows to his midsection and face. His vision became blurry for a moment. He attempted to throw punches at his assailants but quickly realized that he was shackled. Each time he tried to take a breath, his head would bang. He struggled, trying to get the chain from around his neck, but the person pulled it tighter as more punches landed on his body. He felt the chain loosen around his neck as he fell back. He didn't have time to think before he felt something plunge deep into his side and begin to burn.

"Fuck, that nigga got a knife!" someone yelled.

King looked up to see the blade coming at him again, but he blocked it with his forearm. It sliced his skin open, and King punched the dude attacking him in the jaw and continued punching him in the face.

Doc ran over and grabbed King. He threw him in his cell and shut the door. King watched as his boys tried to fight the inmates off and keep them from the door.

The guards were yelling, and a strong chemical smell filled the cellblock. King looked at his side where the blade had entered, and dark red blood oozed from the wound. The room began to spin, and he felt himself falling. The yells and whistles echoed as he fell into darkness.

Carlton sat back in his recliner and stared at the ceiling. Imani had been blowing his phone up most of the evening, and he had been sending her straight to voice mail. He needed her to chill out so he could focus on his and Yogi's marriage. As much as he enjoyed the lovemaking sessions with Imani, his heart was and would always be with Yogi. Carlton just wasn't sure if he totally wanted to break it off with his young lover. So, for now, he was simply trying to ignore her.

Imani stared at the screen for a few moments. She had called Carlton over thirty times and texted him just as many. She screamed and threw the phone against the wall. A knock at the door brought her back to reality.

"Mani, Mani, you okay? Open this door!" Khristian yelled as she pounded on the door.

Imani got up, picked the phone up off the floor, and looked at the screen. It had cracked, but the screen protector was keeping the glass together. She unlocked the door.

Khristian ran in with her switchblade open. When Imani saw Khristian looking like a ninja holding her knife, she let out a loud laugh.

"Girl, what the hell are you doing?" she said laughing.

Khristian exhaled while holding her chest. "I was about to kick some ass. I heard some commotion in here. You okay?" Khristian asked, looking around the apartment.

Imani felt a twinge of guilt, thinking of how she had betrayed her best friend's family by sleeping with Carlton. The girl was standing there ready to go to battle to protect her, and she had not only slept with her father, but was now carrying her half sibling. Tears began to roll down her cheeks. She turned her head in an attempt to hide her emotions from her friend, but Khristian noticed the tears.

"Hey, what's wrong?" Khristian said, pulling Imani to her. "What is it? Tell me," Khristian said as she walked Imani to the couch and grabbed some tissue from the box on the end table.

"I don't know how . . . I'm so embarrassed," Imani moaned.

"Girl, you know we family. You can tell me anything and it won't go any further, nor will I judge you."

"I'm pregnant, Khris," Imani said, sobbing.

"Whoa, shit, are you sure?" Khristian asked, sitting back.

"Yeah, I'm sure. I'm about four months almost five."

"What? And you waited this long to tell my ass. We can't do shit about it now." Khristian stopped and looked at Imani. She had just placed the proverbial foot in her mouth. "I'm sorry, Mani, sorry. I . . ."

"No, that was the right thing to say, and believe me, I considered getting rid of it. I just thought, I mean, I love him so much. I guess I was like the typical stupid female in thinking he would be happy too."

"Well, who is the father?" Khristian asked, holding Imani's hand.

Imani could not look Khristian in the eyes. She looked at the floor, and then in Khristian's direction.

"I don't want to say, Khris. He's married, and now, I'm starting to think he wants nothing to do with the baby."

Khristian exhaled and stood. She smoothed her hair back and began chewing on her lower lip. "Shit, Mani! Well, you know I am here for you as always, and so are my parents. You are like family, and we all will help you. You know you do have another option."

"Yeah, I thought about adoption, Khris, but I don't know if I would be strong enough to do that after carrying it."

"Well, at least you ain't got all big and sloppy yet. You still cute!" The girls laughed and Khris hugged Imani. "Girl, you know I'm here with you 'til the end. At least we get to go shopping and get you some new clothes and some big ass drawers!" Khristian held Imani and laughed.

Imani's heart ached as she lay in the arms of the best friend a girl could have, and of the person she could possibly hurt the most.

"Okay, Sloan, we are going to start it from bar sixteen, okay?" Pitt said before pressing the TRACK button.

Sloan nodded and began singing the verse. She loved this song, and Pitt had helped her tweak it. Over the last few weeks, she had been writing like a maniac.

She wrote songs inspired by her love and devotion for King, as well as her hatred for Deshawn. As she sang the verses of "Truly Royal," she fought back tears, thinking of how much she missed King.

"That is perfect, darlin', perfect. I think we got what we needed."

Sloan exhaled and took off the headset. "Thanks Pitt, this was amazing," she said, opening the door leading to the sound room.

"Girl, you got talent, and that song is hot. Now, think about what I said. I know some artists that would love to buy that song from you. You know writers make a good living in this industry. Think about this business from all angles," Pitt said, holding Sloan's hand.

Pitt was a short, stocky guy with an infectious smile. He had chubby cheeks that made his eyes squint when he grinned. He looked as cuddly as a panda bear. Sloan hugged Pitt and grabbed her bag and keys.

"I will see you in about two weeks, and again, Pitt, thank you for everything."

Sloan walked out of the building. Max was outside smoking his cigarette, which he quickly dropped to the ground and stomped out.

"Hey, you ready to ride, pretty lady?" Max asked.

Sloan smiled and followed him to the car. She coughed as the scent of the cigarette hit her nostrils.

"I will take care of that for you," Max said, as he opened the door to the CL550.

Sloan smiled and sat down in the back seat. She watched as Max took out a small container, sprayed a mist in the air, and walked under it. After a couple of moments, he opened the driver's door and started the car. Sloan sniffed the air and could only smell a minty aroma.

"All right, let's get back to the QC," Max said as he put the car in drive and drove out of the parking lot.

***

Cara checked her watch. She had been waiting for thirty minutes, and now, she was getting restless. Dax had laid down the rules for their relationship, and she needed to find someone pretty and new to team up with to keep his interest. She had a downtown apartment and a new Mercedes payment to keep straight. She checked her lip gloss once again in her compact and chewed her bottom lip. She had finally gotten Khristian to meet up with her, and she was nervous. They had agreed to meet at twelve, and it was almost twelve forty-five. Her phone beeped; it was a text message flashing on the screen. Cara swiped the screen and her heart sank.

Family emergency, brother in hospital will reschedule.

Cara slammed the phone on the table. She growled and buried her face in her hands. She had already told Dax she would be coming by with a friend, and now, she would need to come up with something because she couldn't disappoint him so soon.

King opened his eyes to the bright white lights shining down on him. He tried to sit up, but the movement sent a burning sensation through his right side.

"Aughhh! Fuck!" he said. Trying to hold his ribcage, he realized he couldn't move his arm. He looked over at the handcuffs that restrained his wrists to the bed.

"Mr. King, Mr. King, calm down," a woman said to him.

King turned his head to see a petite red head approaching him. She checked his IV, and gently pushed him back on the bed.

"Where am I?" King said hoarsely.

"You're in the hospital. You were stabbed, and they brought you here. You had a close call. My name is Amber, and I will be your nurse while you are here. And I don't need you trying to move around too much, besides, it's not like you have much of a choice," Amber said, jingling the handcuffs.

The machine beeped as King laid back on the bed. Everything began to hurt all at once and he grimaced.

"What hurts?" Amber asked checking King's pulse.

"Everything," he responded.

Amber laughed. "Okay, I will be back in a moment with something for your pain, and I'll let Dr. Milton know that you are awake."

As the nurse walked out, she nearly bumped into one of the police that was entering King's room.

"Hey, man, how you feeling?" the cop asked.

King looked up to see the detective walking toward him.

"I've been better," King said while Deshawn pulled the chair up to the bed.

"Looks like you got some enemies, my friend," he stated while sitting back.

King studied the detective for a moment. He didn't know what to make of him or why he was being so friendly. One thing he did know was that, from the first time he encountered Deshawn, his gut was telling him that something was slimy about the nigga.

"I am getting in there. That is my damn son!" King heard Carlton yell from outside the room. King felt a sharp pain run up his right side as he tried to sit up.

Deshawn walked over to the door and stepped outside. A few moments later, the door opened, and Carlton and Bolter walked inside. Bolter stopped Deshawn from following them back in and closed the door behind him.

"Son, you all right? These motherfuckers weren't even going to call us to tell us you had been attacked. Shit, you in jail, not the fucking penitentiary!" Carlton said as he sat down.

"I see you dug up Bolter," King said, and smirked at his lawyer.

"I haven't been hiding, King. I've been working on your case, and now, with this attack, I am going to push to have you put in protective custody. Had it not been for your few friends, this would have been a different visit. How the hell did it take the officers so long to get it under control?"

"We got enemies, and those pigs don't make much money. Slide them a grand, and they would let their fucking mother get shanked."

"This was Red's crew?" Carlton asked as he walked over to the window. "It's a good thing Simpson's old ass still on the force. He called us and let us know where they had taken you."

"Where's Ma?" King asked Carlton.

Carlton had his back turned to King. He continued to look out the window at the parking lot. He had tried to call Yogi several times, but it had gone to her voice mail. He started to leave a message but thought better of it. He called his daughter and told her to tell Yogi to get to the hospital. He knew that Yogi would answer her call or text. He was hoping they got there soon to see King before the cops locked everything down. Shit, if it had not been for Bolter, there was a chance he wouldn't have been allowed in.

"So, Bolter, what's up with my bond hearing? I have been locked up for two weeks. What the hell is going on?"

"I don't know. I have been trying to figure that out myself. Look, King, we are working on it, believe me. I am having a hard time getting to this supposed evidence they say they have on you as well. Every time I move forward, some bullshit happens, but I got you. I promise I am working to get this resolved."

"Smells and tastes like a fucking setup to me, boy," Carlton said sitting down. "We need to get the boys out on the streets and find out what is really going on—"

Some yelling outside the room interrupted Carlton's statement.

All the men turned toward the entrance. The door flung open, and Yogi ran inside. She ran straight to King's bedside and began covering him with kisses.

"Oh my God, what happened? Look at these tubes! King, Mama here baby," Yogi said with tears running down her face.

King winced as Yogi embraced him.

"Ma, I'm good, but you are about to hurt me again," King said with a laugh.

Yogi wiped her face and placed her handbag on the table beside the bed. She carefully got in the bed with King and held him. She kissed his forehead and looked at the bruises on his face. "Bolter, you gotta get my baby out of there, I just can't take it. What the hell happened?"

"Just some mess that happens when you're locked up, Ma. I'm all right. I will live."

Yogi wanted to squeeze him tighter, but she didn't want to hurt him again. "Shut up, sounding like your father!" Yogi said, kissing his forehead again.

Carlton touched Yogi's shoulder. He felt her stiffen, so he slowly moved his hand and sat back down in the blue chair.

"Who is your doctor? I don't want no county-appointed quack looking at my baby. I will call Dr. Milton."

"Dr. Milton is the one taking care of me, Ma."

"Okay, okay, I am going to go find him and see what's going on with you. You rest. Okay, baby?" Yogi said, standing. She smiled at King as she grabbed a tissue from the box and wiped her eyes. "Are you comfortable, baby?" Yogi asked as she picked up her purse.

King shook his head and smiled at her.

Yogi turned to Bolter and motioned for him to follow her out. On her way toward the door, she looked back and gave Carlton a scowl.

King waited for the door to close and looked at Carlton. "What's up with you two?" King asked. He could feel the tension in the room rise as soon as Yogi entered.

"Just some stuff man, just stuff. Women," Carlton said laughing.

"It should just be *woman*, as in singular," King said.

He loved Carlton. He was his father in every sense of the word, but he knew that Carlton was also a playa in every sense of the word. There was no doubt that Carlton loved his mother, and would never do anything but love and protect her. King was aware that Carlton liked to taste some other flavors from time to time. He just hoped that if his mother had found out, Carlton would take it as a sign to stop. Yogi loved him, but one thing about her; she was no one's fool. Not even the man she had been married to for the last ten years.

Sloan jumped out of the car before Max had a chance to fully stop in front of the hospital's emergency entrance. She had received a call from Panama, letting her know what happened and where King was. Max had done 120 miles per hour trying to get back up the road as quickly as possible. When she arrived on King's floor, she noticed the police presence in front of his room. She hurried toward the room but froze when she got about six feet from the door. Sloan watched as Deshawn and the officers talked outside of King's room. She wanted to see King and feel his arms around her, but seeing Deshawn had made her pause.

"Hey, Sloan, baby," Sloan jumped as Yogi touched her shoulder. "You okay? I didn't mean to startle you. Come on," Yogi said as she hooked Sloan's arm and guided her to King's hospital room.

Yogi knew that now wasn't the time for separation. When the family had problems, no matter what, they pulled together and showed a united front. So, for right now, Sloan was like her daughter.

One of the young officers looked at the two women and was about to stop them, but the glare from Yogi made him step back. Sloan kept her eyes down as she passed Deshawn. Her heart broke at the sight of King. He was pale, bruised, and looked as if he had lost at least ten pounds. The tubes that were running in and out of him made Sloan's stomach turn. She tried to adjust her facial expression as she approached the bed. King did not need to see how worried she was about him. He only needed to concentrate on getting better and getting out of jail.

"Well, look who I found outside," Yogi said

Sloan kissed King on his forehead and squeezed his hand. "How are you feeling?"

"I've been better, babe, but I will survive," King said, touching her face.

"Boy, we gotta get you out this shit and fast. Bolter, if your ass don't move a little faster on this here, we may need to find someone who can get it done, you feel me?" Carlton said.

Yogi rolled her eyes and gave him a fake smile, letting him know he was trying her nerves.

"Okay, folks, visiting time is over," Deshawn said, opening the door.

"Please, give us a moment. I want to pray with my son for protection," Yogi answered, taking King's hand and Sloan's at the same time.

Carlton and Bolter joined them as Yogi prayed for King's protection and release. Yogi kissed King on his forehead, and everyone began to leave the room. Sloan smiled weakly at King and kissed his lips. She laughed as she reached in her purse and grabbed a tube of Carmex and applied it to his lips.

"King, I . . ." Sloan paused. In her heart, she knew what she wanted to say to him, but she thought better of it. "I will be back, and I will work on getting you out of this situation."

King caressed her face. "Look, I know this is not easy for you, Sloan, but thank you for being by my side."

She grabbed her purse and walked toward the door. Deshawn's glare sent chills down her spine. She quickly broke eye contact with him and hurried along.

As she walked down the hall, she knew that things were only going to get worse for King, and it would be all her fault.

"You leaving already?" Dax asked as he lit his cigar and admired Cara's ass.

"Yeah, I need to get some studying done, and I have to make it to my rental office to pay my rent," Cara responded, holding up the twenty-one hundred-dollar bills Dax had just given her.

"Well, just know it's a lot more where that came from. You see, I take care of those who take care of me, so let your homegirl know just how I do," Dax said with a smile.

He couldn't wait to get her and the beautiful friend she had been telling him about together for a real freak fest. Cara slid her silk red panties over her full hips and turned around to face him. He scanned her flat stomach, toned thighs, and small breasts. Her nipples made his mouth water all over again as he thought about how sweet they had tasted less than an hour ago. He had pounded that ass, and she took it and threw it right back at him. To be so young, someone had taught her well, and the thought of having another just like her made him sweat.

"Look, I'm going to make it even sweeter for both of y'all. Tell your people I got five thousand for y'all to split this weekend if she make it by and spend the night."

Cara's mind began to race. She could give the other girl whatever she wanted, and it wouldn't be no twenty-five hundred either.

"Don't worry, baby, we will be by Saturday to make sure we earn every dollar," Cara responded with a sneaky smile.

Dressed in her True Religion shirt and Joe Jeans, she walked over to Dax and pulled the covers back to expose his partially erect dick. She took it in her hand and began stroking it up and down. Dax's head fell back, and he puffed a perfect circle of smoke. Cara giggled and slid on her shoes.

"Damn, girl, you can't do me like that, then, leave."

"I told you I will be back," Cara said as she walked out the door.

Kareem sat in the green steel chair, staring at his cell phone. He had just hung up from speaking with Yogi, and because he had been at work all morning, he had missed his opportunity to visit King. Tiana had tried to reach him, but his job had a no cell phone policy. On the bus ride over to his mandatory meeting with his probation officer, he had received numerous phone calls letting him know what had happened to his friend. The word was not only traveling in the streets but all throughout the jail. The niggas who had stabbed King up were bragging and talking about how they were going to finish the job as soon as he touched back down. Kareem's blood was boiling, and revenge was the only thing on his mind.

The door opened, and his PO, Ms. Bennett, came inside and walked around the desk. She sat down and opened a blue folder.

"You got somewhere you need to be, Hinson?" she asked, noticing that he was looking at the time on his phone.

Kareem didn't respond. He hated the visits with this bitch, and today, he wasn't in any mood for her shit.

"Put the phone up. You know that is not allowed," his PO uttered.

"Look, I got important things going on with my family, and I need to be by the phone. Besides, ain't shit changed since last week, so why the fuck am I here anyway?"

Ms. Bennett sat back in her chair and looked at Kareem like he was crazy. "Who are you talking to like that? You are on my time, not yours. You need to watch your damn mouth."

Kareem bit his bottom lip in anger and stood up.

"Sit down, Hinson. Don't mess with me. What is wrong with you? Keep it up and I will send your ass back to lock up. You trying to get locked up with your boy King?"

The idea popped into Kareem's head so quickly that he didn't have time to think it all the way through. Instead, he flexed his fist and glared at her acne-scarred face, huge ashy lips, and jacked up lace front wig. Her lips were shining from the cheap Vaseline she had applied, and that damn brown tooth seemed to gleam at him as she laughed. Kareem walked over to her desk and leaned down.

"You need to sit your ass down, now! Don't make me say it again."

Kareem tightened his right hand before he raised it back and slapped her across her right cheek.

Bennett screamed as she fell back against the wall. Kareem laughed and opened the door to the office. Bennett tried to gather herself and follow him out of the door. She grabbed his arm, and Kareem backhanded her with his right hand. She fell to the floor, holding her eye.

Walking out of the door, Kareem nodded to the other parolees in the lobby, who were smirking at Bennett sitting on the floor. He calmly put on his baseball cap. He knew it would only be a matter of time before the cops would be tackling his ass and sending him to the county jail, and that was just what he wanted.

Carlton hurried into the bathroom to finish getting dressed. He had spent most of the morning preparing for Yogi to arrive back at home. He knew everything would have to be just about perfect to get him back into her good graces. Yogi was his wife and the woman he really loved. He knew he was wrong for what he was doing with Imani, and now, the shit had come full circle. Before it tore up his home, he was going to set things straight. He reached down and grabbed his phone, making sure that Do Not Disturb was turned on. Tonight was going to be all about Yogi and their marriage.

He put on one final spray of the cologne Yogi loved as he heard the car engine. Before Yogi could turn the doorknob, he had already opened the door. He stood before her with a smile on his face. Yogi looked at him with a bewildered expression, wondering just what he was up to. Carlton grabbed her hand gently and walked her through the kitchen into the dining room, where he had the table already set up with candles and music playing in the background.

"Carlton . . . What are you up to?" Yogi asked.

"I just want you to know how much you really mean to me. I know that, lately, things have not been going the way that we both would like, and I know that's mainly my fault. I want you to know that there is no one else for me but you. You are the one I love. You are the one I care about, you are the one that I live for. You are my wife . . . You are my life."

Yogi sat and listened as Carlton gave his declaration of love and reconciliation. Although she was still mad as hell at what Carlton had done, she knew that she could not stay mad forever. He had come in and saved her at one of the most trying times in her life. Since the loss of her husband and King's father, Carlton had always been there for her.

Chapter 18

Sloan pulled up in front of Kareem and Tiana's apartment. Tiana had called and asked if she could borrow a couple of dollars for some gas and food for the children. With Kareem locked up again, the little money she had only went so far, and now, she was dead broke. Sloan was about to exit the car when Tiana came out the door and ran up to the passenger's side. She grabbed the handle, suggesting that she wanted to enter the car. Sloan hit the UNLOCK button twice so that she could get in.

"Damn, girl, you didn't have to run out here. I could have come in," Sloan suggested.

"No, you already extended yourself enough, and I had just got the children to lie down. I didn't want to wake them," Tiana uttered in a low voice, knowing that she was lying.

The truth was that the little furniture they had was so old and raggedy, that she and Kareem had thrown it out for the kids' safety. The living room was completely empty except for some of the children's toys. The kitchen set they had gotten so long ago was on its last leg, and she didn't want Sloan to see their living conditions.

"So, is Kareem okay?" Sloan asked, breaking Tiana's thoughts.

"Yes. I talked with him earlier, and he said he would try to give me a call again tomorrow. But I don't have any money to put minutes on my phone, so I'm not sure when I will get to speak with him, at least not until he gets visitation privileges."

"What was going through his mind, Tiana? Why would he do such a thing, knowing he would get locked up again?"

"Are you serious?" Tiana asked, not wanting to go off on Sloan before she got the money she needed.

"Yes, very much so. Am I missing something?"

Tiana studied Sloan for a moment before realizing that she really didn't have a clue. Yogi was right. The girl was as green as newly cut grass.

"Sloan, Kareem is locked up because he loves King more than anybody else in this world, including me and his children. Hell, even more than he loves himself. Once King's life was endangered, it ain't nothin' Kareem wouldn't do for him, and that includes going back to that hell hole and possibly getting killed himself."

"Wow," was all that Sloan could say as Tiana continued her vent about the love Kareem and King shared. It was one that most women couldn't understand; it was the truest love of brothers.

After she had finally finished and Sloan gave her the money, Tiana went back into the house, leaving Sloan to her thoughts. Damn, if Kareem was willing to give his life for King, what did that say about her? All she had to do was sleep with Deshawn one last time, and this nightmare would be over.

Sloan pulled away from the curb, knowing that now was her time to step up for her man, as he had already done for her on so many occasions.

Yogi exhaled as Carlton kissed the small of her back and gently massaged her hips.

"Damn, I missed tasting you, baby. Come here," Carlton said as he spread Yogi's caramel thighs.

His warm mouth covered her belly button, sliding his tongue over it, while the index finger of his left hand caressed her love button.

Yogi caressed Carlton's head as she rode the wave of pleasure his tongue delivered to her creaming peach.

"Oh, that feels so good, don't stop. Please," Yogi said as she grabbed the sheets and bit her bottom lip.

"I'm not going to stop, even if you tell me, baby," he spoke while pulling her clit between his lips and softly spanking it with is tongue.

Yogi arched her back and moaned. Carlton groped her ass and buried his face deeper. Yogi allowed the past weeks to fade from her mind. Her body rippled with two orgasms before she felt Carlton gently turn her over on her stomach. He kissed her neck, shoulders, and the small of her back before sliding his thick pole inside of her and caressing her aching box. Her pussy responded by surrounding his dick and pulling him in deeper.

"Damn, babe, damn!" Carlton yelled as he began to thrust faster inside her. "I love you babe, I love you!"

Yogi held on to the edge of the bed, trying to meet his thrusts. It had been a long time since their lovemaking sessions had been this intense. Yogi wasn't sure if it was the making up factor or what, and at that moment, she didn't care. She just didn't want Carlton to stop, and by the way he was pounding her insides, it didn't look like he wanted it to end either. Those fuckfests with Imani were, now, paying off. He could go for an hour or more with Yogi, especially knowing that he only needed to go one round.

Chin watched the dope boys handle their transactions. He had been scoping out the different trap houses around the city. Red had been a good customer to him, and now that he was in a box, he figured he would scout out the dude who had taken his ass down. One of his men had informed him that the dude was buying his shit from the Colombians that were trying to move in on his shit in South Carolina. With the way the fucking feds had been shutting shit down lately, business was getting light, and he needed to ensure that his funds were flowing from every open river.

Dax had reached out for his help, but before Chin made a move, he wanted to see what he was up against.

"How long we gonna sit here, Chin? I'm hungry and tired."

"Shut the fuck up, Tine, your ass always hungry," Chin said, blowing smoke out his nose.

"Man, we rode four damn hours to get here, and all we did was just look at some damn trap houses. Why we here?"

"We here 'cause I want to be here. Take your punk ass to sleep since you so damn tired. I'll remember that shit when you got your fucking hand out in my face next time," Chin said as he watched the block. "These dudes got a little more organization than I thought up here in the QC. Shit ain't sloppy at all."

Tine sighed and raised the seat up. He had been up all night dealing with a thieving-ass nigga who would not tell them where he had taken the stash. Working a man over was exhausting, and all he wanted to do was get a few winks in. Chin never seemed to sleep and stayed on ten at all times. It was true that business was not flowing like it used to, but shit, they were still making plenty of money, he thought as he watched the dope boys deal and the fiends move in and out.

"This shit looks like any other fucking block in the hood, Chin," Tine said, taking out a pack of gum.

"Nah, nah, it ain't. See, you don't know what you looking at or looking for. Look at them damn doors on the houses. There's a pattern to them. Make note of the fact that you don't see too many hood rats on this block either. Most of the houses look like ain't nobody really in them."

"Man, I seen some females coming through here," Tine said lifting up his left hip to let gas out.

"You a grimy-ass dude, Tine. Damn, what the hell you eat?" Chin said rolling the window down. "I should fuck your ass up for that foul shit. Damn!"

Tine laughed and let out another fart.

"I told your ass I was hungry."

Tine caught wind of his own gas and gagged. He rolled the window down, while trying to control his laughter.

Chin punched Tine in the arm and started the car. He checked his rearview and pulled away from the curb, trying to inhale the air from the outside.

"I hope we going to get something to eat now," Tine said, wiping his eyes.

Chin shook his head and merged onto the interstate.

"Yeah, nigga, we can get something to eat, but first I want to check into a hotel. We got some people to see and business to handle."

Carlton pulled into his circular driveway to see it filled with cars. One car, in particular, made his heart nearly jump out of his chest. It was Imani's white Infiniti parked directly behind Yogi's car. He pulled up beside it and walked slowly to the door. The aroma of bacon, eggs, and French toast filled the air. He stepped into the kitchen where Yogi was whisking a batter in the white ceramic bowl with her yellow apron on.

"It smells good in here," Carlton said as he took a step into the kitchen, all the while scanning the room for Imani.

"Hey, babe, I see we have company this morn—"

"Ms. Yogi, what can I help with?" Imani said, entering from the dining room and cutting Carlton off. "Uncle Carlton!"

Imani ran over and gave him a huge hug.

Carlton hesitantly hugged her back. He was hoping that his outside expression wasn't matching his inside thoughts.

"Good, you are both here," Khristian said with a large smile as she came into the kitchen.

"What's going on, baby girl?" Carlton asked.

"Yeah, what's going on, babe?" Yogi added.

Khristian grabbed Carlton by the hand and led him over to the table. She kissed his cheek and then looked back at Imani.

"Mama, can you have a seat? Imani has something to tell you and Daddy," Khristian said.

Yogi looked at Imani, then Khristian. "Oh Lord, what is wrong now?" Yogi said and placed the bowl on the counter and took a seat on the barstool.

Imani gestured to Carlton to take a seat. His heart began to pound and his palms started to sweat.

"Sit, Uncle Carlton," Imani said with a smirk.

"Nah, baby, I don't need to sit down. What are you girls up to?"

Yogi nervously tapped her nail on the counter. She really could not take too much more from her family. Her nerves were frazzled, and the situation with King had her anxiety level constantly on high.

Sloan walked into the kitchen. She felt the tension flowing in the air and turned to walk back into the dining room.

"Sloan, please don't leave. Come in, I want everyone to hear this. You are part of the family."

Sloan smiled and took a seat beside Yogi.

"Well, Auntie Yogi and Uncle Carlton, you know you are like parents to me, and you have always been there for me whenever I need you," Imani said, fighting back fake tears.

She took a deep breath and lifted the large men's sweater she was wearing, exposing the small bump that protruded from her midsection. "I am five months pregnant," Imani said with tears flowing down her cheeks.

Yogi laughed and clapped. "Oh my goodness, look at that little belly!" She grabbed Imani and hugged her.

"You are not disappointed?" Imani said, looking down.

"Because you are having a baby? Girl, with the type of things that have been going on with this family, trust me, you havin' a baby is a blessing. Now, I would have preferred a ring, but we don't always get what we want."

Yogi kissed Imani's forehead and giggled as she rubbed Imani's belly. Yogi remembered how disappointed her mother had been when she had gotten pregnant with King at an early age, and it didn't help that his father was a drug dealer. Her mother pretty much disowned her, and it was no way she would ever make a young girl feel that way.

"Do we know what we are having yet? I can't wait to go shopping," Yogi said.

"I told them I didn't want to know. Uncle Carlton, you haven't said anything," Imani said, looking into Carlton's eyes.

Carlton flexed his hands. *This little bitch is really fuckin' with me*, he thought. He had to look away from his wife rubbing Imani's belly and steady himself.

"I . . ." Carlton said, clearing his throat, "I agree with Yogi, baby girl."

Imani put on a sad face. "You don't seem as approving as Auntie Yogi."

"He'll get over it, baby. Trust me, none of us are in the position to judge anyone," Yogi said, shooting a glare at Carlton. "So what about the father?"

Imani dropped her head to the floor before speaking. "That is the other thing."

Imani sat down on the barstool. Khristian hugged her and squeezed her hand.

"Baby, don't tell me you don't know who the father is?"

"No, it's not that, Auntie."

"Well, what is it then?" There was a brief pause then Yogi continued. "God, don't tell me he is married." Imani looked at the floor. "He's married? Mani why would you get involved with a married man, baby? You deserve so much more than that!"

"I know, I know, I just love him so much, and he said—"

"Is he older?" Sloan asked, reaching out and grabbing Imani's other hand. Imani shook her head up and down. "You don't even have to tell us what he said. Those kind of men are predators, they know which ones to choose. Did he tell you before you got involved?"

"Yeah, he did, but I thought he loved me so much, and I was so happy. I just—"

"Played the fool," Yogi said.

She took a deep breath and walked to the window. Imani was like her daughter, but, for some reason, she wanted to smack the shit out of her for disrespecting another woman's marriage. She looked back at her and then looked at Carlton, who appeared to have lost all the color in his face. *Yeah, nigga, see what fucking karma does?* Yogi thought to herself.

"Did you tell him about the baby?" Yogi asked.

Imani nodded.

"What did he say?"

"Get rid of it."

"I bet he wants you to get rid of it," Yogi said laughing. "Well, you let him know he doesn't have to do anything for this baby. We got you. Anything the child needs, we can handle it, ain't that right, Carlton? The first thing we gonna do when the baby is born is have his rights terminated. I'm sure he will not protest that!"

Yogi picked up the bowl and began stirring the batter trying to compose herself. King's in the hospital, Kareem's locked up again, and, now, Imani's pregnant by some cheating bastard!

"Ms. Yogi, you okay?" Sloan asked, easing the bowl out of Yogi's hand and stirring the batter for her.

"Yeah, yeah. I just need a moment," Yogi said as she took off her apron and walked into the dining room.

Khristian's phone rang. "Excuse me for a second."

Sloan continued stirring. She turned on the flat grill, and began pouring small circles of batter onto the flat surface.

Imani sat on the bar stool smiling at Carlton.

Carlton checked to see where Yogi was, and walked over to Imani. "Let's go talk down in my man cave, baby girl. Tell me more about this dude."

"I really—"

"I insist," Carlton said, grabbing Imani's arm and pulling her toward the basement door.

Imani snatched her arm away and waited for him to descend the stairs in front of her. She didn't trust that he wouldn't push her down the steps, so she waited for him to reach the bottom. As she took the last step, she noticed Carlton's hand was balled up.

"What, you serious? You actually gonna hit me?" Imani said, taking a seat in Carlton's recliner.

"I told you," Carlton said, pacing back and forward, "I told you to get rid of it. What part of that did you not fucking understand? Then, you tell my wife and daughter? I don't play these kinds of games, little girl!"

"What? Carlton, you are the game master. You been fucking me for over a year, making promises to me, and now, when I need you to come through, you got the fucking nerve to ignore me and treat me like a bitch on the corner!"

"Keep your voice down!" Carlton said, lunging at Imani.

She could feel his breath on her face. The veins on the side of his face protruded and he was shaking. Fear was Imani's first response, but it was replaced with anger.

"Step back, Carlton, or I swear to God, I will start screaming."

Carlton's hands ached, they itched to go around this bitch's neck and squeeze until she turned fucking blue. He pushed himself away from her, walked over to his bar, and poured himself a drink. Imani sat in his chair, rubbing her belly and smiling at him. How the fuck did he mess up this badly, and how was he going to correct this problem? He had to think of something, quick, because. He was not going to lose Yogi and his family because of this little bitch.

Chapter 19

"I see you made it up to the QC, finally," Dax said, shaking Chin's hand.

Chin nodded and sat down in the lounger beside Dax. He inhaled as he viewed the skyline of the city from the rooftop of the building. A young woman wearing a white T-shirt and red shorts smiled at him.

"What can I get you?"

"You know, nothing right now, beautiful. Give me about fifteen minutes," Chin said, scanning her long tanned legs.

The girl smiled and squeezed his left shoulder before she sauntered off.

"Your city has a lot of little desirable things in it. I see potential," Chin said, licking his lips.

Dax laughed and sipped his gin. "So it does, my friend. So it does. You should've come sooner."

"Yeah, well, you know I don't like being too far away from my money, and from what I see, I could be making this my second home. I scoped your boy's scene out. He pretty organized, and he ain't green. That is for sho, system flowing without a hitch."

"Yeah, he got his shit together, but everything has its weak spots. Red found that shit out the hard way and paid for it with his life," Dax said, rubbing his goatee.

"So, what you want from me, Dax? I got you on the weight all day and night. You got Red's business, and from what I hear, ya got his bitch, too."

Dax looked over at Chin and, then, back at the sky. "Let's stick to business, Chin. What I want is to form a strong partnership. I'm about to put King out of business for good. My people nearly did just that a few weeks ago, but the nigga managed to stay alive. He won't be so lucky next time. I am offering you King's part of the city," Dax said, sitting up. "Well, part of his part. I will keep buying my shit from you 'cause it is good quality and out of respect. But . . ." Dax said, reclining as the waitress placed another drink on the small table.

"But what?" Chin tightened his jaw.

"There's two problems that must be dealt with. First, things are real tight out here now, with the feds on niggas asses. The fiends don't care about how tight the supply is right now, but they do care about quality. King's shit is potent, man, and his customers are loyal only for that fact. Yo shit good, but they prefer his to yours, and I need my partner to understand that."

"Don't fucking threaten me," Chin said, swirling his gin in his glass without looking at Dax.

"I don't threaten men. I simply have conversations, Chin. We are simply having a conversation. Besides, I have a gun connect I think you would be real interested in. This ain't no regular shit, this some top of the line, Pentagon type shit."

"Oh, yeah?" Chin asked, now sitting up in his chair. The gang with the biggest firepower always ruled the streets. It was no different than the armies of the world. The bigger the weapons, the greater the power. "So, you got my attention. Now, what's the other problem?"

"I got a dirty cop that Red was dealing with, and now, he on my ass to move some dope for him. Nigga giving me bullshit, but I still have to pay him. I can't get no local nigga to take him out, so I was thinking maybe you could assist me in handli—"

"Nah, I don't fuck with no cops, brah. You can count me out on that part, but I got you on the other shit all day, my nigga."

Deshawn smiled at himself in the mirror. Sloan had finally given in to his offer, and he planned to make the most of it. The large suite at the Hilton Hotel was one of the finest, with gold adornments throughout and a view that would cause the hardest woman to cave. He had the staff ensure that the colors of blue and pink were everywhere in the room, along with blueberry scented candles.

There was a soft knock at the door. He checked himself one last time in the mirror and clapped his hands as he made his way to the door and opened it. Sloan stood there wearing his favorite dress, a Chanel strapless cocktail dress he had bought for her when they were dating. He loved how the dress hugged her curves and how the soft blue color brought out the flecks of gold in her complexion.

"Damn, baby, you look beautiful," he said, standing to the side. "Please come on in."

Sloan walked into the suite and sat down in the large brown wingback chair. Without a smile, she sat on the edge of the seat.

"I have dinner for us being delivered in a few minutes. Do you want something to drink?" Deshawn asked.

Sloan shook her head.

He sat on the small coffee table in front of her. "Sloan, you are so beautiful, and I've missed you so much," he spoke while caressing her face.

"Where is it, Deshawn? Before I do anything, I want the evidence like you promised," Sloan demanded with a hardened expression.

"Sloan, this evening is—"

"This evening is nothing more than blackmail. That is it. My God, I can't believe I am doing this! How could you ask someone who you say you love to do this? You have no soul or conscience!"

"You loved me, Sloan, and I know you can love me again. Why are you into this little thug?"

"That thug, as you refer to him, has honor, and I don't have to share him with anyone."

Deshawn felt the room begin to spin. He tried to focus on his breathing, but he wanted to wrap his hands around Sloan's neck. She was being foolish, and he wanted to slap her until she realized how dumb she was being.

"Okay, okay, I don't want to talk about him or anybody else, baby. I will keep my word that I will have the evidence against him disappear. Tonight," Deshawn said kissing the back of her neck, "tonight is about us."

Sloan fought back tears as his hand traveled up and down her body. She swallowed the bile and closed her eyes, praying for strength to make it through the night. She had to do this to help King. She owed him, and she wanted and needed him back in her life.

Carlton smiled as he and Yogi walked into the lobby of the Hilton Hotel. Yogi had on a beautiful camel-brown wrap dress, with the new diamond necklace he had just bought for her. They headed to the bar, took their seats, and he ordered them some drinks. Carlton kissed her hand and studied her flawless skin. In that moment, as he stared into Yogi's eyes, he couldn't figure out what had made him risk losing her with his latest affair, an affair that, if he didn't get his hands around it, could end up costing him not only Yogi, but his whole family. There was no telling how Khristian would respond if the truth came out about who had fathered Imani's baby. Then, there was the major problem of King's reaction. King was Yogi's son, and the business side of their empire would be drastically affected if there was a falling out. No, Carlton knew he needed to get this problem handled soon and permanently.

"You okay?" Yogi asked, seeing that Carlton was in deep thought and appeared to be worried.

"Yeah, babe, I'm fine. You just making me nervous, got me feeling like I'm sixteen years old again."

"What are you talking about? Don't be silly." Yogi blushed as she responded.

"Damn, I'm for real. Got me wanting to skip dinner and go straight to the dessert."

Yogi grabbed his hand and held it to her cheek, before releasing it with a soft kiss on his palm.

"Maybe, we should go to the suite and order room service there," she whispered in his ear.

Carlton extended his hand to her, and Yogi paused for a moment. She took a deep breath before following him. Carlton was really trying hard to win her heart back, and it was working. As they got on the elevator, Yogi stared at their reflection in the doors. Carlton was still a very handsome man, standing six-feet-three with dark brown skin, high cheek bones, a bald head, broad shoulders, and a V-shaped physique, even though he was about to hit fifty.

Yogi followed him down the hall to room 825. He opened the door for her, and she walked inside and looked around the suite. Carlton had rose petals scattered throughout the large room. Yogi had told him he was going to have to put in work to get back her love, and Carlton was proving he was ready to do just that.

The next morning, Sloan sat on the edge of the bed. She slipped on her shoes and combed her hair back.

Deshawn snored softly as he slept. She quietly grabbed her purse and keys.

"Hey, you leaving?" he asked as Sloan walked toward the door of the bedroom.

"Yeah, it's morning. I got things to do," Sloan responded as she grabbed the black duffle bag off the floor. "Keep your word, Deshawn," she added without turning around.

"I said I would, although I shouldn't," he answered, now sitting up.

Sloan sighed and walked out the door.

"Oh, you will, nigga, or else. You are not the only one who can hold shit over people's heads."

She smiled as she looked down at her Samsung phone. She went to the video and watched as Deshawn appeared on the screen, holding the evidence against King. Sloan placed the phone in her purse and checked the duffle bag. Now, all she needed to do was wait and see if Deshawn upheld his part of the deal.

Leaving the lobby of the hotel, she wore her Chanel shades as the morning sun beamed down on her. She handed the valet her ticket and waited for her car. Her phone buzzed and Yogi's picture popped on the screen.

"Good morning, Ms. Yogi," Sloan answered.

"Good morning to you as well, young lady. How are you?"

Sloan was about to speak when she realized that Yogi sounded a lot closer than the phone. She turned around slowly to see Yogi standing behind her. Her stomach dropped and she felt the blood stop in her veins.

"Ms. Yogi?"

"Yes, good morning. She will get her car later," Yogi said, handing the valet a twenty and taking Sloan's ticket back. "So you look . . . caught."

Yogi struggled to keep her composure. She had allowed the relationship between her and Sloan to become close because she knew how much King loved her and needed her during this trying time. But now, here she was, with her little trifling ass, up in a hotel, while her baby was lying in a hospital. This was why Yogi knew she wasn't the right woman for King. The little bitch couldn't even hold him down for this short bid. Her fist tightened up, and she wanted to slap that lost look off Sloan's face so bad, but she held her temper. She couldn't wait to hear what excuse Sloan would try to use to clean up being caught red-handed.

"You know they serve an excellent breakfast here. Come on, let's have some and talk."

Sloan looked at her wide-eyed.

Yogi gave a fake grin and walked back inside the hotel. "Come on, girl."

Sloan followed Yogi, her stomach flipping as the hostess led them to a table.

"Look, Ms. Yogi, this isn't what you think."

"Is that right? Well, why don't you tell me what I should be thinking. Because right know, I think that I was right about you not being the one for my son."

Sloan began to tear up and took a deep breath before sliding Yogi the black duffle bag. Yogi looked at the bag, then, back at Sloan. Those crocodile tears were not going to work on her. She placed the bag on the table and slid the zipper back.

"What the fuck is this?"

"It is the gun and watch the police recovered from the murder scene."

"How . . . How did you get this?" Yogi whispered, closing the bag. "Sloan, how did you get this?"

Sloan tried to fight back the stream of tears, but Yogi seemed to stare into her shame. "I . . ." Sloan began to sob and tell Yogi the truth. She started from dating Deshawn to sleeping with him last night in order to get the evidence to free King.

Yogi was quiet for what seemed like forever. She inhaled and slid her chair close to Sloan and took her in her arms.

"Oh, babe," Yogi said holding her. "I wish you would have come to me."

"I thought I could handle him on my own, and I have. He says he is going to make everything shift from King and get him released." Sloan wiped her eyes with the white cloth napkin. "If he thinks he can go back on his word, well, I have something that will ensure he does what he promised."

Yogi sat there holding her. Sloan had stood up and sacrificed for King. That was something Yogi couldn't deny. Maybe, she had been wrong about her. Maybe, she was just what her son needed, a woman who would give her all for him.

"Come on, let's get out of here. I will fix us breakfast at home, okay? I know you want to shower."

"I need to take several showers," Sloan said as they exited the restaurant into the hotel lobby.

Yogi shook her head and took Sloan's arm. "I know, honey, I know."

Carlton lay back on the king size bed in the hotel suite. Yogi had called to let him know that Sloan had called, and she was going to go and check on her. She would meet him back at the house later. This was the alone time he needed to plot how to properly handle the Imani ordeal.

He grabbed his cell phone from the nightstand. Scrolling through his list of contacts, he pressed the name, Ox. Carlton knew he needed to bring in someone he could really trust to take care of this problem with discretion and professionalism. Ox was just the man for the job. Although he had gotten a little older, he was still one of the best at making problems disappear. The other great thing about using an older head was that they didn't share the problem most of the youngsters had of running their mouths and bragging about everything they did.

Chapter 20

Two weeks later. . . .

King sat on the side of the bed, and for the first time, the room didn't spin as he moved. Bolter had stopped by last week and informed him that the charges against him were being dropped. He had no other details besides that the investigation was going in a different direction. King didn't give a shit. As long as this was over, and he could get back to his family and his business, he was cool for now. He hadn't seen his baby girl, Malani, in over a month, and it was killing him. He missed her terribly, and he knew she missed him.

Bolter also had informed him that Kareem's crazy ass had gotten himself locked up by slapping his PO, and he was going to have to finish out the last three months of his sentence.

Panama had swung through and guaranteed King that Kareem was good, and he had made sure the guards were keeping an eye on shit. It had cost them a pretty penny, but he didn't want his boy to end up where he was or worse. As soon as he was released, he was going to go down and check on him.

"Mr. King?" The door opened, and Nurse Petty smiled at him. "How we feeling this morning?"

"Like I am ready to go home."

"Well, yeah, I know you are. Shouldn't be too long now. Glad to see you lost the county jewelry," Petty said, looking at King's wrist.

King nodded and lay back on the bed.

"Yeah, they love shackling our boys more than educating them. I have always tried to keep mine out of that type of situation, so I am glad to see that yours got straightened out," she said as she checked King's pulse. She gently pulled up his gown and checked the dressing on his wound. "All right, I will be back in a couple of hours to change that for ya. You need to rest, how are you on pain?"

"I'm okay."

Nurse Petty patted his shoulder and walked out of the room. King looked at the box of his things that Bolter had brought to him. His cell phone was in there, but he didn't have his charger. Panama had given him a report on his trap houses and the business. To his surprise, Red's people had been quiet.

King pressed the button to raise his head. He stared out the window. Sloan had not been by in a couple of days. She had called, and King could tell from her voice that something wasn't right. Sloan was so beautiful, smart, and a beast in the bedroom. She was, also, the type of girl who was not accustomed to guns, bodies, and blood. However, she had been a trooper for him and had remained by his side through all of this shit. His mother was not thrilled with the fact that he decided to date someone like Sloan. King knew that Yogi was right; Sloan adjusting to their way of life would be difficult, if not impossible.

Hell, he was tired of this life. He was in the hospital, coming back from an attack that damn near took him to his grave. Since he had been locked up, his business was still pulling in about three hundred stacks a week. The club was doing well, and Sloan was in the studio putting down tracks for her album. He had gotten "Falling" played on the local station, and it was received well by the local market. It was making its way up the iTunes chart, and her Web site was getting hits and comments. She had sang a couple of hooks on some rap songs, and she was working with a voice coach. King had spent time and money on Sloan. Not just because he loved her, but because she truly had talent. Music had always saved and soothed him. It was what he and his father had bonded over, and he hoped it would be what would get him out of this life.

All that time King had spent in jail had him horny as hell, and Sloan could tell by the way he was watching her undress that the royal crown needed to be polished. She didn't say a word. Sloan just unzipped her blouse in a slow and seductive way and, then, stepped out of her Louboutin shoes. He grabbed her by the waist and pulled her body against his. She looked up at him for a brief second before their lips connected. They kissed each other passionately and gently. The love they shared for one another was evident. Tasting the sweetness of her tongue as she swiped it across the tip of his, King backed her up to the bed, softly pushing her onto it and, then, reached for her pants.

Sloan assisted, arching her butt up so he could pull them and her panties off at the same time.

His jeans were next, and when he dropped his boxers, Sloan took a deep swallow, nearly choking on her own spit at the anticipation of feeling him inside her. King stood there with a seductive grin on his face, knowing that he had a lot of lovemaking to give her for his time away.

"It's gonna be a long night for you," King teased as he climbed on top of her.

King's legs began to go limp as the sensation of the tip of his dick penetrating her warm, soft womb began to take effect.

Sloan looked up at him with wide eyes as he slowly pushed his pole deep inside of her, inch by inch. Her head went backward, mouth shot open, and she dug her nails into his back. It was too much for her to handle, but she did it anyway, loosening up her walls as much as she could to allow him to push the rest of it in. She needed him to fill her up, to clear away any traces of Deshawn. Her body welcomed him home, and not for a second did she regret the sacrifice she had made in order for them to have this moment.

"Shit!" she yelled out, biting down on his shoulder.

Slowly, King dipped in and out of her drenched, tight tunnel of passion. He looked into her eyes before letting his lips find hers. His strokes were long and deep, and every time his dick pressed against her back wall, Sloan's body jerked.

"*Kinnnggg*," she moaned between strokes.

They made love off and on until dusk. Between their passionate lovemaking, Sloan would sing some lyrics of her new songs. Finally, at around seven in the morning, they fell asleep in each other's arms. Both bodies were soaked in sweat and sticky from the exchange of erotic juices.

Chapter 21

The block was on fire with music, laughter, and food. King sat back in the patio recliner, sipping on pineapple Cîroc. His mother and Carlton were throwing him a coming home party, and everyone had come out to celebrate.

"Hey, bro, you looking like you nice right now," Khristian said, taking the empty glass from King and handing him another.

"Yeah, little sis, I'm good. You seen Sloan?"

"She is in the kitchen with Ma."

"In the kitchen with Ma?" King repeated. "Damn, I must be drunk."

"No, they been cool since you been locked up."

"No, shit? Well miracles do happen, huh? So how you doing? How's school? I hear old girl knocked up by some married nigga."

"School is almost over, and then, it is out in the real world. Everything good, bro, especially now that you're home and safe."

Khristian smiled and took his hand. Seeing him in the hospital like that had shaken her to her core. The thought of him being so weak scared the hell out her. King always seemed bigger than life, and the sight of him in that hospital bed, looking like a mere human, terrified her. Superheroes don't go down; nothing hurts them. To her, that is what King was, immortal. She always felt safest with King, and the thought of him not being there with her was something she did not want to consider.

"Yeah, well you know I'm Teflon, sis," King said laughing.

Khristian's phone buzzed. She swiped the screen saver.

Hey, call me. I'd like to take you out later.

Khristian bit her lip. Cara was persistent if nothing else.

Doing the family thing right now, call you later?

"Hmm . . . what nigga texting you?" King asked and slid his sunglasses down.

"What? Why you say that?"

"Whatever!"

"So when Kareem getting out?" Khristian asked, trying to change the subject.

"Well, it cost a pretty penny, but Bolter got him a deal and he will be out in a couple of weeks." King winced as he tried to place the glass on the ground.

"Still hurting, huh?"

"I'm cool. So tell me about this dude that got Imani expectin'."

"I don't have anything to tell. Never met him, and she doesn't talk about him much to me. She seems to be doing okay, though."

"She ain't said this nigga name?"

"Nothing. I don't want her to feel like I'm snooping. She will tell me when she wants me to know. I think she is inside lying down. Seems like all she does is sleep."

Carlton laughed as he flipped the burgers on the grill. He was happy to have his whole family home, but, at the same time, he felt a little uneasy with Imani lying up in his house. He and Yogi had worked everything out, and that part of his life was going great.

Carlton placed a burger on a little boy's bun.

"Thank you, Mr. C." The boy smiled at him with two missing front teeth.

Carlton patted his head and watched the child run to one of the tables.

"Mmm, those look good. I want mine well-done," Imani said, smiling seductively at Carlton.

He squeezed the spatula as he turned to her.

"A'ight, one well-done coming up, little mama." Carlton was trying his best to keep everything cool between him and Imani, for fear of what she might expose if she got angry.

"Mhm. We are really hungry," Imani said, touching her stomach. She was glowing. The jumpsuit she wore seemed to accentuate all the best parts of her figure. Her breast had gone up at least two cup sizes, and her ass seemed a little fatter.

Imani knew that look. She had seen it so many times in his eyes. She slowly licked her lips and rested her right hand on the small of his back.

"Mani, stop playing with me. Not now," Carlton said, stepping away from her.

"What? I just want my meat."

"Damn," Carlton said as he felt his dick begin to react to the site of Imani's cleavage.

"Hey, Daddy," Khristian said and kissed his cheek.

"Hey, baby girl. You having a good time?"

"Yeah, it is real nice, Daddy. When you putting on the steaks?"

"In a minute. Tell Ox to check the lobsters in the pot over there."

Khristian nodded and hip bumped Imani. The girls giggled. Imani looked at Carlton and then followed Khristian.

Ox walked over to the grill. "What up, Big C? Ain't no lobster in them pots yet, just the water. You want me to turn the burner on for ya?"

Ox was a large man. He was Russian and black with wide shoulders, huge biceps, and meat hammers for hands.

"Yeah, man. I need to discuss some business with you." Carlton placed the last steak on the grill and closed the top. "Come on over here, and let's talk. I got something that needs to be handled, and it needs to be quick and quiet."

Across the yard, Yessenia, King's ex, watched her daughter, Malani, as she played on the swing set with the other kids. She waved to her as she smiled and slid down the slide and, then, ran after another little girl. Yessenia had on a large white sun hat, a pink fitted tee, and white leggings. She sipped some spiked lemonade as she sat on the lounger. Since she and King had been broken up, she usually just dropped Malani off so she didn't have to see his ass. But this was his coming home party, and the nigga had survived being stabbed, so she felt it was only right for her to celebrate with the family. She also wanted to see who this bitch was that he had put up on a damn pedestal. Her girlfriend, Dinky, had told her that "Falling" was the bitch's song, and it was blowing up on the local hip-hop stations. Yessenia had to admit that even she found herself humming along to it. Her girl, Candy, had been at the club the night Sloan performed. The pictures that Candy had shown her were of a beautiful woman who had talent and who didn't belong with King. She was too prissy and uppity. King needed a woman that could handle her business and his.

Yessenia had to admit King was a handsome man. Any woman in his vicinity had no choice but to admire him.

His swag was deadly and addictive. It was the kind of swag that was natural; nothing was forced or fake. She had heard that King inherited his charm from his father, along with other things.

Yessinia shook her head as she adjusted her Chanel shades and looked at King. She recognized Sloan from the pictures that Candy had shown her. Her hair was pulled back in a neat ponytail, and she only wore a light pink lip gloss. Sloan leaned down and kissed King. As she kissed him, the sun shone off the pendant around her neck. Malani ran over and jumped in her father's lap. King winced for a brief moment and, then, squeezed his baby girl.

Yessinia felt a bit nostalgic as she watched Malani interact with King and his new woman. King had pulled a package from his pocket and handed it to a giggling Malani. She clapped her hands and pointed to Sloan's necklace. Sloan took the small box from Malani and removed the necklace, which she placed around the little girl's neck. Malani kissed Sloan on the cheek and ran over to Yessinia.

"Look, Mommy! Look what Daddy got me."

Yessinia touched the diamond butterfly pendant and smiled.

"It's just like Sloan's! Sloan is pretty, huh Mommy? Daddy said we are going to the zoo next weekend!"

"Oh, he did?"

"Yep," Malani said before running back toward the swing set.

Yessinia watched King caressing and kissing Sloan. She had never seen him smile so much. His mood seemed lighter, and she could not believe that he was not constantly looking at his phone. That's something he couldn't resist doing when they dated. Usually at family functions, King would have skipped out by now to go "handle business," and Yessinia would be left alone to worry about his return.

King seemed settled. His relationship with Sloan looked real to Yessinia. A slight ache pierced her heart as she watched them. She knew that ache was from the last hope she had for their relationship crumbling before her eyes. King was happy with Sloan, and maybe it was time for her to find some happiness of her own.

Chapter 22

"Oh, I think I should have picked him up," Tiana said, pacing the floor of King's townhouse.

After three long months, today was the day Kareem was to be released, and King had convinced her to allow him to pick him up from outside the prison walls. He had also persuaded Tiana to have the coming home party at his house because he knew how much Kareem enjoyed the swimming pool and Jacuzzi in his complex. It was an easy sell because Tiana was barely keeping food on the table for her and the kids. The last thing she could afford to do was throw a party.

"Girl, sit down, they will be here in a few minutes," Sloan said as she stirred the punch.

"Hush, heffa," Tiana said with a laugh. "You were the same way when it was time for King to come home."

"Actually, I was worse," Sloan said as she opened the oven, took out her crab cakes, and placed them on the stove.

Yogi walked in with all the kids. Keana, Kareem's eight-year-old daughter held Malani's hand. She helped the child sit on the couch and remove her sneakers. Kordell, Tiana, and Kareem's youngest were fast asleep in Yogi's arms. Twelve-year-old Kareem Jr., who everyone called KJ, had stayed outside shooting baskets.

"I think the sun beat all of them down," Yogi said, laughing.

Tiana took the child from Yogi and began taking off his shoes.

"Sloan, can I lay him down?"

"Are you really asking me that?" Sloan said with a laugh.

Yogi walked over to the sink and washed her hands. She observed the crab cakes and inhaled the aroma of the coleslaw.

"Need me to help with anything?" Yogi asked.

She and Sloan's relationship had changed over the last few months. Yogi had a new respect for the girl who had made such a huge sacrifice for her son. A situation they still needed to handle, but that would come in due time.

"I think I got it, Ms. Yogi, unless you want to peel those eggs for the deviled eggs," Sloan responded.

Yogi smiled, placed the pan in the sink, and turned on the cold water. The doorbell rang, and Tiana almost sprinted to the door. She swung it open to see Imani and Khristian smiling at her.

"Oh, hey," Tiana said.

"Well, damn, hey to you, too," Imani said waddling inside.

Her pregnancy had been one from hell. Everything that could swell up had swollen, and she was constantly hungry. Being hungry made her gain weight and live in the bathroom. She stepped down the steps from the foyer to the living room, holding her back.

"Hey, Tiana, thought we were Kareem?" Khristian said hugging her. Tiana shook her head. "He's coming, don't worry."

The door opened again, and Carlton stepped inside.

"Hey, beautiful ladies. Your majesty is here, and he is thirsty."

"Hey, Daddy," Khristian said, kissing Carlton on the cheek. "I will fix you a drink."

"Thanks, baby girl." Carlton walked over to the counter and sat down on one of the bar stools.

Sloan placed chips and dip on the counter.

"Hey, Mr. C, you okay?"

"Yeah, baby, I'm good. I hear that you are going to be opening up for Marsha Ambrosius. That is major!"

"Yeah, I'm excited and nervous. This is a national tour. It is surreal for me, but King has promised to be there for me every step of the way. He just signed two new artists, and they are fiyah."

"Oh, yeah? He didn't tell me that. He serious about this music thing, huh?" Carlton asked, dipping the cracker into the dip. "Mmm, whew! What is this?" He said, dipping another cracker in the dip. Khristian placed Carlton's drink on the counter. "Baby girl, taste this," Carlton said, placing the dipped cracker in her mouth.

"Mmm, that is delicious!" Khristian said taking a spoon and placing some of the dip on a plate and grabbing some crackers

Imani struggled to get up from the chair. She walked over to the counter and took a cracker from Carlton. She made sure her breast and stomach rubbed against him.

"Taste the strawberry after you eat the cracker," Sloan said with pride. She enjoyed watching people eat her food. Her cooking skill was something she had inherited from her grandmother.

"Mmm, look at Sloan being all Food Network!" Khristian said, munching on the cracker.

Sloan laughed.

"Glad you guys like it. It is a family recipe. Simple and easy to make, but you gotta know how to layer your ingredients."

The women began talking about the recipe. Carlton's attention turned to Yogi, who had taken a seat on the patio. He stood and headed toward the French doors.

"Where you going?" Imani said, smiling at Carlton as he passed her.

"To talk to my wife, Imani."

Imani grabbed his hand and placed it on her belly. "You feel that, you feel your child?" Imani whispered.

The baby kicked Carlton's hand. Feeling the baby kick stirred something within Carlton, but it wasn't anything fatherly. He gently pushed Imani to the side and opened the door to the patio. Yogi was reclined back on the large yellow chair, relaxing in the sun. Carlton almost stepped outside, but he stopped when he felt his phone buzz on his side. He looked down to read the incoming text.

Still on?

Carlton glanced beyond him and quickly responded.

Yep, I will text you when the bird is out of the nest. Clip the wings quickly.

The doorbell rang. "Got it," Carlton said as he walked to the door. He knew it was not King because they rang the doorbell.

"What up, bro in law?" a boisterous voice said.

"Pauly? Boy, when you get in town?" Carlton pulled Pauly inside and hugged him.

"Man, I just rode in. Look at you, nigga!"

"Get on in here. Why didn't you call us to let us know you were coming to town?"

"I didn't know I was coming until I hit ninety-five, eighty-five, and seventy-seven. You know how I roll, man. Where my big-head sister?"

"Uncle Pauly!" Khristian said, running to him and giving him a hug.

"This Khristian? Well damn, look at you all grown up."

Pauly hugged Khristian as the sliding glass door of the patio opened, and Yogi stepped inside.

"Hey, sis."

"Pauly? What are you doing here?" Yogi said as she embraced her brother.

"I decided it was time to check in on my favorite little bratty sister."

Yogi took Pauly's arm and led him into the kitchen to meet Sloan.

The door opened and King stepped inside with Kareem.

"'Bout damn time. Where y'all been?" Carlton said to King.

"They were on some bullshit for a minute, Unc, but we got it straight," Kareem said, pounding Carlton.

Tiana ran from the kitchen. She smiled at Kareem and ran into his arms, showering him with kisses.

"Kareem! Welcome home, son." Yogi kissed his cheek and squeezed him tight.

Everyone went out on the deck. King started the grill and began grilling food for everyone. They sat at the table toasting to Kareem and King's freedom.

Imani had grown tired and decided to make it an early night. After closing the door to King's condo, she began walking toward the elevator. She sighed as she saw a maintenance person working on it. He turned to look at her and forced an apologetic smile.

"Sorry, but the elevator is down temporarily," he explained.

Imani smacked her lips and headed to the stairwell. She really did not feel like walking down steps, but she wanted to get home and put her feet up. It was only four flights of stairs, and she needed the exercise anyway. She held onto the railing as she walked down the stairs. The lights in the stairwell flickered, and Imani sighed again. She thought she heard a door open, but she looked back and didn't see anyone. Relieved, she continued down the second flight of stairs. As she gripped the railing, it pulled away from the wall.

"Shit! This place is falling apart!" Imani said, trying to steady herself.

"No, bitch," a woman said from behind her. "Your ass is falling."

Imani turned around and was met with a punch in the face and, then, a kick in the stomach.

Imani screamed as she fell backward down the stairs. She felt her arm snap as she bounced against the concrete, trying to protect her stomach as best she could. Each time she crashed against the hard stairs, she saw flashes of blue until she finally stopped falling. She heard a crack as her head hit something metal. Flashes of colors filled the stairwell and, then, darkness.

Carlton, Khristian, Pauly, Yogi, Kareem, Tiana, and the kids all stepped onto the elevator. As the doors closed, Carlton's phone vibrated. He unsnapped it from his belt and smiled at the screen.

Wings clipped

Carlton held the button for the doors so that everyone could get off the elevator. He lingered behind, allowing the group to walk to their cars.

Carlton knew that he should feel bad about what had just occurred, but it was necessary. He had always been able to contain situations like this without issue. Just a stack, and his problem disappeared. He hated that Imani had to be dealt with in this manner, but the girl was playing games with him and his household. Shit, maybe his life. Yogi definitely would have shot his ass for this one.

"Daddy, I will see you later, okay?" Khristian said, waving to him as she got in her car.

He waved back as he opened the door to his Range for Yogi. Smooth jazz flowed from the speaker. He put on his shades and pulled out of the parking space.

Kareem placed his little man in his car seat. He kissed the forehead of the sleeping child and got into the driver's side of the Avalanche. He smiled at Tiana and kissed her hand.

"Whew, it feels good to be home, baby."

"Kareem, we are glad you're home, and I hope this time it's for good. What you did was stupid," Tiana said as Kareem pulled out onto the street. "Like I said to you before, what were you thinking? You just left me and the kids out here to fend for ourselves."

Kareem tried to focus on driving and ignore Tiana's nagging.

"We been through this, T. It wasn't the best move, but it was needed."

"Needed? We needed you, Kareem, your babies and me. King is a grown-ass man. He can take care of himself. I told you, this street shit is going to get you killed. Hell, it almost got King this time for good. Just like always, you followed his ass." Tiana stopped talking and stared out the window. Tears rolled down her cheeks. When Kareem decided to slap his parole officer, she knew that she and the kids were always going to be second to King and the streets for him.

Kareem turned down Park Road. He turned up the radio and began bobbing his head. He was feeling good, and Tiana's nagging wasn't going to ruin his mood.

"Where are we going? The kids need to get home and be put to bed."

"I know. We going home," Kareem said.

Tiana looked out the window and then back at Kareem. "Are you drunk? This is not the way home."

He took Tiana's hand and kissed it as he turned on the right signal and pulled down Cinnamon Row into the driveway of house number 4037.

Tiana looked back at Kareem as he pressed the garage door opener on the visor. "Kareem?"

He laughed as he pulled into the double car garage and pressed the opener again. The door closed behind them and he opened his door and got out. KJ and Keana got out of the car, as well. They were curious about where they were, but they knew better than to interrupt their parents.

"Kareem! What are you doing? Whose house is this?"

This was the reason King wanted to pick up his best friend. He had this house and the truck waiting for him.

"Grab Kordell and come on," Kareem said.

Tiana took Kordell out of the car seat and followed Kareem into the house. Kareem guided her through the laundry room and into the kitchen.

"So how do you like it? There are four bedrooms and three baths."

"Kareem, I don't understand," Tiana said, walking into the great room.

"Tiana, this is our new home, baby."

"What?"

"Yep, our new rent-free, mortgage-free home. Come on, let's show the kids their rooms," Kareem said, opening the first bedroom door.

"Oh my God! Daddy, is this for me?" Keana yelled as she raced past Kareem into the room.

The room was a little girl's dream. The pastel pink walls were decorated with hot pink and purple shooting stars. The white canopy bed had a zebra striped comforter with hot pink satin trim. A dresser with an oval mirror, a desk, and a purple furry rug completed the décor.

"Yes, baby girl, it's all yours," Kareem said proudly.

Tiana looked on with tears in her eyes. Her children had been through so much, and, although she still had so many questions, she decided to just accept this blessing for now. She wouldn't take this from them.

"What about me, Dad? Can we see my room now?"

"Let's put Kordell down first. Okay, son?" Kareem said and took Kordell from Tiana's arms.

"No problem, Dad."

The five of them walked across the hall to Kordell's bedroom. He was still asleep, but when Kareem laid him down on his new Lightning McQueen bed, he shot straight up. He was confused for a moment as he looked around at the Lightning McQueen curtains, toy box, and TV/DVD combo. However, being the typical four year old, he quickly got his bearings and headed straight for the Radiator Springs play set in the corner of the spacious room.

"Well, I'm going to assume he likes his room," Tiana said with a chuckle. "Okay, KJ, you're up next, baby."

Kareem led them to the end of the short hallway and opened the door. With a huge smile, he stepped back and let KJ into his new room.

"No way!" KJ whispered as he looked around the room.

He was the oldest child, so he actually remembered when they had lived this way before his father went to prison. The dream of their former life had all but faded during the hard years without Kareem. The young boy walked over and sat down on his queen size bed, which was covered with a Charlotte Hornets comforter. He loved his room. It wasn't a baby room like Kordell's, and it featured his favorite thing in the world—basketball. He had a walk in closet, with a basketball hoop over the sliding door, and the espresso wood desk held a Charlotte Hornets lamp and a brand new Macbook Air.

"So, what do you think?" Kareem asked.

"This is cool, Dad. Thanks," KJ replied.

Kareem had hoped that he would be as enthusiastic as the other children were, but he knew that he had a lot to make up for with KJ. He knew that he had let him down with his time in the streets and in the pen. It would take time and patience to rebuild his trust, but he was committed to doing so.

"I'm glad you like it. I'll let you finish checking out your spot while I show your mom the rest of the house," Kareem said and headed out of the door.

Tiana followed Kareem with her mouth open. "Kareem . . ." she began.

Kareem kissed her and caressed her face. "Hey, Tiana, stop nagging and worrying. We deserve this, okay? We can go shopping tomorrow for living room and dining room furniture."

"Okay, Kareem. I am going to follow your lead on this one. Just know that you hold our family's future in your hands."

"I know, baby, I know. I got us. Trust me. Trust your man . . . please."

Chapter 23

"Ma'am, ma'am, can you hear me?" the petite Asian woman asked as she checked Imani's pulse. "Yes, yes, hello? This is Dr. Hmong. I'm at 2945 Center Lake Drive. I have a young, pregnant African American female who appears to have fallen down the stairs. Please, send medics quickly!"

"Shit!" Dr. Hmong felt Imani's pulse dropping. "Come on, honey, stay with me, stay with me." Dr. Hmong noticed Imani's stomach move. "Okay, okay, little one. We are going to get you help.h ang on. Help! Help!" the doctor screamed.

The door to the stairwell opened.

"Oh my God!" a woman said, running down the stairs. "What happened?"

"I don't know, looks like she fell. Can you make sure that the medics know where we are?" Dr. Hmong said to the young woman.

The woman nodded and ran back up the steps.

Dr. Hmong noticed a purse lying below the girl on a step. She kept her hand on her wrist and stretched to reach the handbag. This had been quite a day for her. She usually jogged from the first floor up to the fifteenth floor through the stairwell. Most people were too lazy to take the stairs, so it made her workout easy and uninterrupted. Seeing Imani lying on the steps shocked the shit out of her and made her heart race from fear instead of exertion. She didn't want to move her due to the potential damage to her neck and spine. The door flung open and two EMTs made their way down the stairs.

"Come on, she is in pretty bad shape, and she looks to be about seven or so months pregnant. We need to move fast, guys," Dr. Hmong said.

She stepped back while they worked on Imani. Taking a stethoscope from one of the EMTs, she listened to Imani's heart.

"Do you know what happened, Dr. Hmong?" the female EMT asked.

"No, I just found her here. Open the IV full-blast on her, I mean wide open! She hasn't been responsive to any pain stimulant." Dr. Hmong held the IV bag as the EMTs placed an oxygen mask and a neck brace on Imani.

She opened Imani's purse and found her driver's license and her phone, but the screen was cracked. Dr. Hmong pressed the call button, hoping that it would work so she could contact the last person Imani had spoken to.

"Hey, girl, where are you?"

Dr. Hmong was silent for a moment.

"Imani? Imani, can you hear me?"

"Umm, yes. Hello, this is Dr. Hmong."

"Dr. who?"

"Dr. Hmong. I found your friend. It appears she's had a nasty fall. We are taking her to Presbyterian Hospital. Can you contact her family and let them know?"

"What? Oh my God, is she okay?" Khristian yelled, grabbing a pair of leggings.

"Are you a relative?"

"Shit, what is wrong?" Khristian asked as she slid her feet into her Nike sandals.

"All right—on three. One . . . two . . . three." The EMTs placed Imani on the stretcher and began taking her up the stairs.

"I won't know that until I get her to the ER, but you should advise her family to come."

Khristian grabbed her keys and ran out of her apartment.

"Come on, quickly," Dr. Hmong said, watching the monitor. "Where is my ultrasound, people?" she yelled while cutting off Imani's dress.

Looking down, Dr. Hmong saw Imani's stomach moving, and she felt a little relief. Imani had suffered several blows to the head, and the oxygen they supplied through the mask was maintaining her oxygen levels.

Dr. Vincent viewed the ultra sound while Dr. Hmong attempted to stabilize Imani, whose heart rate kept dropping.

"Okay, we need to take this child," Dr. Vincent said.

Khristian rushed inside the ER and ran to the desk.

"Umm . . . yes . . . hi, my friend was brought in. A doctor called me, and . . ." Khristian stopped to fight back tears.

The nurse touched her hand. "Okay, what is her name, honey?"

"She's pregnant, and umm . . ." Khristian's mind was racing and she could not gather her thoughts.

"Okay, okay. Take a breath, and we can check on her. I need her name."

"Imani Davis," Khristian said trembling.

The woman smiled and checked her system. She picked up the phone as Khristian paced back and forward.

"Okay, ma'am. Janet," the woman said to a chubby young lady wearing a candy stripe uniform, "please take this lady to floor twelve. They are waiting for her. What is your name?"

"Khristian."

"Okay, Khristian, Janet will take you upstairs."

Khristian shook her head and followed the teenager to the elevator. She took out her phone, but she could not get a call to go through.

"You won't get a signal in here. All the technology we have, but, for some reason, they can't make a phone that will work in an elevator, huh?" Janet said smiling.

Khristian bit her lip. She watched the numbers on the screen change, stopping on floor ten. A couple got inside. It seemed the air became heavy inside the elevator. She began nervously tapping her foot. The elevator dinged again, and Janet held the door for her. She walked up to the receptionist's desk.

"Hey, Glenna, this is Khristian."

"Thank you, Janet. Khristian, if you would have a seat right there, Dr. Hmong will be out to see you in a few moments."

Khristian exhaled and walked over to the waiting area. She tried to sit down but stood again and walked to the window. She took out her cell phone and dialed King's number. It rang a few times but went to voice mail. Khristian felt her heart begin to beat faster. She tried his number once more, and, again, she was sent to voice mail. After bringing up her text screen, she pressed the VOICE COMMAND button on her phone.

> "King, I'm at the hospital. Something has happened to Imani. Please come."

"Khristian?"

Khristian recognized the voice from the phone call. She turned quickly and paused. Although the doctor attempted to maintain a stoic face, Khristian could tell that whatever she was about to say was going to be devastating.

***

"I'm glad my boy is out, now things can get back to normal," King said as he kissed Sloan's neck.

He felt her body stiffen. She kissed him and began taking off her socks. King fell back onto the bed and watched her pull her hair up into a ponytail. "What's wrong?"

Sloan took off her diamond studded hoop earrings and placed them in her jewelry box. She was happy to have her man home and happy for Tiana that Kareem was finally out. Still, Sloan had trouble sleeping at night. The secret she was keeping from King weighed heavily on her. Memories of Deshawn touching and defiling her body hung over her psyche like a dark cloud. She thought that giving in to him would be the end of it, but it seems it was just the beginning.

Her phone buzzed. She looked at the screen and saw the number, 9191. Sloan cursed under her breath for even thinking about this dude, and, now, he was calling her. She swiped IGNORE on the screen. Immediately, the phone chirped with a text message.

Call me.

Sloan deleted the message and walked into the bathroom.

King watched her place the phone down. He had noticed over the last few weeks that she would walk out of the room when her phone rang, or that her attitude would change at times without cause. Her phone chirped again. King inhaled and turned on some music. He heard the shower running, and could tell by the way the water sounded that Sloan must have stepped in. Her phone chirped a third time.

King was on his way to changing his life, but he was still bothered by what his mother had said about Sloan in the beginning. It was always in the back of his mind that his lifestyle would be too much for her. Sloan was from a world where the most violent thing she may have seen was one grocery cart hit another. Although she had not really spoken about her family that much, he knew that she came from a "normal" background. Her phone chirped again, four times back to back. King sat up and stared at the phone across the room on the charger.

"Who the fuck is blowing up her shit like that?" King asked quietly.

King had been with many women in his lifetime. He had been far from faithful with any of them, but when he met Sloan, he put all of them on ice. For the first time, he was in love with a woman and faithful. The thought of Sloan not being devoted to their relationship made him feel nauseous with anger. Or was it hurt? He wasn't sure what he was feeling. At the moment, he felt he should look at the text messages that were coming to her phone. As he stood to walk over to the dresser, his phone rang. He looked at the screen and saw Kareem's number.

"Man, where you at?" Kareem asked, sounding out of breath.

"I'm at home. Why? What's up?"

"Khristian been trying to call you. Imani in the hospital."

"What? What happened?"

"I don't know. I'm running inside now. Come on down, we at Presby." The phone clicked.

King grabbed a pair of jeans and a white T-shirt. As he walked toward the bathroom door, Sloan's phone chirped again. He stopped with his hand on the doorknob and looked back at the phone. Taking a deep breath, he opened the door. Sloan squealed as he entered.

"Geez, babe, you scared me!" Sloan said as she picked up the towel.

King stared at her. She was everything he'd ever wanted–beautiful, elegant, educated, and talented. His hand squeezed the doorknob as he thought about another man trying to take her from him.

"What's wrong?" Sloan said as she slid her boy shorts up her long legs.

"Umm, we gotta go. Imani is in the hospital," King said.

"Is she having the baby early?" Sloan asked, walking out of the bathroom and into the closet. She grabbed a pair of jeans and a blue satin tank top, and then slid her feet into a pair of blue flip-flops and grabbed her purse.

"Well, damn, that had to be a damn record. I have never seen a woman get dressed that fast in my entire life," King said laughing.

"Shut up, what is wrong with Imani?"

"Kareem didn't say."

King checked his call log and noticed he had six missed calls from Khristian.

As they headed for the door, King paused by her phone. "Hey, you want your phone?"

Sloan didn't hear him, so he grabbed the phone and placed it in his back pocket. They had to check on Imani, but King was going to find out who was blowing up his girl's phone and put a stop to it.

While Kareem and Khristian sat in the waiting area, the doctors informed them that Imani needed emergency surgery. Her parents were out of town, as usual, and she did not have any blood relatives. Time was of the essence, so Dr. Hmong decided to move ahead with the surgery. First, they would perform the cesarean. Then, Imani would be taken for an MRI scan to see what was causing the swelling in her head. It appeared she had fallen down the stairs, but doctors couldn't be sure.

"Why would she take the stairs? The elevator worked, and she was complaining about her legs hurting her. It just doesn't make any sense," Khristian said, pacing the floor.

Kareem sat back in the uncomfortable blue chair and rubbed his goatee.

Yogi entered the room, and Khristian ran to her. Yogi consoled her and looked at Kareem for answers, knowing that Khristian was too upset to make coherent sentences.

"She is in surgery," Kareem said, getting up and helping Yogi sit Khristian down.

"What happened?"

"I'm not sure. They said she fell down the stairs."

Yogi kissed Khristian's forehead. "I don't understand. What stairs?"

"The stairs in King's building."

"Why in the world would she take the stairs? The elevator was working."

"Yeah," Kareem said looking off. "Yeah, that is the million dollar question. Y'all want some water, tea, or coffee? I'm going to head down to the cafeteria."

"Yeah, some coffee would be good, baby."

Kareem almost bumped into King as he headed to the elevator.

"Hey, man," King said, looking over at Khristian. "What's going on?"

"Come on, I'll fill you in. I was about to go get something for your mom and sister," Kareem answered.

Sloan walked over to the women and sat down, taking tissue out of her purse.

King and Kareem walked down the brightly lit hallway. "What the fuck is going on?" King asked again.

"Imani fell down the steps after the party. A doctor was doing her run or some shit and found her in the stairwell of your building. They taking the baby right now. Then, they're going to try to stop the bleeding in her brain."

"What the fuck she doing taking the stairs?"

"I don't know, man. Sound fucked up to me. Don't make any sense."

"Shit, I know we got cameras in the building, but I'm not sure about the stairs."

"I'm sure the police are on it. I saw your boy down there talking to one of the doctors earlier."

"Who?"

"The detective you said had been at you. You know . . . the undercover nigga."

"Oh, yeah? Detective something," King said as he leaned against the wall.

"Yeah, he eyed me as I went into the room with Khristian. He stuck his head in the door a couple times. I guess he saw Khristian was too upset to talk, so he said he would be back later."

"For what? We don't' know what happened," King said, taking out his phone.

He realized he had taken out Sloan's phone, and stared at the eight text messages missed on the screen. He knew that swiping the screen could and would be a mistake. Ignorance was bliss, but curiosity was about to kill him. He leaned against the vending machine and swiped the screen.

Call me.

Don't fucking ignore me, you know I can have your boy put back in the cage.

I want to see you, and it will need to be soon.

Are you at the hospital?

King stared at the screen. He was trying to process the messages, but instead of having answers, he had questions. It didn't sound like someone hooking up with Sloan, but then again, he couldn't be sure. He scrolled back to the one about "putting her boy back in the cage."

"King!" Kareem said, handing him a cup of coffee. "What up, dude? Something else popping off?"

"Umm, I don't, I uh . . ." King stared at the screen again. "Nah, thangs are cool, man. How long you been here?"

"I was on my way in when I called you. Tiana and the kids are at home. I'm gonna call her when I get this to Ms. Yogi and Khristian."

King and Kareem made their way back to the waiting room and saw Sloan walking around the corner with the detective. Sloan's face showed that she was uncomfortable or upset. King walked into the waiting room. As he handed his mother her coffee, he noticed that Khristian seemed to have calmed down.

"Thanks, baby." Yogi took the cup. "I hate hospitals."

"Yeah," King agreed. "Where did Sloan go?"

"I don't know. She was just here a second ago," Yogi said before sipping her coffee.

King took out her phone. He could hear his heartbeat. He walked out of the waiting area and down the hall where he had seen Sloan and the detective walking. He was about to turn the corner when he heard Sloan's voice.

"Look, Deshawn, you have to stop. I held up my part of the deal, and this is over."

Deshawn grabbed Sloan's arm.

"Sloan, I let your boy go, but you know I can put him back in. Along with his boy. You don't belong with these motherfuckers. These niggas ain't nothing but drug-pushing killers. Hell, he may not have killed Red, but I know his hands got blood on them. You better than this shit. Damn, I love you, and I'm not going to stand by while you be with this nigga," Deshawn said, sliding his hand down Sloan's back.

Sloan slapped him and walked away.

Deshawn laughed as he watched her march away.

King stood back as Deshawn walked toward the waiting room. He wasn't sure what to do. His heart was telling him to kill this nigga on the spot, but his head reminded him that it takes two to tango. So, before he placed this nigga six feet under, he needed some answers; and he needed them soon.

Tiana scrubbed the kitchen floor with a brush. She loved her new house and was anxious to make it a home. The kids were playing in the backyard, Kareem was out, and she had taken out the meat she was going to prepare for dinner.

Kareem had called her from the hospital last night to tell her what had happened to Imani. Her heart ached for the girl as a mother but not as a woman. There was something about Imani that had never set well with Tiana. Something was sneaky and fake about her. Tiana peeped the way Imani used to look at Khristian when she wasn't looking, and that was unsettling to her.

She rinsed the brush off and walked into the bathroom with the bucket of dirty water. King had the house cleaned before they moved in, but it wasn't clean enough for Tiana's standards. She smiled at the box that lay in the yard; the kids' swing set inside. She planned to call her cousin, Thomas, to come over and put it together. Kareem was too pre-occupied with the Imani situation to think about anything else. She was going to make sure that no matter what he faced in those streets, he would have a home to come to at the end of the day.

Kareem still being in the game made her nervous, and she wished that he could go legit. He had tried and failed, but she would keep praying that God would deliver him from the streets before it was too late. She was going to start working from home next week for a call center. One of them had to have a legitimate job in case something popped off. It was time for the kids to start daycare and learn how to play with other kids.

She was determined to make life appear as normal as possible for them, and she prayed that one day it would be a reality. Her sister, Pumpkin, was supposed to come over and watch the kids so that she could go to the hospital, but as usual, her fat ass was late. Tiana smacked her lips as she placed the bucket in the garage. The doorbell rang. She wiped her hands on her pants and closed the garage door.

"It is about time you showed up," Tiana said, opening the door for Pumpkin.

"Girl, what you got to go do? Shit, I had to get my nails done," Pumpkin said, holding up her hands.

"I do have things to do, which is why I asked your ass to come over and watch the kids. I need to run some errands, pay some bills and stuff," Tiana said, grabbing her keys and bag. "You need Kordell's car seat in case y'all go out?"

"We ain't going nowhere," Pumpkin said as she kissed the kid's foreheads. They squealed and returned her kisses. "Dey love them some Aunt Pumpkin, don't you?" Pumpkin said, tickling Kordell.

Tiana smiled as she watched Pumpkin play with the kids. Pumpkin wanted kids of her own, but thanks to some bullshit niggas who thought it would be fun to rape a twelve-year-old, she wasn't able to carry a baby full-term. She knew that when Pumpkin fussed about watching them, it was all an act. She loved Tiana's babies like they were her own, and besides Tiana, there was no one better to take care of them.

"I'ma stop by the hospital to see what is up with Imani."

"Hospital? Wuz up?" Pumpkin asked sitting down on the couch.

"I'm not sure. Kareem left last night, saying she was in the hospital. She had some kind of accident."

"Ah, shit, is the baby okay?"

"They had to take the baby last night," Tiana said putting on her pink lip gloss.

"Oh, no, that is horrible! I will pray for her."

"I will tell her. Be back later," Tiana said as she walked out the door.

Chapter 24

Kareem slowly pulled up to the front of King's apartment complex. Tonight was the night that they would put all the whispers on the street to rest. In Kareem's mind, the streets had been buzzing about what had happened to King for far too long, and it looked like no one was going to be held accountable. King had convinced him not to seek revenge while he was locked up. It was too dangerous. Even if Kareem had been able to get close enough to take care of the guy who had stabbed King, he would still be risking his freedom, considering that there was always some jailhouse snitch who would love to give someone up in order to get their time cut or be switched to another yard.

King had a young runner named Black, who had been working for him for the past two years. He had given King a call about three days ago to let him know that a guy named Freeze, who was King's supposed stabber, had just gotten out and was living at a halfway house off Remount Road. He was due to be in by 6 p.m. every day, but just three days out of the pen, he was already violating the halfway house agreement. The nigga was hanging out with one of his ex-girlfriends, a young chick named Mel. She lived in the same hood Black was hustling in. Black had seen Freeze a couple times and begged King to let him smoke the nigga to get revenge for the crew. But King wanted to make sure that anything that was done to Freeze came by his hands, and by his hands only.

King grabbed the door handle of Kareem's truck and jumped inside the vehicle.

"Yo, what up, my nigga?" King asked.

"It ain't shit, brah. You know I'm ready to put this work in and quiet these bitches who out here running they mouths."

"Yeah, it's been a long time comin', my nigga!"

Kareem put the truck in drive and began heading toward the Southside Homes neighborhood, which was located right off of South Tryon and Remount Road. As they drove along, the car was quiet, except the tunes from Young Jeezy that played on the radio.

King stared out the window. He had so many things going on, and so much of it was good, that he wondered if now was the right time to be getting into some shit like this. Why the fuck should he risk the possibility of losing his freedom by putting in this work? He could have easily had someone else do it, especially since Sloan was on the verge of getting a major recording deal. She was receiving so much great airplay. Not only was she getting big in North and South Carolina, but now, the whole East Coast was talking about her latest single. King was as close to his dream as he could have ever imagined, but he also understood that the majority of the money he was using to finance Sloan's career and his new record label was from the work on the streets. There was no way that he could continue if the streets didn't respect him, so everyone needed to be reminded of the repercussions of trying his gangsta. And now that he had his best friend and partner back, he knew that he had the one person who he could trust with not only his life, but the life of everyone he loved.

As they pulled into the apartment complex, Kareem's senses heightened. He knew anything could go down at any time. Junkies ran toward the truck when they saw its lights. The young hustlers were trying to peddle their goods to nearby residents. Most stopped in the middle of their transactions to observe the approaching vehicle. Once they realized whose truck it was, they went back to handling their business.

King pointed to the second parking lot on the right. When he saw Black and a couple of the other young hustlers hanging out with him, Kareem slowly pulled the truck over in front of them and rolled down the passenger's side window.

"Yo, what up, youngins?" King motioned for them to come over so he could speak with them directly.

Black walked over to King's side of the truck and gave him some dap. "Yoo, what it do, big homie?" he asked in a laidback tone.

"Shit, just ready to handle this little situation. Y'all ready?" King asked, looking down at Black and his boys.

"Hell yeah, we ready," the three said before climbing into the back of Kareem's truck and giving him directions to the apartment were Freeze was laid up with his old girl.

It took less than three minutes to find the building, and as they pulled up, they noticed that lights were on both upstairs and down.

King turned to the back and asked, "So, Black, are you sure this nigga always leaves around midnight?"

"Yeah, I'm sure, homie. He's done that every night for the last three nights. Right around twelve o'clock, some nigga in a white Impala comes to get him. Shit happens just like clockwork."

"A'ight, cool. Kareem, find us a nice little place to sit, so we can wait for this bitch to come out," King instructed.

"Fuck that, big homie, let me go up in there. I'll blast every motherfucker inside," one of the young cats hollered from the backseat.

King and Kareem looked at each other at the same time. These young boys had no respect for the way the game was supposed to be handled. There were rules to this shit, and they needed to be followed and understood. Most of the young hustlers had never had any OGs to break it down for them.

"Look, my niggas, those people up in there could possibly be women and children. They have nothing to do with what we got going on. We signed up for this shit. We soldiers. So, in battle, soldiers know that they may have to kill or be killed. But, my nigga, we don't kill civilians. Ever. That's how we can sleep at night. We start violating that rule, the whole order is broken, and before you know it, it's total chaos. Always remember: this game is about the money, not about the murders. The more murders, the less money."

Just as Kareem was about to add his two cents to the lesson, a white Impala pulled up in front of the apartment complex. "Yo, Yo!" yelled Black, "that's the car right there . . ."

Kareem started the engine of the truck. "Yo, niggas, get your shit and make sure them bitches is locked and loaded."

Everyone gazed down at their weapons, making sure the safeties were off and bullets were in the chambers. Kareem put the car in drive and waited for Freeze to come out of the house. They only had to wait a few seconds and, just like Black had said, here came the nigga boppin' down the steps as though he didn't have a care in the world. Just as he began to open the passenger's door of the car, Kareem punched the gas pedal of the truck and slammed it into the back of the Impala.

The door brushed harshly against Freeze. King, in one swift motion, jumped out and stood with his pistol cocked and pressed directly to Freeze's skull.

"Nigga, you know what this is!" King barked.

Freeze stood frozen like a deer caught in headlights. He didn't know exactly what was going on, so his first thought was that this was a robbery.

"Yo, kid," he laughed, "I just came home, and I ain't got no money. So, robbin' me—shit, you just doing this for practice."

King matched his laugh as he looked at Freeze. This nigga really thought that being robbed was the only thing he had to be worried about. He pressed the gun harder into his temple.

"Nigga, I'ma ask you one time, and one time only. Who else was with you when you decided to push that metal into my side?"

Now, Freeze didn't have to think about what or who this was. Although he had stabbed many people during his prison stint, he knew there was only one nigga crazy enough to come to this hood at this time of night with this type of backup. . . . It had to be King.

"Yo, man, I don't know what you talkin' 'bout. You must got me confused," he said, trying to hold his composure, hoping that just maybe he could talk himself up out of this shit.

King was having no part of it. He looked over at Black and the other two young soldiers with their guns drawn on the driver and another passenger who was sitting the backseat.

"Nigga, I told you, you only had one time for this, homie. Do me a favor, and say hello to ya boy, Red."

With that, King cocked back the hammer, took a deep breath and let the trigger fly. All of Freeze's brain matter splattered onto the car. The driver and other passenger damn near shitted themselves. Even though Freeze was their man, neither one of them wanted to end up like him. Both began to frantically beg for their lives.

"Yo, man, I swear I'll tell you anything you want," the driver, Jeff, desperately uttered.

"I just need the name of the niggas who was with him."

Jeff wasn't sure of exactly who was with Freeze that day, but he wished he did know so he could get himself and his little cousin, Brian, up out of this situation. Jeff was only fuckin' with Freeze because Freeze had told him about a connect he could get some good weed from.

"Look, we don't know who it is. But I promise you, if you let us live, I will go to work for you like I'm a private detective to make sure that I get you the information you need."

Black, now standing directly in front of Jeff, put the pistol down toward his side.

"My nigga, this is your lucky night. Now, do yourself and your people a favor, and find out who the fuck is responsible. Put this number in your phone. Call me as soon as you get that info, and maybe I'll put y'all down on the right team."

With that, King and the crew jumped back into the truck. "Y'all niggas hungry?" he asked.

"Hell yeah," Black and the two young gunners replied.

"Waffle House it is."

Sloan hummed along to the music as she wrote the lyrics to her new song. She had been hearing the melody in her head for a few days.

His love is the most painful that I've ever felt. Mhmm.
But a little hurt ain't nothing, 'cause I can't love nobody else.
I can't find another to fill this hole in my soul.
This man, oh this man y'all, is all my heart knows. . . .

"That is pretty, who is it about?" King said as he sat down on the couch.

Sloan smiled at him and pulled her ear buds out. "Sorry babe, didn't hear you."

"I said, I like that. Who is it about?" King repeated, forcing a smile as he thought back to seeing Sloan and the detective in the hospital.

He had decided to wait for his emotions to stop kicking his ass before he confronted her. He wanted to go into it with a clear head. King had never been played; that shit was for dudes who didn't keep their head on straight and see shit for what it was. Although his heart had Sloan on a pedestal above any reproach, the thug in him knew that a bitch is a bitch. Some just clean up better than others.

"It's not about anyone, babe. Just something swirling in my head, is all. Everything okay? You haven't been around a lot lately."

"No, everything is good. You know, working on these deals and trying to get the spot in Atlanta set up," King said. "It's not like you been around much lately, either."

"Yeah, I have been at the hospital with Imani, taking shifts with your mom and your sister. She doesn't like being alone."

"Yeah, I got my people trying to find out who did that shit, but they haven't turned nothing up. It's like this person is a damn ghost. I know Imani shouldn't have any enemies. I always keep her and Khristian far away from mine and Carlton's business. I don't know why anyone would do that to her."

"Well, maybe it isn't you guys. Where is the father of the baby? He has yet to show up to check on Imani or Caleb. He is such a precious baby. One look into those big brown eyes, and you are in love with him," Sloan said smiling. "Babies just make the world seem better, especially when you do it the right way."

"Yeah, what way is that? First come love, then come marriage, then comes Sloan with the baby carriage?" King sang the nursery rhyme and laughed.

Sloan threw a pillow at him, and as he listened to her laughter and watched her smile, he almost forgot how she had betrayed him.

Six weeks later. . . .

"I need this handled, and it needs to not have no fuck up this time," Carlton said as he sliced his porterhouse steak. The heavyset older man that sat across from him wore a face devoid of expression. "I paid you well for last time. Shit, I may as well have gone and hired Henry the crackhead to handle this shit for me."

"There will not be any issues this time. I will personally take care of this for you."

"Ox, make sure you do. This bitch is wreaking havoc on my damn life. I want her ass to be a memory. She living in my house, having my wife take care of her. She is way out of pocket."

"Yeah, that is some disrespectful shit. I got you on this one. Like I said, I will personally take care of this bitch."

"Ox, no fuck ups. You got me?"

"I got you. Trust me, C man." Ox nodded to Carlton and put on his shades. "This little issue will be done by tomorrow afternoon."

Imani smiled at her handsome little man. Despite the way he had entered the world, he was perfect. She held him against her bare skin and inhaled his scent. As she rocked him back and forth in the chair, Kareem walked into the room with his arm full of blankets.

"Hey little mama, how you feeling? You want me to take him?" Kareem said as he placed the blankets in the large wicker basket.

Yogi had turned one of the spare bedrooms into a nursery, and she made sure that it was on Gucci level. The crib was filled with little bears and rabbits, and the walls were covered by FatheadsIt was more than any baby could ask for, and Caleb was only seeing a little of his godmother's generosity.

Imani winced as she stood and placed Caleb in the crib. Kareem stood beside her and stared down at the child with her. Imani still had a large bruise on her shoulder from the fall, which was odd to Kareem. He had not talked to her much about the incident. She had talked to the police about it enough, and he was sure she wanted to put it behind her.

"So, how you feeling?"

"Like I'm going to go crazy if I don't get out of this house," Imani said, placing the baby's clothes in the small basket on the changing table.

"You can't go too fast, girl," Tiana said, entering the room. She kissed Kareem on the cheek and playfully smacked him when he squeezed her butt. "Trust me, that first kid does something unholy to your body. And you had extra trauma, so the best thing for you to do is sit your butt down."

Imani sighed and sat down in the rocker. She looked over at Caleb and smiled as the child watched his mobile. She was so glad that he came out healthy. He was a little underweight, but the doctor said that he should gain his weight with no issues. Tiana and Kareem had been with her all night, but they didn't know she had gone to the convenience store last night to get a bag of Andy Capp Hot Fries. It was difficult getting in and out of the truck, but the fresh air on her face felt wonderful.

"Babe, I need to run and check on the kids. I will be back in a little bit," Tiana said, checking her watch. "Imani, your car is blocking mine. Give Kareem your keys so he can move it."

"Girl, it ain't no need to do all of that. You just take my car. I filled it up with gas last night, and I ain't going nowhere today," Imani responded.

"Yeah, I knew you took your butt out last night. You need to work on your sneakiness," Tiana said as she grabbed the keys.

"Please, I am plenty sneaky," Imani said and nodded toward Caleb.

Tiana looked at Kareem and shook her head. "I won't be too long."

Although Imani was wounded, and likely not thinking about a man right now, Tiana still didn't trust her around Kareem. She took Kareem's hand and led him out of the room.

Imani smirked at the sneakiness comment. She knew that in the book of women, she would be defined as the most ratchet of bitches. She loved Yogi and Khristian, but her desire for Carlton overruled the love she had for the both of them. She also knew that if Yogi ever found out about her and Carlton, there would be no hole deep enough for her to crawl into and hide from her wrath. Although the fear of Yogi finding out about her and Carlton was scary, her fear of Carlton was paralyzing. She had not told anyone about the nightmares she had been having since she was pushed down the stairs. The dream was recurring and terrifying. She was falling down the stairs, and as she fell, she looked up to see Carlton smiling down at her, holding the baby. Then, he throws the baby down the stairs, as well. She always woke just before the child hit the ground.

Over the last few weeks, she had seen a darkness in Carlton's eyes that chilled her to the bone. At times, when he was around her, she felt the temperature drop a few degrees from his icy glare. She made sure that when she did go to sleep, the door was locked; and she placed a chair in front of it for extra security.

Caleb had drifted off to sleep, so she reclined the rocker and closed her eyes. She needed to get some sleep while Carlton was out of the house, and now was the perfect time with Kareem just outside.

"You know that onion looking tasty in them damn jeans," Kareem said as he groped Tiana's butt and lifted her up.

She laughed and wrapped her legs around his waist as he carried her to Imani's truck. "Girl, don't be squeezing my damn waist like that. I will throw you on top of this hood and . . ." Kareem bounced her up and down while kissing her neck.

"Kareem! Stop, Ms. Yogi's neighbors!"

"Shit, I don't care about them. They will learn some shit."

Tiana giggled as Kareem opened the door and placed her on the seat.

"You know I'm gonna work that pussy tonight, right?"

She had been with Kareem for years, but she still blushed when he said dirty things to her. "Boy, you are crazy. Stop now before you start something," Tiana said, checking her lip gloss in the mirror.

Kareem slid his hand between her legs and rubbed her clit through the denim. Tiana gasped. His hand was strong. She tried to resist grinding against it, but her clit was aching. He bent down and slid his tongue over her lips. Tiana moaned as he thumped her clit with his index finger.

"Y'all better take that shit somewhere before my mama pull up," King said.

"Nigga, damn, how long your nasty ass been standing there?"

"Long enough to see Tiana 'bout to—"

"King!" Tiana shouted, feeling her face burn. She quickly closed the door as King burst into laughter.

Kareem licked his finger as Tiana started the Lexus truck and put it in reverse. She rolled the window down and blew a kiss to Kareem. "Love you, see you later. Bye King," Tiana said, flipping him the bird.

She put the truck in drive and headed down the street. King slapped Kareem on the back as they shared a laugh. All of a sudden, a loud boom filled the air, and the earth beneath them shook. As they attempted to turn around, pieces of hot debris rained down on them, causing Kareem to fall back on the flowerbed. King winced as something sharp pierced his side. He couldn't hear anything but loud, high-pitched ringing in his ear. Time stopped as he focused his eyes to see a ball of orange and white in front of him.

"Tiana! Tiana!" Kareem screamed.

King tried to grab Kareem as a second explosion sent both of them flying on their backs again. Although King's ears were ringing, he could hear Kareem's screams.

"Tiana, Tiana!"

King grabbed Kareem by his waist before he could stand and reach the car.

Flames leapt from the windows of the SUV. The truck was completely engulfed. Imani ran from the house and saw Kareem and King lying on the ground. She looked back at the truck, and her head began to pound. She tried to breathe, but the air would not enter her lungs. Her vision was blurry as she tried to dial 911. The sound of sirens approaching made her look up again at her truck. The neighbors were on their lawns. One man tried to use his hose to put the fire out, but that seemed to make the flames leap out at him. The firetrucks pulled up to the scene, along with the police. Police pushed the onlookers back, and the firefighters began fighting the blaze.

King held Kareem in his arms. Kareem had stopped moving and blinking. He stared at the driver's side of the truck. His body was cold, and his heart felt as if it had stopped beating. He watched the firefighter spray the truck, and he waited for them to pull his baby out.

"King, they gotta get her out, they gotta get my baby out!" Kareem yelled, sobbing.

King held his boy close as tears ran down his own cheeks. He didn't have any words to comfort him.

Carlton swung his club and watched the white ball sail through the air.

"Boy, you on point today, old man," Parker said as they got into the golf cart.

"Yeah, this is what I needed–to get out here and relax. Shit been so crazy lately, that I haven't had much time for enjoying myself."

"How are things with you and the queen?"

"Everything is wonderful, and it is only going to get better. Having the new baby in the house got Yogi feeling like she a new mother all over again. She out shopping now," Carlton said, grabbing his golf bag.

His phone rang and King's name flashed on the screen.

"Hey son."

"Pops, you need to get home now. Something bad has happened."

"What's wrong?"

"Just get home." King's voice trembled.

"Is it your mama?" Carlton asked as he waved to Parker.

"No, but I need to call her. Just get here."

The phone disconnected, and Carlton ran to the parking lot. He reached his SUV and waved his foot under the tailgate. The back opened. He threw his clubs inside and hurried around to the driver's side. As he pulled out of the parking space, he heard a phone beeping. He opened the glove compartment and grabbed the burnout phone. There was a video message. He pressed PLAY. Imani's truck backed up, and seconds later, it exploded. The video ended, and Carlton pulled back into the parking space and laughed. The air in the car seemed to become lighter. He wanted to get out and run a few laps around the course.

Carlton put the car back in reverse and pulled out of the space. He grabbed his aviator shades and searched for the appropriate song, "It Ain't Nothing to Cut That Bitch Off."

"Hey!" Carlton sang along with the song as he pulled out onto the road.

Chapter 25

Detective Johnson shook his head as he stared at the charred frame of the Lexus SUV. The poor girl did not have a chance. He prayed that she went quickly, but there was no real way of knowing. The young man that sat on the ground of the driveway was clearly distraught. His gaze had not left the smoldering frame of the truck since Johnson had arrived. He managed to get some information from his friend. He found out the young lady in the car was the young man's fiancé. He had refused medical help, even though he had a large gash from the debris hitting him in the face and on his arms.

"Damn, this is some fucked up shit, huh?" Deshawn said, looking at the car. "This is definitely not the work of some street dude. This shit was done by a professional. They made sure that no one would even have a chance to survive."

Johnson pretended to write in his notebook. Deshawn was a bastard. His clout with the station was only due to the fact that he was married to someone of status and political importance. He spent most of his time taking credit off the brows of other detectives.

"Yeah, it is pretty sad. Mother of three, no criminal record," Johnson said, closing his notepad.

"She may not have a criminal record, but her fiancé and his friend definitely do. They've been in some trouble over the last couple of months. It seems their shit is spilling over to their females. A few weeks ago, a pregnant young lady was pushed down some stairs, and now, one is blown up."

Johnson turned around to look at Kareem. "Who are they?"

"That is Ronnie King and Kareem Henson, two majors in the drug game here and in surrounding areas. We had King on a murder charge, but we couldn't get it to stick. He took out another major in the city, so this shit right here is probably retaliation," Deshawn said, walking around the truck.

"Well, this is my case, and we will figure out what the hell happened. I will contact my boys at the DEA and see what they got for me," Johnson said, watching Kareem. "That boy right there is done. I don't care if you a killer or not, seeing the mother of his children go like that had to destroy his soul."

A white Audi SUV pulled up to the curb in front of the house. Detective Johnson watched as Sloan kneeled down in front of Kareem. He was still unresponsive. She stood and looked around the street. King walked over to her and embraced her. Johnson could not make out what they were saying, but he saw the young lady turn to look at the truck. She covered her mouth and fell to her knees.

"Why? I don't understand what the hell is going on? This is all too much, King. First Imani, now Tiana? I just don't understand. Oh God, I told your mother I would call her back, but I don't know what to say to her. This is horrible," Sloan said, sobbing.

King pulled her close to him and kissed her forehead. Sloan was right; the last few months had been nothing but one thing after another. As he comforted her, King looked into the streets to see the so-called detective, Deshawn, watching them. Immediately, King's left hand began to itch as he helped Sloan up.

"Hey, baby, I will call Ma. Can you go inside with Imani?"

Sloan nodded and walked toward the house. King stiffened his hand trying to stop it from reaching for his gun.

"Mr. King?" Detective Johnson called, gasping for air as he walked up the driveway. "I'm sorry to do this, but I really need to get your statement. I don't think your friend is going to be able to help us, and we need to get on this as quickly as possible."

"You are handling this, correct?"

"Yeah, I am the lead detective," Johnson said, following King's glare toward Deshawn. "Can we talk inside?"

King nodded but looked back at Kareem. "I need to try to get him inside first."

"I think the medics should take him. He is not going to move on his own," Johnson said.

King nodded to the two EMTs that had attempted to treat Kareem earlier. They followed him over to Kareem. His eyes were swollen and red. King touched his shoulder as the female EMT quickly pressed the needle into his arm and pushed the plunger down. The male EMT brought the gurney over.

"Hey bro, they gone take care of you, a'ight?" King said as he felt Kareem's body begin to go limp from the sedative.

King slid his arms under Kareem's armpits and helped the EMTs place him on the gurney. Kareem continued to stare off into space as they loaded him into the ambulance.

"We will take him to Carolina Medical Center, main hospital," the female EMT said to King.

"A'ight, we'll be there in a few." King watched the EMT close the doors of the ambulance.

As he turned to walk up the driveway, he saw Deshawn standing near the gate of his mother's house. King fought the urge to feel the grip of his .40-cal in his hand. He tried to concentrate on his breathing and walked past Deshawn without acknowledging his presence.

Detective Johnson was sitting in the family room with Imani and Sloan. Imani had her head on Sloan's shoulder. She was trembling so badly that Sloan's body seemed to tremble with her.

Detective Johnson stood and walked out of the family room. King walked into the kitchen and had a seat at the counter with him.

"Can I get you something to drink?" King asked, getting up to grab a soda from the refrigerator.

"No, no, I'm good. So the young lady, Imani Davis, tells me that the truck was hers."

"Yeah," King said, opening the soda.

"Now, if I understand, someone pushed her down the stairs about a month ago?"

"Yeah, you think that might be connected?" King asked as his brain finally started to come out of the fog.

"It is a hell of a coincidence. She was pretty shaken up, so I want to give her a little time. Do you know anyone who would want to harm her?"

"No, she just had a baby. She's a college kid. She works and goes to school," King said.

"Any issues with the father of the child?" Johnson asked.

"I really don't know much about the father. Mani doesn't talk about him much," King said, remembering her saying he was married.

"So you don't know if they are on good terms or if there are any issues?"

King stood and leaned against the counter. He had never really questioned Imani about the nigga that got her pregnant. She didn't say anything about him at all, except that he was married and not happy that she kept the baby. King sat down on the barstool. He knew that was a conversation they were going to have to have real soon.

"Did you think of something?" Johnson said, studying King's face.

"Umm no, just thinking about my boy is all."

"I know it is hard to talk about this, but we find that it is best to get statements as soon as possible. I will give you some time and will talk to you tomorrow. We should have everything cleared up in just a while," Johnson stated.

King stood and walked him to the door. Johnson nodded and walked down the driveway toward the other policemen and forensic technicians.

Sloan walked out of the bedroom and encircled King's waist. He touched her arms and looked out of the window at Deshawn talking to Johnson. He took a deep breath and turned to Sloan.

"Bae, you know that I love you, right?" King asked, tilting her face so that he could see her eyes. "I can't even think of anything else most of the time, other than making you happy. I have never allowed any woman other than my mother to be this close to my heart." Sloan caressed his face and kissed his lips. "Getting inside here was something that not even Yessinia could do, which is why we are not together now."

King walked around Sloan. He gently moved her to the window and pulled the sheer curtain back. "I'm only going to ask you this once. And I pray, for the love of God, that you give me an answer that will not make me regret you being planted so deep in my heart that pulling you out would literally kill me, Sloan." Sloan was confused as King inhaled and kissed her neck. He kissed behind her ear and whispered, "Tell me about that nigga, Sloan."

Sloan stared out the window. She felt like someone had a vice grip on her throat. King had pointed to Deshawn.

She stared at the men talking for a few moments. King's grip on her waist tightened. "Sloan, please," King said, trying to control his anger.

The door opened and Carlton walked inside.

"What happened? Is your mother okay?" Carlton asked, walking over to King and Sloan.

King loosened his grip. Sloan didn't realize she was trembling until the support of King's body was no longer behind her.

"Shit, I forgot to call her back," King said taking out his phone.

"I talked to her, King. She called me earlier. That is how I knew to come over here. She should be here in a few minutes." Sloan was afraid to take a step away from the window. She could feel King's eyes on her. Feeling dehydrated, she licked her lips and slowly turned to walk over to the couch.

Imani walked into the room carrying Caleb. She was wobbly from the sedative she had been given. Sloan stood quickly and grabbed the child from her arms.

Carlton turned to see Imani still alive and King helping her to the large wingback chair.

"Imani?" Carlton said, unable to hide his shock at her being alive and breathing.

King was so distracted, trying to make sure she made it in the chair, that he didn't notice the color drain from Carlton's face.

Carlton turned and walked out the door. As he stepped outside, Yogi ascended the driveway.

"What the fuck is going on?" she asked.

Carlton couldn't even respond. His mind had just been given a punch that had left him dizzy. He placed his hand on the doorknob to open the door for Yogi.

"I think you better let King and them tell you."

Carlton then turned and walked around the house to the backyard. He sat down in the patio chair and took out his cigarettes. He needed to call Ox but thought better of it for the time being. He only had a few minutes to get over the shock of seeing that fucking bitch still breathing, and now, he had to find out who was driving her truck.

Chapter 26

"He's sleepin', and he probably won't wake up for a while," the nurse said.

"Thank you," Yogi responded as she sat down beside Kareem's bed. She took his hand and kissed it. The nurse looked around the room. "He really needs his rest. You guys have five minutes."

"Someone should be here when he wakes up," Yogi said.

"I'll stay here with him, Ms. Yogi," Imani said.

"No, baby, you need to be at home resting. You're still recovering, and Caleb needs you there."

"I'm fine, Ms. Yogi. Besides, the police are right outside the door. I will be safe here. I won't rest at home, anyway. They have this comfortable recliner, so I will be fine," Imani said, looking at Carlton.

"I just think—" Yogi began.

"Please, let me do this. You guys go on home. If it's too much, I will call."

Yogi sighed and kissed Kareem's forehead. She grabbed her clutch and walked out the door.

"How is he doing, Ma?" King asked.

"He's resting, baby. Imani is insisting on staying with him."

"What? She should rest," Sloan said.

"Let her stay, she says she can handle it," Carlton said as he closed the door.

"I just want to go home. I need to process this mess," Yogi said, kissing King and Sloan's cheeks.

"Well, has anyone spoken to Tiana's family?" Sloan asked.

King dropped his head and cursed.

"Hey, I'll go see Naomi, King," Carlton said. "I know this won't be easy. I'll try to take Pauly with me. Go home and get some rest."

King nodded and took Sloan's hand. He had delivered news to some of his boys' families in the past when they had been shot and killed working for him. They were about that life, and their people usually were about that life or understood what the game could do to your lifespan. Tiana wasn't like that. Her parents were hard-working people who raised her to be a good girl. They did not like her dating Kareem, at all, but she loved him. Over time, they tolerated him for the sake of their daughter and grandchildren. Now, their worst fears had come to pass. He looked over at Sloan. Her hair was pulled back in a smooth, taut ponytail. Her profile was something that King could stare at for years.

The elevator doors opened. King held the doors for her, and they walked to the SUV. He opened the door and allowed her to get into the car. Then, he went around to the driver's side. They sat silently for a few moments.

King looked at Sloan and took her hand into his. "Sloan, we need to talk about what I asked you about earlier."

Sloan looked out the window. Telling King the truth would be dangerous, but lying to him could damage their relationship beyond repair. So much had happened over the last few months that she hadn't had a chance to catch her breath or wrap her mind around the new reality she was currently living. King treated her like a queen. He had given her the keys to her dreams, the dream of having a place to showcase her voice and someone to give her heart to.

"King, I love you, and that is something that I didn't really think was possible a few months ago. You know your lifestyle is not one that I would have knowingly become a part of. When we met, my heart was hidden behind so many walls that I would check it sometimes, to see if it was still beating." Sloan smiled weakly and caressed King's face.

King felt adrenaline rush through his body. He tried to steady himself but found that he was trapped between fear and anger.

"Before I met you, I dated that detective. We went out for a while until I found out that he was married. Once I found out, I broke it off with him." Sloan broke her gaze from King's face. "He has had a hard time letting me go and has been stalking me ever since we broke up."

King listened to Sloan. She told him about Deshawn killing Red to set him up and about how he blackmailed her into sleeping with him for King's freedom. Sloan wiped the tears from her eyes. They were both quiet. The car seemed to have had the oxygen sucked out of it.

"I'm sorry, King. I just wasn't sure what to do. After you were stabbed, I just panicked. And all I knew was that I had to do whatever it took to get you out of there. Please, please, forgive me. I love you, I just . . ."

King pulled her close to him and kissed her forehead. He held her tightly, unable to speak. His entire body felt like it was on fire. He just wanted to pull her inside of him to take away the pain and protect her. They both sat in silence, clinging to each other. King felt his heart crack. Sloan had sacrificed herself for him. She made a sacrifice that could have destroyed her and made her hate him, but she had done it and stayed with him.

"Damn, Sloan, I wish you would have told me." He stopped, not really having the right words to say to her. "I love you, baby," King said as he caressed her back.

She kissed his neck and closed her eyes. They both needed a moment to escape from their chaotic reality. King knew that he had just added another name to his to-do list. He would make sure that Deshawn paid with his life for violating Sloan.

Chapter 27

Carlton parked in front of the house where Tiana's parents lived. Pauly had sold him out, so he had to come alone. He had known Naomi for years, and they had a brief fling back in the day. Things were fucked up. Imani was a grimy bitch with nine fucking lives. Why did Tiana take her damn car? Carlton took a deep breath and opened the door to his truck. He could hear a television playing as he rang the doorbell. After a few seconds, he rang the doorbell a second time.

The door creaked as Naomi opened it. He had known her over twenty years and could not remember ever seeing the woman smile.

"Hey, Nae Nae," Carlton said, putting his keys in his pocket.

"Hey, come on in."

Carlton looked around the small, neat living room. Pictures of Tiana and the kids were on the table by the door. Carlton followed Naomi into the living room and sat down on the floral print couch.

Naomi pressed the mute button on the remote and sat back in the blue recliner. "I ain't seen you in a minute, so that must mean something is wrong. What, Kareem back in jail again?" Naomi said without changing expression.

"Nah, he not back in jail," Carlton said looking at his hands.

"He dead?" Naomi asked sitting back in the chair.

"Naomi . . . Tiana is dead. She was killed in a car accident."

Carlton's voice was flat. It didn't reflect the pain he was feeling. He wasn't good at being empathetic, and in this particular situation, he felt guilt.

Naomi's eyes widened, and she sat on the edge of the chair. "What, what did you say? What did you just say to me?" Naomi asked, unsure if she had heard him correctly. "Did you say my baby is dead? Did you say my baby is—"

Carlton tried to find the tone and the words to match that would calm Naomi down, but she was becoming more and more hysterical as the thought of her youngest child being dead began to sink into her psyche.

"Look, Naomi, don't you worry about a thang. Me and Yogi will make sure that everything is paid for and that there will be no expenses spared."

Naomi looked up at Carlton with a strange glare. "Do you really think I give a fuck about some damn money or about some funeral expenses? If you want to do something for me, get my baby back!"

Carlton began to second-guess if he should have allowed King or someone else to come over and give the news to Naomi. He thought because of their old relationship, he would be better at handling the situation. Perhaps he had chosen the wrong words.

"Naomi, I apologize. You know I didn't mean it like that. I just didn't want you to worry about nothin'."

"Worry about nothing? I just lost my baby! My grandbabies just lost their mother. What in the hell else could I be worried about, huh? Some fuckin' money?" Tears began to pour out of her eyes like raindrops.

Carlton could see that her body was becoming unstable, so he grabbed her just before she fell to the floor. "Naomi, I'm sorry. I'm so sorry . . . I'm so sorry."

Hearing her cries and feeling the hurt in her body made Carlton began to think about his own daughter. What if it was Khristian who had gotten in the truck? What if it was

Yogi? The more he thought about it, the more guilt began to set in, knowing it was his fault that this young girl had lost her life. He began to cry as he held Naomi. After a few moments, their cries subsided. Just then, the door opened as Jack returned home from work.

Jack was Tiana's father, an honest, hardworking man who had been a mechanic all his life. Some people would call him a "square." He would get up every day and go to work. Jack worked twelve- to fourteen-hour days so Naomi didn't have to work and could, instead, stay home to provide a stable environment for their children.

"What's goin' on?" Jack asked, seeing the hurt and distress on his wife's face, and Carlton looking like he had been crying also.

Carlton tried to find better language than what he had used on Naomi, hoping that it would produce better results.

Before he could put the sentence together, Naomi shouted, "She's gone! She's gone. Our baby is gone!"

Jack looked at her in confusion. "Who's gone, baby?"

"Tiana, Jack. She's dead! Our baby is dead."

She ran over and embraced him. They held each other tightly, realizing that their daughter was now gone.

Carlton, realizing that there were no words he could give to help ease their pain, decided the best thing he could do was leave.

Chapter 28

Dax let the smoke from the Black&Mild swim in his lungs for a few moments before releasing it through his nostrils. Chin drove up next to Dax's SUV and killed the lights.

"Dax," Chin said as he opened the door.

"What up, Chin?"

"You tell me."

"Brah, yo, that was a hell of a move you made the other day against the competition. I hope your ass gonna stick around to deal with the fall out," Dax said, leaning against his truck.

"What the fuck you talkin' about?"

"Blowing up the truck with King's man, Kareem's woman in it," Dax said rubbing his hands together.

Chin stared at Dax as if he had grown a second head. "What the fuck you talking about?"

"Come on, man, it's just us here. You blew up King's right-hand man's girl. It was on the news. That shit was savage, dude."

"I don't know what the hell you are talking about, Dax. I ain't blow up nobody." Dax studied Chin's face for a moment. He could see the sincere confusion.

"Damn, you really didn't have shit to do with that?"

"No, man, I don't fuck with dudes' females," Chin said. "I ain't seen the news, so what the fuck is up?"

Dax took out his phone and keyed in the news Web site. He handed it to Chin and leaned back against the truck.

"Damn, that shit is out of control! You said old boy's girl was in the truck?" Chin asked.

"Yeah, man, I ain't had shit to do with that there. That is a problem. You know them niggas on lock and load right now," Dax said opening the driver's door to his SUV and sitting down.

"Shit. Shots fired, and somebody returned fire for you. Ain't nothing left to do now but suit the fuck up."

"Yeah, but we still got a problem. There is another playa in this shit, and we need to find out who the fuck it is," Dax said, taking his phone from Chin.

"Yeah, but in the meantime, we need to hit some traps while these niggas down. This is the best time. Get your crew together. We need to strike this shit hard. There is money laying there for us. The world don't stop 'cause one life is gone. Let's move on it now," Chin said smiling.

Dax nodded in agreement and began making phone calls.

A few days later. . . .

After Sloan placed the white flower in her hair, she took Keana and Kordell's hands, and walked down the hall to the living room. Kareem sat in the recliner staring off into space. He had barely spoken or eaten anything since Tiana's death. Carlton finished tying his neck tie and helped him put on his suit jacket. He smiled briefly at his kids as they ran over to him.

Yogi kissed Kareem's forehead and stroked his jacket with the lint brush. The driver from the funeral home entered the room and advised everyone that it was time to go to the church.

Sloan reached for the children and walked them out the door. The funeral director nodded to her as she walked toward the limo. Yogi put on her hat and grabbed her black gloves. She walked over to Kareem and squeezed his shoulder.

"Come on, baby. Mama Yogi is here."

King put on his jacket and stared at his boy. For the first time since his father had passed away, King felt helpless. He didn't know how to console Kareem or how to fix this shit, but they would start by making sure that whoever was responsible would be dealt with swiftly and ruthlessly.

"Y'all go on. I got him," King said to Yogi and the rest of the family.

The women looked at Kareem and then, at King. Caleb cooed in Imani's arms, as they walked out the door.

"King," Kareem said without looking up. "She said this shit was gonna get me killed. She said we was going to die in the streets, and she was terrified of being left alone without me. You know, I would hear her say that shit and think, 'you gonna be a'ight without me. I'm gonna make sure of it. You and my kids gonna be straight.' Man, I never thought it would be the other way around. Brah, I made peace with the fact that a fucking bullet had my name on it. You know what I'm saying? But, brah, T was a good girl, man. She was a good girl. She didn't deserve this shit, man. Fuck, I did this to her, brah . . . I killed the only woman I ever loved," Kareem said crying.

King sat down beside Kareem and held him. "Reem, you didn't do shit. My nigga, we going to find out who is responsible for this, and they gonna pay. I put that on my life, brah, they going to pay for this shit.

"Man, kill me because this shit on me. I did this, fam. . . . I did this to T."

King grabbed Kareem by the face and stared into his eyes. "Brah, look at me. We will get through this, and when you are strong enough, we gonna make sure that whoever did this to your wife and my sister is going to pay with their lives. It ain't gonna be quick and painless either. You know you my brother, and everything you feel, I feel. Right now, we need to say our good-byes to T, and we got to be strong for the kids."

Kareem took a deep breath. He nodded to King, and the two of them walked out the door to the waiting car. Kareem slid inside. The burn marks from the car were still in the road. The fire was so hot that it had melted the asphalt.

Kareem took a deep breath as the car backed down the driveway and over the black spot. King felt a chill go through him. They were going to a funeral where there would be no physical body. Tiana was cremated, in a sense—in the car, but her ashes were destroyed by the efforts made to save her.

Kareem stared out the window. He looked at King for a moment and, then, back out the window.

"We need to show these niggas that they have crossed into another dimension with us, fam. A fucking eye-for-an-eye type shit," Kareem said as he put on his aviator shades.

King nodded and patted his shoulder. They were burying one of the innocents today, and for that, King was going to make sure they felt the weight of dirt as well.

Once they had arrived at the church, the large presence of the news and media outlets was ever noticeable. A mixture of Sloan's newfound popularity and the social media attention brought on by a video that had surfaced of the explosion had the church filled to capacity. Kareem and KJ sat on the front row with Tiana's parents, along with King, Sloan, Yogi and Carlton. Imani and Khristian sat directly behind them with Keana and Kordell, not wanting to have them scared by all of the crying. Naomi was already going full-throttle, and the service was just getting started.

Carlton gazed over at her, not wanting to look her or Jack in the eyes. It looked as if both of them had lost significant weight in just the few days since his visit to give them the news of Tiana's death. As the preacher asked everyone to take a seat, Carlton was taken from his thoughts.

"Family, I want to welcome you all to the home going service for our beloved Tiana. We will give everyone a chance to share a special moment about our beautiful sister. We just ask that you keep your remarks to no longer than five minutes."

Person after person came forward and shared stories of Tiana's goodness and kindness. The more they spoke about her, the more upset her parents and Kareem became. So much so, that the pastor decided it would be best to bring the service to a close. He didn't like to put that much emotional distress on the family. King and Yogi were shocked at the amount of hurt that Carlton expressed. He got up to say a few words, but broke down halfway through his speech. King had to go up front and help him back to his seat. The more he witnessed his loved ones' hurt, the more hatred King developed in his heart for the person behind Tiana's murder.

Finally, Sloan got up to sing Tiana's favorite gospel song, "Jesus, I Love Calling Your Name."

"When my troubles surround me, I didn't have to despair.

Lord, you told me that you'll be right there.

Oh Jesus, oh Jesus, oh how I love calling your name."

Cameras were flashing, and everyone had their cell phones out recording Sloan's rendition of the gospel song. There wasn't a dry eye in the building, and there weren't enough ushers to handle all the people giving praise and falling out. The preacher made one last statement and extended the right hand of fellowship to anyone who wanted to come forward and accept Christ as their savior.

Yogi almost passed out when Carlton released her hand and walked up to receive prayer and accept Christ. At that moment, guilt had his heart heavy. He was hoping that God could take some of the weight off of him.

After the funeral was over, King didn't want to leave Kareem alone. He knew that his boy was filled not only with hurt but also with anger. Although payback was definitely in order for the death of Tiana, King wanted to make sure that it was done to the right person and in the right manner.

"Hey, bae, can you do me a favor, and let Mom drop you off? I want to stay with my boy for a while."

"I can stay with y'all and make sure you guys don't need anything," Sloan offered.

"Nah, bae. I think, right now, he just wants to be alone and have some distance. I just wanna be there to make sure that he's okay. It's cool, you can go home. I'll be there later," King responded.

Yogi pulled Sloan by the arm, realizing that it was King's way of saying that this was a time for just him and his boy to be able to express themselves. Both had tried their best to hold back their tears and emotions during the funeral, but Yogi knew that it was only a matter of time before Kareem broke down again; and he wouldn't want anyone else around but King when that time came.

As Yogi and Sloan drove toward King's condo, they enjoyed being able to slide their feet out of their high-heeled shoes. It had been a long, emotional day, and neither of them had a chance to grab something to eat. Although there was food at the church, the guests had eaten nearly all of it by the time the family made it to the fellowship hall. There was no way Yogi was about to eat some picked-over chicken, and Sloan was too busy talking to people who were complimenting her on her solo.

"Hey, you want to stop and get something to eat? I know a great sushi spot about two blocks up the road," Yogi said, looking over at Sloan.

She agreed, and fifteen minutes later, they sat enjoying their first meal of the day. Sloan was so glad her and Yogi's relationship had taken a full 180-degree turn. She actually enjoyed spending time with Yogi; and the joy it brought King to see them getting along was a feeling he hoped to have for a very long time.

"Ms. Yogi, how did you know that Mr. Carlton was the one?" Sloan questioned with a mouth full of fish.

"Well, I didn't know with Carlton, but with King's father, I knew he was the one from the first time I met him. I would get all nervous and sweaty whenever he came around. I had never been like that with any man, but it is just something about them King men that make a woman act all different, you know?"

"Oh yeah, I definitely know," Sloan responded and the two ladies enjoyed a laugh.

"Speaking of Carlton, I think it's time I make it on home before he get to worrying. With all this craziness going on, we have to be on high alert."

They paid the bill and started toward the condo. When Yogi pulled into the front circle of King's building to drop Sloan off, she realized that she wasn't going to make it home in time. Though it was good going down, the sushi was, now, fighting her stomach. She and Sloan hurried up the elevator and into the apartment. Yogi made a beeline to the bathroom, and she was just in time because her stomach muscle couldn't hold the steamed fish any longer. When she was done, she placed her phone on the sink so she could wash her hands. Sloan jokingly knocked on the door to ask if she was okay.

Yogi opened the door to give her response. "Girl, my momma always said better out than in, and you know your bougie butt going to be right behind me," she said and laughed.

Yogi said her good-byes to Sloan and headed down to her car.

Sloan twisted a lock of her hair around her finger as she got ready to take a shower. She had undressed down to her undergarments, and she was ready to relax under the hot, steaming water. The doorbell rang. She knew it had to be Yogi. She had found her phone sitting on the sink when she went in to start her shower. Not wanting to let all of the hot water run out, she grabbed the phone, ran to the door, and opened it. Her heart nearly stopped when she saw Deshawn standing there.

"Now this is what I'm talking about. This is how you greet me, baby."

Sloan tried to hurry and slam the door back shut, but Deshawn overpowered her. He came in and slammed it behind him.

"Oh, let me guess, you was expecting that little nigga, huh?"

"Deshawn, what are you doing here? You better leave before I call the police!" Sloan threatened.

"Be my guest," he teased, showing her his badge.

"Deshawn, leave me alone. I told you that I don't—"

"You don't tell me shit! Damn, why can't you see that you belong with me and not that garbage you laying with? That nigga ain't going nowhere but, either, the ground or a fucking cell! What is he doing for you that I can't? That singing shit ain't nothing real! That is just some shit kids do. You ain't gone make no real career out that shit! You need to be focusing on something real in your life, like me. Now, look, I had that nigga locked down before, and I can do it again. I was giving you time to come to your fucking senses, but you want to keep acting like a dumb bitch. I know what is best for you, even if you don't!" His anger echoed with each word he spoke.

"Please, just leave me alone. Leave King and I alone. You have a wife, and that is who you should be—"

"Shut the fuck up and listen. You got a week to get your shit and move back to your apartment, or the next funeral you sing at will be that nigga's!"

Sloan stood, shaking like a leaf.

Deshawn moved close to her and tried to put his arms around her. She attempted to pull away, but he locked his hands around her. Her skin felt so soft and warm, he immediately became aroused.

"Sloan, I'm doing this because I love you. In the long run, you will understand that we belong together. I love you," he whispered while trying to kiss her mouth.

Sloan raised her knee directly up into his groin. The shock of the blow forced Deshawn to curl over. She tried to hurry and sprint to the bedroom door, but he reached out and managed to grab her feet before she was able to make it.

With one hand on his nuts and the other on her foot, he pulled Sloan to the floor and climbed on top of her. His anger was now boiling at such a temperature that he no longer was paying attention to the pain he felt in his genitals. Now, all of his focus was on making Sloan pay for her stupidity in not accepting his love. He raised himself up to his feet, grabbed Sloan by the hair, and slung her into the bedroom.

"Is this where you let that thug disgrace your body at?" he screamed, pointing to the bed.

Sloan was crying hysterically and trying to think of some way to escape.

"Well, it's time I help you come back to your senses, even if you don't want to," Deshawn continued while removing his pants and gun holster.

He let both fall to the floor before stepping all the way into the bedroom. Sloan, realizing there was no way out, remembered that King always kept a pistol under his pillow. She just needed to get to it before Deshawn could grab her.

"Baby, I'm sorry I was so foolish. You know I'm just a young, stupid girl. Can you forgive me?" she asked in the most seductive tone she could muster up.

His eyes widened. This was all he had been asking for, and Sloan had finally come around.

"Baby, of course I can forgive you," he answered. He walked up to her and kissed her neck.

Sloan was sickened by his touch and kisses, but she played along, trying to make her way to the bed. She grabbed his chin and pulled his face up until their eyes met.

"Baby, please make love to me," she said as she walked toward the bed and lay back.

While Deshawn removed his shirt and underwear, Sloan inched herself up the bed and slid her hand under the pillow. She felt the cold steel and made sure to release the safety like King had taught her.

Deshawn was so excited that, by the time he looked up, Sloan had the gun drawn on him.

"Now what are you going to do with that?" he questioned, not believing she had the courage to shoot him. "Do you know what happens to cop-killers? You think because you been around King that you are some type of killer now? Well, let me see you pull the trigger."

"You are no cop, and when they see the video I have of you, they will know that!" she responded, trying to get her courage up.

"Well, we will just see about that. Come on, shoot me, Sloan, if you're ready to spend the rest of your life behind bars!" Deshawn screamed while walking toward her.

Sloan's hands were shaking. She was trying to work up enough strength to pull the trigger, but it felt like her hands had frozen in place. Before she knew it, Deshawn was close enough to extend his hand to grab the pistol.

Three loud blasts sounded as Deshawn fell to his knees, then, to the floor. Sloan couldn't believe what she had just done and started to question if this had all been a nightmare. Just then, she saw Yogi standing there with Deshawn's gun in her hand.

King sat in Kareem's living room while Kareem got some sleep. He had watched three episodes of *Love & Hip-Hop Atlanta* and was starting the fourth when his phone rang. He looked at the screen and noticed it was Sloan calling.

"Hey babe, I shouldn't be much longer. Imani is on her way, and Reem is sleeping now," he stated.

"King, baby, this your momma. We need you to get home quickly and—"

"Is Sloan all right?"

"She is just a little shaken up, but yeah, she okay," Yogi responded.

King felt relieved to know that she was okay, but now, curiosity was setting in.

"So what is it, Ma?" he questioned, now totally confused.

"Just bring someone with you. It's some trash that needs to be taken out. That's all, baby."

Final Chapter

Kenny sat on the couch watching TV and sipping on a 99-cent forty ounce. He had been drinking since that morning, and the liquor had done nothing to ease his tension.

"Addie! Addie!" a woman yelled, walking up and opening the screen door.

Adele, or Addie, as everyone called her, was his wife and the neighborhood beautician.

"We back here, Nan," Adele said.

A tall woman wearing a peach halter-top and denim capris sauntered in. Her long, brown box-braids swung past her waist.

"Damn, girl, how many times I done told you to take them braids loose before you get here? I'm going to start charging your ass extra," Adele angrily stated.

"Girl, you know you be spoiling me," Nancy said, winking at the other client that was sitting in the chair.

Nancy took a seat in the other empty chair. She wasn't paying Addie's complaints any attention. She knew that Addie needed the money, and if she had to remove some hair to make it, she would do just that. Kenny had not worked in years since he was released from prison, so the weight of the bills fell on his wife.

"Girl, I came prepared for your slow ass," Nancy added while placing her tablet on her lap.

She started scrolling through Facebook and stopped on a video that she had already watched about twenty times.

"Hey, have y'all seen this video right here? This bitch can sing her ass off. She blowing up right now."

Nancy hit play on the screen and Sloan's tribute to Tiana, her version of Shirley Caesar's song blared through the small apartment. Everyone's ears and eyes tuned into the soulful songstress.

"Umph, that girl got a beautiful voice," the other client said.

Addie kept her eyes on the hair she was braiding, but her ears told her there was something familiar about the voice that flowed from the speakers.

"Damn, that girl can sing, and that voice will have you mesmerized," Nancy kept saying. "And she pretty too. She gonna do well. She is going to be opening up for . . . umm I can't think of her name, but she heavyset."

"What is her name?" Addie asked.

"It's Sloan something," she answered.

Zooming in on one of the pictures, Nancy placed the tablet where Addie could get a good view of the singer.

Addie had to adjust her eyes. She exhaled as she stared at the beautiful girl with large eyes and an enchanting smile. She looked toward the wall at a picture of a little girl with pigtails wearing a plaid school uniform holding her grandmother's hand.

"Deja," Addie said smiling. "So you call yourself Sloan, now? Looks like you are doing pretty well for yourself too," Addie whispered to herself.

She wiped her hands on the dirty towel and walked into the living room where Kenny was sitting.

"Hey, baby, you will never guess who I found," Adele said, laying back on the couch. "I found our baby girl, and she seems to be doing very well. I guess we know where we can get the money for my new shop from."

"Did you call Kareem?" Yogi asked King as he and Sloan sat on the couch.

The house was filled with the smell of the Sunday dinner that she, Imani, and Khristian had spent the previous night and morning preparing. With all the things that had happened over the last few months, Yogi just wanted her family around her and back to a somewhat normal schedule.

"Mom, they pulling up now," King responded.

A few minutes later, Kareem and the kids entered the house.

"Dang, you got it smelling good up in here, Ms. Yogi," Kareem yelled.

"We got it smelling good up in here," Imani added, letting Kareem know that she had put in work as well.

"Let me find out you doing some cooking around here, little girl," he responded jokingly.

"Well, little girls have to grow up at some point, especially when they have a child," Imani said as she walked into the dining room.

Everyone sat down. They were all about to start grabbing for food when Yogi made them halt. "Now y'all know we going to bless this food before anybody's lips touch one crumb. Carlton, honey, you want to do the honors?" Yogi asked.

"No, baby, you go ahead," he responded.

"Okay, well, everyone grab hands. Lord, I want to thank you for all you have done for my family and the blessing you have and continue to give to us. Jesus, we also thank you for the heartache because we know you never put more on us than we can bear. We pray that you strengthen us and keep us safe in your arms, and we ask that you give that special angel of yours a big hug from her earthly family, and tell her that we miss her and love her. Amen."